DEADLY DIRTY WORK

Jeremiah Buie knew what his police superiors thought of him.

They didn't like him. They didn't like the way he bent the rules to lay down the law. They didn't like the way he took their orders and trashed them. They didn't like his amazingly perfect record that kept them from getting rid of him. His enemies were everywhere.

But now the son of a police major's fiancée had been savagely slain after a brutal sexual assault. And the major picked Buie to head the hunt for the perp.

Buie knew that this time nobody was going to keep him from taking the gloves off . . . as he went after a vicious madman killer who had racked up too many victims and followed too many agendas for terror and murder. . . .

RUNNING DEAD

Robert Coram

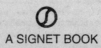

A SIGNET BOOK

SIGNET
Published by the Penguin Group
Penguin Books USA Inc., 375 Hudson Street,
New York, New York 10014, U.S.A.
Penguin Books Ltd, 27 Wrights Lane,
London W8 5TZ, England
Penguin Books Australia Ltd, Ringwood,
Victoria, Australia
Penguin Books Canada Ltd, 10 Alcorn Avenue,
Toronto, Ontario, Canada M4V 3B2
Penguin Books (N.Z.) Ltd, 182-190 Wairau Road,
Auckland 10, New Zealand

Penguin Books Ltd, Registered Offices:
Harmondsworth, Middlesex, England

First published by Signet,
an imprint of New American Library,
a division of Penguin Books USA Inc.

First Printing, April, 1993
10 9 8 7 6 5 4 3 2 1

For Jeannine

ACKNOWLEDGMENTS

The idea came from Ron and Judy Metcalf.

At the Atlanta Bureau of Police Services, thanks be to Major Vernon Worthy, Captain Calvin Wardlaw, Lieutenant Mickey Lloyd, Sergeant Dean Gundlach, and detectives Sidney Dorsey and J. W. Knox. For walking me through the protocols of an autopsy and teaching me about the dead, I thank Dr. Randy L. Hanzlick of the Fulton County Medical Examiner's office. Information about forensic odontology came from Dr. Thomas J. David.

Caren Mayer's research demonstrated both her persistence and her brilliance.

Part of this book was written in a cabin on the farm where I was born. For allowing me to return to the old homeplace, I thank Linda and Julian Morgan of Coleman, Georgia.

A special thanks to Sandra and Richard Price.

Guide us in the straight path,
the path of those whom Thou hast blessed.

—The Koran

1

Tony the Dreamer did not want to say his prayers while he was covered with blood.

He placed his *jambiya*, the curved Arab fighting knife, on the floor of the shower, turned on the water, and stepped inside. He showered thoroughly, taking his time as he removed the blood caked in his hair, pooled in his ears, and congealed in long streaks down his legs. Blood was even in his nose.

He adjusted the shower until the water was blistering hot and clouds of steam filled the room. Tony used his toe to move the *jambiya* about, ever careful of the razored edge. With each movement the knife released another gout of semi-congealed blood.

As Tony watched the blood flow down the drain, he remembered every detail of what he had done to the boy. Killing the son in the same fashion he had killed the father had excited him beyond anything he had ever known. Now only the mother was left, and soon she would meet her son and husband in their Christian paradise. She would die within the next few days.

Tony stared at the water running down the drain.

He waited until it no longer was tinged with bursts of red or hints of pink, then he squatted, the water pelting off the muscles of his back, picked up the *jambiya*, and turned it back and forth, examining it in minute detail, occasionally placing it under the water or scraping the curved blade and the rhino horn hilt with a fingernail until he was satisfied that every trace of blood had been washed away. Then he held the blade in his right hand and pulled it along the fingernails of his left hand until the nails were cut to the quick. He did the same with the nails of his right hand, pausing occasionally to make sure all the cuttings were flushed down the drain. Afterward, he used the tip of the blade to scrape the soft pink flesh to the quick. He did not wince.

It was unlikely that he would be arrested in connection with the murder of the boy—the Atlanta police did not know he existed—but if he were, scrapings from his nails would yield nothing.

He wiped the floor of the shower with his hand. No pieces of fingernails remained. He stood up and turned off the hot water. He made no sign, not even a gasp of breath, as the sudden shock of cold water sluiced down his body. For long moments he stood there, face uplifted under the cold water, not moving, then he turned off the water. With a towel he wiped the blade and the hilt of his *jambiya* until the knife glistened. He toweled his lithe, muscular body. He was forty, but had the face and physique of a man in his early twenties. Only his eyes, burning pools of oil almost hidden between thick eyebrows and prominent cheekbones, revealed his age. His thin, rectitudinous lips were pressed together.

The towel with which he had dried off was stuffed into a paper bag atop the shirt, pants, underwear, and socks he had worn the night before. In a few moments he would take them behind his house, douse them with gasoline, and burn the lot. He was not worried about the police investigating a small, brief puff of smoke. Shootings, lootings, robberies, fires, and general mayhem went on twenty-four hours a day in the neighborhood around Clark–Atlanta University where he lived. Even the cops had given up trying to regain these streets.

For a moment he considered tossing the black tennis shoes he had worn the previous night into the bag. But they were new. He put them aside.

Tony dressed quickly in loose-fitting gray trousers and a soft white cotton shirt. Barefooted, he strode into the living room. The only furniture was a wooden chair and a small table. A telephone sat on the table. The walls were bare except for a yellowing newspaper clipping tacked up near the door. The clipping from *The Atlanta Constitution*. Occupying most of the page was a story about a new mosque in east Atlanta and how it symbolized the growth of Islam in the city. The reporter had written that Islam was the fastest-growing religion in America and that soon it would surpass Judaism and become the second largest religion in the United States.

The reporter had been wrong; Islam now was the *largest* religion in the United States. *The Koran* had been dipped into the Atlantic and the faithful, almost seven million of them, ranged from coast to coast.

Below the story about the growth of Islam was a much smaller story about Atlanta synagogues lowering their dues in order to attract young people. A rabbi was quoted as saying that unless more young people came into the synagogue, Judaism was in danger of dying.

Tony liked the long story about the growth of Islam and the short story about the decline of Judaism, and he was doing everything he could to bring to fruition the rabbi's prophecy. If all went well during the next few weeks, Israel and the Jews would be nothing more than a bad memory.

Tony's house was small and nondescript, but it had one advantage: living room windows with an eastern exposure. Tony always said his prayers facing these windows.

The first faint blue-gray hint of the new day was appearing beyond the city, backlighting the downtown skyscrapers along the ridge of Peachtree Street. It was dawn, time for the first prayer of the day, and the obligatory purifying ablutions had been performed. As Tony the Dreamer kneeled on his prayer rug, he rejoiced in the thought that Islam was on the edge of its greatest victory. The Jews were finally, irreversibly, irretrievably about to be removed from America's protection. In only a matter of months the country would cease to exist.

Tony stretched out his hands and leaned forward until his forehead touched the rug. His bare feet and forehead on the rug demonstrated his submission and proved his belief that before Allah he was as the dust. He began to pray:

In the name of God, Most Gracious, Most Merciful. Praise be to God, the Cherisher, and Sustainer of the Worlds; Most Gracious, Most Merciful; Master of the Day of Judgment. Thee do we worship. And Thine aid we seek. . . .

2

Occasionally, on the shank end of a black-dog night when there was more scotch in him than in the bottle, when memories swirled in his head like dark Celtic storm clouds, and when laughter was buried so deeply in his heart he thought it might never again rise to the surface, Jeremiah Buie would wrap his kilt about him, tenderly retrieve his bagpipes from a red velvet-lined case, step outside his small house in Inman Park, and, with head high and shoulders square, march up and down the street, around and around the block, playing his heart out and seeking absolution in the ragged skirling of the pipes.

Last night had been such a night. It began with a drink of scotch. Then another. And another. Jeremiah was fifty, and when a fifty-year-old man drinks too much scotch it causes the years to rush and tumble over each other like shifting tectonic plates; it reminds him that more of his life is behind him than before him, and it reminds him of all that remains undone and probably will remain undone.

The mixture of scotch and the pipes always lured unbidden thoughts of Jeremiah's daughter and sent those thoughts rampaging through his head. Sue was the only child of a long-dissolved marriage, and he had not seen her since she was seven years old. Now she was twenty-two and he realized for the thousandth time that he had missed all the mile posts in her life. He had *wanted* to be there, God knows how he wanted to be there. But Sue's mother, in whose veins coursed the bile of a rejected woman, had threatened to sue him if he visited, wrote, or called. Overflowing with guilt, he acquiesced, and by the time he realized the magnitude of his mistake it was too late. He had written Sue the day she turned eighteen. He fully expected her to say now that she was an adult who made her own decisions that she would see him.

Instead she told him to stay out of her life.

Remembering made him want to forget. So he thrust aside the memories and turned to his pipes. For a while he played softly—as softly, that is, as the pipes can be played. A few reels and marches. Then he put on his kilt, stepped outside, and began playing "Flowers of the Forest," the Scottish lament for the dead.

The sound of bagpipes shredding the early morning hours tends to anger city dwellers. It makes them call downtown and raise hell. And that, in turn, disturbs the patrolling police officers, who take such things personally. So it was an impatient cop, a female uniform officer, who confronted Jeremiah on a street corner at 4:00 A.M. The cop, an attractive blonde named Arnett, recognized him. Regulations dictate that when a uniform cop encounters a drunk sergeant, the cop is to call a superior officer. This one stepped from the car, hitched up her belt, and shook her head.

"Hello, Nessie," Jeremiah said with a disarming grin.

When Jeremiah was drinking, all women were called Nessie.

The uniform officer's mouth tightened. Buie was one of the old-timers in homicide. He was a legend. She could cut him a little slack.

"Sergeant," she said, "people are complaining. You gotta go home. You gotta stop making that noise."

Jeremiah was indignant. He ripped off a few notes as he patted his foot in time with the music. He leaned forward, eyebrows raised, and said, "That 'noise,' as you refer to it, is the most glorious music in the world." He groped for the mouthpiece and was about to launch into another march when she waved for him to stop.

"Sergeant, you gonna force me to call the lieutenant?"

Jeremiah stared at the cop. He suddenly realized she was trying to give him a break. He stared at her name tag a moment then bowed—an exaggerated sweeping bow with his right arm extended. "Arnett, excuse me. No more noise from me tonight."

Arnett stared at him for a moment, then nodded. She hitched up her belt again. "Thank you, Sergeant. I suggest you take it home." She stepped back into the patrol car and drove away.

Jeremiah stared after her fading taillights for a moment. Like all the older cops, he did not like female officers. But now they were everywhere, throughout the department. Women even drove motorcycles. Ridiculous. A person who rode a bike should be able to pick it up when the bike took a spill. But when female motorcycle riders took a spill, they got on the radio and made a special call. It meant, "Help, I've fallen and I can't get up. Will somebody come pick up my bike for me?"

Jeremiah sighed. It was too late to go to bed. So he marched down the street to his house, where he showered under cold water, shaking his head and waving his arms as he tried to push aside the effects of the scotch. He dressed and drove a few blocks to the Majestic Grill on Ponce. A hodgepodge of people mingled there in the early morning hours: drunks, hookers, pimps, and Emory University students on the way home; blue-collar workers and businessmen on the way to work; and homeless people who sat in their little bubbles of pride and defiantly chewed their food.

A few people looked up as Jeremiah entered the restaurant. He instantly was identified as a cop, and it was not just by the hand-held radio he carried or the bulky mass of the fifteen-shot 9mm pistol stuck under his belt. There was something else.

First, he stopped upon entering the door. Most civilians never slow down upon entering a restaurant or bar. They simply walk in, find a chair, and sit down. But an experienced cop, when he enters a room, always stops, steps to the side, and looks around before he proceeds. His eyes sweep over the faces of every person as he imprints their features on his mind. He catalogues them, remembers where they are sitting, and some of them he watches with a wary eye.

Then there was Jeremiah's attitude. Like most homicide cops, he owned every building he entered. An aura of self-confidence spread from him like the bow wave of a battleship. He was so self-confident he would not accept a blessing from the pope.

Jeremiah was a big man, six feet tall with wide shoulders and a trim waist. From the back, if one ignored his white hair, he appeared to be a wiry and athletic man of about thirty. He was a vibrant and virile man whose white hair and laugh lines around his eyes were the only signs of his age.

Jeremiah walked toward a booth near the back of the restaurant. As he sat down he adjusted the pistol in his belt. Only the old cops, those who had worked vice, eschew holsters and stick their reversed pistols in the waistband of their pants. Wearing a strong-side holster causes the hammer of the pistol to abrade the lining of the coat. The first thing a savvy prostitute does is check the inside of a john's coat. If the lining along the hip has been roughed or torn, she laughs and tells the vice cop to get lost. Jeremiah also avoided the other sure sign of a cop in civilian dress—cheap wing tips. He wore loafers. Highly polished loafers that were not run down at the heels.

Jeremiah read *The Atlanta Constitution* while he slowly ate a greasy breakfast—grits, eggs, sausage, and toast slathered with butter.

"More coffee, hon," the waitress said. It was not a question. She sloshed coffee into his cup and began walking away before the cup was full, leaving a trail across the table.

Jeremiah looked around his folded newspaper. "Thank you," he said. He paused as he caught sight of a roach on the far end of his table—a young, slim, and very nervous roach whose legs and antennae twitched nervously. The roach darted a few inches and stopped, all aquiver, before darting another few inches. Jeremiah was in no mood for urban charm. Arms spread, he shoved the newspaper across the table, trapping the roach underneath. With a triumphant grunt he began slapping the paper with both hands—slapping hard, cutting off all avenues of escape. He sat back, hands poised, waiting for any sign of movement. The newspaper was still. Slowly and carefully he lifted the edge of the paper, peeling it away from the table until he found the remains of the roach. He nodded in approval.

"Got him," Jeremiah said to no one in particular.

He stood up, tossed a bill on the table, picked up his radio, and walked down the narrow aisle toward the door.

Less than five minutes later he was in the police station, part of the gigantic old Sears building a few blocks west on Ponce. In the mid-1990s the building became City Hall East.

Now it was seven and the full weight of the previous night rested heavily upon Jeremiah. He looked around. The morning watch guys were gone. No one else was in the office except Dean Nichols, a day-watch detective who always came in early to update his scrapbook of homicide victims.

Jeremiah did not go to his small office. He sat down in the squad room and leaned over the keyboard of a computer, sighing frequently and frowning as he stared at the list of homicide cases his squad was investigating. Twenty-four open cases. Atlantans were killing each other in record numbers.

The telephone rang.

"Homicide. Sergeant Buie."

"Buie, this is Major Worthy. Zone Three. Is your captain in?"

"No, sir." Jeremiah was relieved. This phone call was about administrative stuff and not about another homicide.

"What about the lieutenant?" The major's voice was tight.

"No, sir. They probably won't be in for another hour."

"I'm at one-one-one-zero Rosedale Drive and I got a forty-eight here."

Jeremiah paused. It was a homicide. But why was a zone commander reporting it? "Major, I haven't heard anything about this on the radio."

The major's voice was sharp. "That's because I'm the first officer on the scene and I didn't put it on the radio. Get over here. Now."

"One-one-one-zero Rosedale?"

"Affirmative. That's east of North Highland. Down at the bottom of the hill. Now move it."

"Yes, sir." But the major had hung up.

Jeremiah opened his desk and reached for several notebooks and his fingerprint scanner. "Hey, Nichols," he said over his shoulder.

Nichols looked up.

"You're up. We got a forty-eight at one-one-one-zero Rosedale."

Nichols picked up the telephone and quickly punched the numbers that connected him with the radio room. "Nichols. Homicide," he said. "Start me a setup. Call the M.E. and the ID techs." He quickly reeled off the address, slammed down the telephone, and stood up. His smile was beatific.

"Another one for my scrapbook," he said.

3

His prayers completed, Tony the Dreamer oiled and wiped with a soft, dry cloth the knife he had used to cut off the boy's head.

Then he sat down to a breakfast of fruit and cheese.

Afterward, still hungry, he went to the refrigerator and pulled out two lamb chops he had brought home from his favorite Middle Eastern restaurant. He wolfed them down and began chewing one of the bones, careful to avoid the tooth he had broken two days earlier while crunching another rib. The tooth was painful, but Tony was reluctant to go to the dentist. He had been only once in his life. However, if the pain did not subside, he would soon have to have the tooth repaired.

He savored the lamb bone. It reminded him of home. But lamb was difficult to find in Atlanta. Southerners preferred pig meat. He knew this all too well. At the empty lot on the corner, only five or six doors from his house, a man known as Old Black Joe cooked barbecue and brunswick stew and chitterlings. The cooking was over a pit and in enormous black pots under a carport-like structure open on all sides. At the rear of the vacant lot, against a high wall, was a decrepit shack where Old Black Joe stayed in inclement weather. He was at the empty lot Wednesday through Sunday of every week and had been for as long as anyone could remember. In the late afternoons, cars filled with white people lined up sometimes for a full block as they waited to buy barbecue.

Old Black Joe was said to have put four daughters through college on the proceeds from his barbecue. If that were true, the old man should retire. Let the fires die down and cook no more barbecue and no more chitterlings.

Tony hated the odor of pig meat. The idea of eating chitterlings, which he was told were the intestines of pigs, he found repugnant. And when he found the chitterlings were cooked in lard—the rendered fat of a pig—he almost vomited. He kept his windows closed to avoid the odor.

As Tony sucked and chewed on the bone, he picked up the sheaf of papers he had found behind a carved wooden mask in the woman's house. He began thumbing through them. The report was entitled "OPERATION BILAL" and stamped "TOP SECRET."

Only a few pages later, Tony was so transfixed that he put down the lamb bone, wiped his hand on the tablecloth, and devoted his full attention to the report.

It was all here. Everything was here. Everything. How Operation Bilal was to be financed, the execution of the plan, even the details of the elections.

Tony the Dreamer realized for the first time just how good the Nigerian colonel of intelligence had been.

The only thing missing from the report was the

most important part, the part about the Jews. But because the Nigerian colonel's frame of reference had been the Americans, he did not understand how Operation Bilal revolved around the Jews and that the American elections—first the U.S. Senate and then the presidency—were only the means to an end.

The report had been prepared in 1985 by Colonel Christopher Gowon, chief of intelligence for the Nigerian army. That it should fall into Tony's hands now, short weeks before the senatorial elections, was proof of the control Allah wields in historical events.

Only two days before, a friend in the Atlanta government, a friend sympathetic to his cause, told him the report had surfaced; that a Nigerian woman had given it to a police major who wanted to open an investigation.

Tony thought rapidly. Then he told his friend, "Have the major return the report to the woman. Make sure there are no copies made. And there must be no investigation."

Tony was pleased with the way he had handled the surprising development. The entire affair would have ended the previous night if the woman had been at home. But soon he would find her and she would learn that the terror of the day is greater than the terror of the night.

Allah was opening the way for the success of Operation Bilal.

Tony the Dreamer closed the report and looked across the skyline of Atlanta, the city where, for more than a decade, Operation Bilal had been nurtured; the city that, for him, had assumed an importance exceeded only by the three holy cities of Islam. As he stared at the skyline, he remembered the night before.

The boy had been an unexpected pleasure. Tony slumped in his chair, smiled, and began to replay the events of the previous evening at a slow, leisurely pace, savoring once again the pleasure he had known.

It had been about 3:00 A.M. when he parked his car under the sprawling limbs of a giant oak tree, hidden in the black shadows where the hard glare from the streetlight on the corner could not reach. Two blocks away an occasionally fast-moving car could be heard, but on Rosedale Drive, a quiet residential street in the Virginia–Highland neighborhood of northeast Atlanta, all was quiet. Only one car had passed during his vigil and the driver had not noticed him.

It had been forty minutes since two young men wearing sleeveless T-shirts and cutoff jeans had sauntered down the hill, arms around each other, heads together. He had seen them when they were a block away. He sat unmoving, eyes staring into the rearview mirror as they approached. His eyebrows rose slightly at the skimpy clothing and the overt display of affection between the two men.

Tony slowly wiped the sleeve of his black shirt across his face. It was October, a time of year when the temperature should have begun to abate. But even at this early morning hour the temperature was in the high seventies.

The two men sauntered slowly past. Tony dismissed them out of mind. He lowered his eyes and looked at his watch and then, without moving his head, glanced up and down the street again. He had the skills of a professional hunter; he knew that movement revealed a hiding place quicker than anything else. Even though the streets were empty, he took no chances.

He sighed in anticipation. It was the darkest hour of night, the time just before dawn, the time when the woman would be in deepest sleep.

His eyes checked the street a final time, and then he slowly opened the car door. No light came on, for he had removed the bulb from the dome light. He turned and walked toward a house three doors down. A certain lupine quality was apparent in the alert and wary fashion in which he carried his head, and the way in which his burning eyes endlessly roved. To a superb degree he had developed what soldiers call "situational awareness," a sense of who was around him and whether or not they were in position to do him harm.

When he reached the small frame house, he turned and walked down the driveway. On one side, against a fence which was the property line, was a thick border of late-blooming canna lilies.

Beyond them was a neatly maintained yard. The heat and smell of the lilies caused a rush of memories to overwhelm Tony—memories of hot and steamy nights long ago in Lagos, nights when the harmattan blew and when the ineffable sweetness of tropical flowers occasionally surged triumphantly above the stench of human waste, rotting garbage, and sewage-filled ditches.

He shrugged the memories aside and stepped onto the porch.

Two small tools enabled him to enter the house

as quickly as if he had used a key. He closed the door, stepped to the side against a dark wall, and listened. His senses were so alive that he almost trembled.

He crossed the living room, which spanned the width of the house, needing no light as he quietly threaded his way through the furniture and then down the hall toward the rear bedroom.

The bedroom door was open and caused him to pause. People usually close their bedroom doors when they settle down for the night. He looked inside. Even in the darkness he could see that the spread across the bed was smooth and unruffled.

The woman was not here.

He felt a quick flash of anger. Twice the previous morning, only an hour after he had heard from his friend in City Hall, he had driven past the house. He came back in the afternoon and again in the early evening. The woman had been at home then.

Tony withdrew a penlight from his pocket and pointed it across the room. A narrow beam of light confirmed that the bed was empty.

The man paused. He was not used to having his plans thwarted. For as long as he could remember, every event in his life, and in the life of those he knew, had been planned in such infinite detail, with every possible contingency considered, that there had been few surprises anywhere along the way. When surprises did arise, it was his job to correct them.

Because the planning had been so thorough and because his own work had been so implacable, all of the players were in place. The stage was set. The ending, only a few weeks away, was a forgone conclusion.

Tony looked around the room. He was disappointed the woman was not at home. But he would complete the second part of his mission. He would find what he sought.

A moment later Tony felt the pull of a vague disquietude. It was as if another person was in the room with him. He never ignored such feelings. He turned off the flashlight and slid it into his pocket. From inside his shirt, his right hand pulled the *jambiya*, the knife that was never drawn except to taste blood. He walked across the room toward a closet, pausing in a brief frozen tableau as a board squeaked loudly underfoot. He rested a hand on the knob of the closet door, turned it slowly, and pulled the door open. No one was there.

Tony tensed. Suddenly he knew, knew beyond any doubt—someone else was in the room. In a move so fast as to defy description, he spun around. He held the *jambiya* neither in the hammer position nor the icepick position—favorites of amateurs—but rather in a loosely clenched fist braced between his thumb and forefinger, a position that provided maximum reach and made the knife a virtual extension of his arm.

The uncovered beam of the flashlight revealed a slender young man, a boy, really, standing at the door, hands up and attempting to ward off the light. He wore only a pair of white cotton briefs.

Tony realized the boy must have been asleep in one of the guest bedrooms. Because the woman lived alone, he had passed the doors without opening them. Careless.

"Who are you?" asked the young man in a tremulous voice. "What do you want? I shall call the police."

"You are Nigerian?" Tony said, surprised at the crisp over-pronunciation of the young man, a speech so unlike the blacks of Atlanta and so like that of the people of Lagos. Except, except, there was something else. The boy's speech was even crisper than that of a Nigerian—more like the English.

The young man blinked, said, "Yes," and then caught himself. "Who are you?" he repeated.

"Some call me Tony. Tony the Dreamer." His voice was very soft. He took a step closer.

The boy's brow wrinkled. His thoughts were obvious. Tony the Dreamer? What sort of name is that?

Tony's mind was racing. Who was the boy? Could he be . . . ? He was about the right age. He must be . . . But it had been fifteen years.

"You have lived in the U.K.?" Tony asked.

The boy paused, confused by the question and the soft voice of the intruder. "Yes, I lived in London until . . ." He caught himself and his voice rose in determination. "What do you want?"

Now the man was almost certain. "I seek Glory. Glory Gowon," he said as he moved a half-step closer, the knife hidden behind his leg.

"You know my mother?"

It *was* the son. Tony was elated at what Allah had placed before him. He reversed the knife and thrust his hand forward. The rounded pommel of the Yemen-style knife shoved into the boy's solar plexus with such force that the boy gasped and slumped to the floor unconscious. The flashlight roamed over the boy's body for a moment. Then Tony turned off the light and slipped it into his pocket. The knife was returned to its resting place inside his shirt.

He stooped, pulled the boy's left arm around his neck, then stood up, carrying the limp figure across the hall and through an open door. He twisted and allowed the boy's body to slump across the bed. He turned on his flashlight and placed the light atop a dresser so that the beam shone over the bed, bounced from the wall, and cast a soft penumbra throughout the room.

The boy did not move when Tony reached down and slapped him hard on each side of the face. Tony looked around. A glass of water stood on a table near the bed. He picked up the glass, tilted it, and trickled water across the boy's face.

After a moment the boy stirred, squinted, and shook his head in fear. His eyes widened. His mouth opened. Before he could shout, Tony leaned forward, one hand tightly squeezing the boy's slender neck.

"You will make no sound," he said softly. The quiet malevolence was more intimidating than a threat.

The boy, eyes wide, nodded.

"Where are the papers? Where did your mother hide them?" the man said. He slowly removed his hand from the boy's neck.

The boy coughed. "Papers? I don't know . . ."

"Papers left by your father. I know they are here. Where are they? In which piece of art?"

"My father?" The boy was confused. "He's been dead—"

"Fifteen years," the man interrupted. "To be precise, fifteen years and two months."

The boy stared, almost in horror. "How do you know that? Who are you?"

The man's stiffened fingers suddenly jammed into the boy's solar plexus, not hard enough to render him unconscious but hard enough that he gasped in pain and curled into a fetal position.

"Where are they?"

The boy sobbed. "I don't know. I have no way of knowing. I've only been here—"

Tony interrupted. "When did you arrive from London?"

"Two days ago." The boy appeared relieved to be asked a question he could answer. He rushed on, anxious to appease the intruder. "I've been sleeping most of the time since I arrived. Mother is out tonight with her fiancé. She left me a note. May I show it to you?" He rose to a sitting position.

"Fiancé? Fiancé?" For the first time Tony's voice lost its softness and became harsh and indignant. "Your mother is a whore. A Christian whore sleeping with a policeman." He said *policeman* as if it were an epithet.

"Don't you say—"

Tony backhanded the boy, knocking him to the pillow. He pulled the knife from inside his shirt, walked across the room, and cut the two cords that adjusted the drapes. One of the cords he used to lash the boy's wrists together. It was done quickly and expertly.

"Why . . . ?"

Tony smiled. He doubled the other cord and slipped it over the boy's head. Then he twisted the cord, winding it in a thick spiral until it began to squeeze the boy's neck. He tugged hard. The cord bit into the boy's neck and caused him to gasp for breath.

Tony released the pressure. The boy coughed and choked and drew in long gulping drafts of air.

The boy was terrified. His legs suddenly pumped in fear as he attempted to crab across the bed. Tony jerked hard on the cord, pushed the boy's face into the bed, pinning him, holding tension on the cord, ignoring the muffled gasps.

The boy's body jerked a few times, then stopped. Tony released pressure and rolled the boy's head to the side. He waited until the boy's eyes opened.

"You will do as I say," he told the boy. His voice was soft, almost caressing.

The boy looked over his shoulder, and his eyes widened in bewilderment when he saw the man was undressing. The man leaned over him, one hand maintaining tension on the cord, the other shifting the boy's body. The boy whimpered.

Tony the Dreamer smiled, leaned forward, held his breath for a moment, then sighed in pleasure.

"God is great," he whispered.

4

Jeremiah was not in the best of moods when he arrived at the crime scene. Cars were the cause of his simmering anger.

First, there was his car, a dingy old 1990 model of indeterminate color. It could have been black or it could have been dark blue or it could have been dark brown; it was impossible to say. Faded was the only color that leaped to mind. The car smoked and belched and wheezed and surged, and looked as if it occasionally had been used for a battering ram, which it had; and it drove as if most of its innards were about to suffer a catastrophic breakdown, which they were. The sergeant who drove the car during the morning watch was six feet, five inches tall and weighed three hundred and forty pounds. His weight had broken the back of the seat and caused it to recline at a forty-five-degree angle. In order for Jeremiah's feet to reach the brake and clutch and his hands to reach the steering wheel, he had to drive with the seat pushed all the way forward. But even then he was leaning back so far that when he turned to look out the side window, he was, in fact, looking out the window of the rear door. By contrast, the passenger side of the front seat was normal. Dean Nichols sat there with his knees forced up under his chin.

The second reason for his anger was a white unmarked car—the sort of car assigned to majors in the Atlanta Police Department—and two black-and-white squad cars. A small number "3" on the sides of the black-and-whites identified them as being patrol cars from Zone Three, Major Worthy's zone. Uniform officers from Zone Three had secured the crime scene, and Vernon Worthy, commander of Zone Three, was present. And still there had been nothing on the radio.

What was going on?

If Major Worthy said there was a forty-eight here, somebody was dead. And if somebody was dead, this was homicide country. A zone commander had no authority there. Jeremiah Buie owned the homicide scene, and it did not matter that Vernon Worthy was a major.

But in the Atlanta Police Department it was not always wise to defend one's turf too vigorously. Jeremiah had been burned badly by the major many years before and was wary of him. The major was a longtime friend of both the chief and the mayor. In fact, the chief had restructured Zone Three several years previously at the request of the major. He gave the gentrified areas of Inman Park and Virginia–Highland to the major so he would have a "relief pocket." Until then Zone Three had been the roughest in all Atlanta, a twenty-one-square-mile sewer that reached from burglar-infested Grant Park in the north through the hell stretch of McDaniel Street and rambled on through the numberless pustules of crack-infested apartment houses near I-75 and over to the federal pen. And now, right in the middle of the major's relief pocket was a homicide, one for which he, for some unknown reason, was the first officer on the scene.

As Jeremiah and Nichols stepped from the car, one of the uniform officers waved and grinned. "Hey, Sergeant," he said. "Still wearing your dress?"

Jeremiah ignored him and continued across the lawn toward the porch, where Major Worthy was waiting. But Nichols slowed and looked at the uniform cop—his name was Steve Newberry—and grinned. Nichols slowly stuck a forefinger to his temple, eased his thumb back, and said, "Pow."

Newberry's grin disappeared. He made a grimace of distaste and turned away.

Newberry had once worked in homicide. But he was demoted to the uniform division after a suspect in his custody pulled a hidden gun and committed suicide by blowing his brains all over the squad room. Whenever other officers saw Newberry, they clenched their fist, stuck an extended forefinger to their heads, and said, "Pow." It was called the Newberry Salute.

Jeremiah walked up on the porch where Major Worthy waited. "What's going on at my crime scene, Major?" he said to the tall black officer.

"My fiancée lives here. She stayed with me at my house last night. When I brought her home she found the victim—her son—his name is Christopher Gowon, Jr., dead. He's back there in a bedroom." Major Worthy paused. "What's left of him."

He paused. Then he said, "I didn't put out any-thing on the radio because I don't want news peo-ple around here."

"You hanging around," Jeremiah said. It was not a question.

"I'll come inside when you finish."

"Major, I'm going to have to print you."

Major Worthy nodded. He understood.

Jeremiah turned to go inside.

"Hey, Sissy."

Jeremiah stopped. He looked over his shoulder. Only his closest friends called him Sissy, and he and Vernon Worthy were not friendly.

"Yes." His voice was flat.

"This is more than a homicide. A hell of a lot more."

5

It was almost noon when Jeremiah and Dean stepped outside. The air was hot and humid and no wind was blowing. Jeremiah took a deep breath and slowly exhaled. Nichols chewed his cigar, then peeled off his rubber gloves and said, "Ummmmm. Ummmmm. Ummmmm. Another fucking tragedy."

Dean stuck the rubber gloves in his pocket. Usually homicide detectives dropped the gloves wherever they finished with them, but Dean was very much aware of the major's presence.

When Jeremiah did not respond, Dean tried again. "Smelled sweet in there, didn't it?" he asked.

Jeremiah nodded. After he and Dean had done everything they had to do in the room where the homicide had been committed, Dean walked out and closed the door, leaving Jeremiah alone. Jeremiah liked to sit with a body for a while and try to feel through some ineffable fashion what had taken place. Dean heard him several times talking to the body, talking in a soft, cajoling voice. And he heard him humming "Just a Closer Walk With Thee."

Dean did not find it odd that his sergeant had solitary conversations with the dead. He only wondered what Jeremiah talked about. In this case it probably was blood. The overriding impression at this homicide was blood. Blood was everywhere. Ceiling. Walls. Floor. It was difficult to imagine that a human body could contain so much blood. And the blood smelled like copper sulphate; it had a metallic odor, a sweet odor. It clung to Jeremiah's clothes and filled his nostrils.

As always when leaving a crime scene, Jeremiah felt an overpowering urge to stand under a hot shower. He would settle for being able to scour his hands. An oppressive miasma, the invisible cloud present at every homicide, left him feeling clammy and grimy.

Jeremiah had never seen such horror as he saw in the small bedroom. But over and beyond the horror of what had been done to the victim was something—he did not quite know what—that nagged at the back of his mind.

"Look at that," Nichols said, nodding across the lawn toward the street. The detective chewed on his cigar and stared balefully at the crowd that had gathered—neighbors and television crews.

"Runners or floppers?" Nichols said. "You the boss. You get first choice."

"Floppers," Jeremiah said. "Five bucks."

"You got it."

"By the way," Jeremiah said, "when I was in the room with the body, were you in the bathroom?"

Dean nodded.

Jeremiah shook his head. At every homicide Dean used the nearest bathroom. He was like a dog in a new yard.

A commotion was taking place on the lawn. Jeremiah's presence caused the television crews to shoulder their cameras as the newspaper reporters and artificially attractive television reporters shouted questions and motioned for him to come down to the yellow crime-scene tape that held them back.

The presence of television was causing several black neighbors to begin profiling and showcasing. Nichols stared balefully from the porch and realized for the hundredth time that homicides involving black victims are different from those involving white ones. When a white person is killed, the neighbors peep through their windows or stand silently looking over the fence, but they almost never intrude. And rarely is there any overt public display of emotion.

But when the victim is black, then the black neighbors became very much involved, especially in the presence of television cameras.

Jeremiah and Dean watched as several black men stalked up and down the sidewalk in front of the cameras, poking their chests out, clenching their fists, and growling about "white motherfuckers what did this." They apparently came from the apartment house two doors down the street.

"Willy is getting excited," Dean said.

Willy is a collective name that Atlanta cops apply to black people.

Women from down the street began doing the chicken: waving their arms, hopping about in circles, and caterwauling. When women do the chicken, it takes one of two forms—floppers or runners. Floppers simply fall down or twirl in a circle and flop their arms. Runners go berserk. They dash up and down the streets while screaming and wailing.

The two women rolling around on the sidewalk were definitely floppers. Nichols sighed, pulled out his wallet, and passed Jeremiah five bucks.

Jeremiah wondered who fed the most off television: neighbors or criminals? Where would it all end? Atlanta now had so many homicides that most people were inured to them; surprise and outrage had disappeared and the only thing remaining was the macabre magnetism.

Jeremiah turned to Nichols. "Remember not to smile," he said.

The captain had issued instructions that no homicide officers were to smile or crack jokes when television cameras were anywhere in sight. Nor were they to shake hands with any corpse and make jokes about the physical characteristics of any corpse. A long lens and a sensitive microphone could pick up such mannerisms. If the grieving family of a homicide victim turned on the television and saw a smiling, wise-cracking detective standing over the body of their loved one, all hell would break loose. So homicide detectives were to be, in the captain's words, "responsible and professional."

Nichols turned to Jeremiah. "Boss, you know I never smile."

Jeremiah nodded. Nichols was dour and brooding. His normal expression was a baleful stare. And his elbows always stood slightly away from his muscular body, almost as if he were an over-inflated blow-up doll. Some homicide detectives believed that every morning on the way to work, Nichols stopped somewhere to get pumped up.

Unconsciously Jeremiah ran his left hand inside his coat pocket and touched his notebook. He never used a tape recorder as did some of the younger homicide cops—he did not trust tape recorders. His notebook was filled with charts and diagrams and drawings and notes.

The ID techs had photographed everything. Tomorrow he would have pictures. The medical examiner's office was so over-burdened that it would take several months to get the official medical report, but he would go down the following day for an unofficial version.

Jeremiah and Nichols stayed on the porch. The television people were still shouting questions, and the two women were still flopping about. It was turning into bedlam.

Major Worthy sensed the growing unease and stepped away from the slight, aristocratic-looking woman with whom he had been softly talking. He nodded for his lieutenant to take his place, raised his right arm, and in a loud voice said, "Okay, people. Listen up." His size and his voice, combined with his command presence, caused the floppers to settle down and the television crews to become silent.

The major paused and made sure he had everyone's attention. Then he continued. "This is a crime scene where official police business is being conducted," he said. "You people will conduct yourselves in an orderly manner or you will disperse."

His eyes roved over the group of people for a moment, then he slowly walked across the lawn. Behind him was silence. The two cops on the porch walked to meet him.

"What you got in there?" Major Worthy asked.

"Job security," Nichols said. He rolled the cigar around in his mouth and stared at the major.

Major Worthy snapped a sharp look at Nichols. Homicide cops are ghoulish hotdogs, chroniclers and cataloguers of the dead. They boast of working longer hours than other detectives, of facing greater stress, and they say that a sense of humor is the only way to survive. But the major, like most cops who had never worked homicide, thought they were prima donnas and that their humor was perverted.

Take Buie. Most cops, if they reach Buie's age and sense retirement and a pension just around the corner, become superstitious and careful. They use drive-in windows at banks because they are afraid—if they use the front door—that they might walk in with a radio in their hand just as a holdup man is coming out with a gun. Not Buie. One of his favorite stories was how, after two cops were killed in the space of several weeks, a superstitious cop who believed such events happened in threes, took a vacation. He did not want to be the third. While he was on vacation, his wife killed him.

Buie did not believe it was his destiny to die on duty. He still wore the mantle of invincibility that cops usually shed either the first time they are shot at or by their thirtieth birthday. Buie was unique. He had the canny street smarts of a guy who has been on the street twenty-five years, mixed with the invincible aggression of a kid just out of the academy.

Buie was an old-time cop who never covered his ass. He was interested only in results. Several years before, the police department had been on the lookout for a fugitive who had killed two people. Buie kidnapped the fugitive's sister, then called the girl's mother, and said, "I have your daughter. You can have her back when you tell me where your son is." Nine hours later the mother gave up her son.

Arresting a dangerous fugitive usually means a commendation. Buie was relieved of duty for a week.

And then there was the time he extracted a murder confession by taking the suspect out near the Chattahoochee River, handcuffing him to a tree, placing an apple on his head, and shooting at the apple until the man begged to tell all he knew.

Buie had been a cop long enough to know that all too often the only justice is that meted out by the arresting officer. He loved being a cop, but he also liked to help out the juries and the courts.

As for Nichols, he was considered weird even by other homicide cops. Him and his scrapbook. He enjoyed taking the scrapbook over to Manuel's Tavern, where he drank beer, hummed mindless little ditties, and thumbed through the pictures of those who had been shot, stabbed, run over, poisoned, drowned, or hanged. In considerable detail he talked about each victim.

"This is what we call a floater," he would say as

he pointed to the puff-pastry face of a drowning victim.

"This guy got popped in the cabbage," he would say as he showed a gory close-up of a person whose head had literally exploded from the hydrostatic pressure of a bullet.

Nichols measured civilians by how many pages they could look at before they turned green and walked away in disgust. Any one who could look and listen through the entire book was an okay guy.

At one homicide scene Nichols started a betting pool about which neighbor would do the chicken for the longest time. At another, a particularly messy one where two brothers had shot and killed each other with shotguns, the father of the victims asked Nichols if the homicide squad would clean the blood and gore from the walls and ceilings of the room where the shootings had occurred. Nichols flipped out his gold shield and said, "Mister, this says I'm a detective, not a garbage collector."

Major Worthy was dealing with a couple of wild horses.

He sighed, turned to Jeremiah, and asked, "Buie, what happened in there?"

Before Jeremiah could answer, Dean looked at Worthy and said, "Major, that boy pissed off somebody big-time."

6

"You and your fiancée found the body?" Buie asked Major Worthy.

"That's correct." The major paused. "Was the crime scene disturbed?"

Jeremiah nodded. "Either you or your fiancée stepped on a couple of the perpetrator's footprints." Jeremiah paused. "But blood was so thick on the floor that the first few footprints weren't that good. I think we got a couple of good ones down the hall when he was leaving."

"We can measure the depth of the footprints," Jeremiah said, almost as if talking to himself. "Then measure the length between the prints and come up with the approximate height and weight of the perp."

Major Worthy was embarrassed. Majors do not contaminate crime scenes. He nodded. "Did you get any prints?"

Jeremiah grabbed his coat pocket to make sure he had picked up his fingerprint scanner. It electronically transmitted images of fingerprints to his car, where a satellite uplink tied it into a national data bank. In seconds the name and last known address of the subject appeared in a window of the scanner.

Jeremiah spooled through the information in the window of the scanner. "Four prints. One is a Glory Gowon. That your fiancée?"

The major nodded.

"Second print is one Vernon Worthy." He looked up from the scanner. "That you?"

The major nodded. "Get on with it."

"We got two unknowns. One clear and one may be an identifiable partial. One might be the victim and the other the perp."

Jeremiah looked at the major. "There were several suitcases in the victim's room. Did he live here?"

"No. He just got here a few days ago. He's been in school." He paused. "In London," he added.

Jeremiah nodded. That would explain why the prints were not in the data bank. But it raised a difficult problem. Most murderers know their victims, and they kill, more often than not, either for profit or for revenge. Those who kill strangers, or those who kill for fun, are difficult to identify and arrest.

"What time did you arrive?" Jeremiah asked.

"Couple of minutes before I called you. About seven." The major stared at Jeremiah. "What'd they do to him?" he asked. "Give it to me straight."

Jeremiah looked away. Before he could answer, Nichols took his cigar from his mouth and in his flat, emotionless voice said, "His head was cut off and jammed atop one of the bedposts. You saw that. The other bedpost was shoved up his ass. His penis and testicles were cut off and put in his mouth like Christmas tree decorations. Major, he is one fucking mess."

"Don't hold back, Detective," Major Worthy said sarcastically.

"Major, we need to know these things," Nichols said. "The choice of weapons says a great deal about a perp. This guy used a knife and a bedpost. That tells us something."

"You're making bricks without straw."

"Major, how long were you in the house?"

"Only a minute or so." The major looked across the lawn toward his fiancée. "When we went in the house she walked back to her bedroom and saw that it had been ransacked. Her artwork was all over the floor. She found her son, screamed, and ran out of the house. I called you and followed her."

"Did she notice if anything was missing?"

Major Worthy knew where Jeremiah was going. It is axiomatic that there are no perfect homicides, only imperfect investigators. Criminals bring something to a crime scene or they take something away. Always. They bring guns and knives and clubs, and they take away money, jewelry, television sets—whatever they find. Sometimes they take weird stuff: a broken umbrella or a paperweight. The idea is to know what was taken away and to find what was left behind.

Major Worthy looked away. "I'm not sure," he said vaguely. "She mentioned some papers. A file."

Jeremiah waited. But the major did not explain. "A file? What sort of file?"

"Tell me what else you got in there."

Jeremiah paused. The major was not answering his questions. "The pieces don't fit," he said.

"And they never will again," Nichols said. "Not after what that guy did to him."

Major Worthy ignored Nichols. "What do you mean?"

"The same thing you meant when you said this was more than a homicide. The nature and extent of the violence don't fit the circumstances. Burglars don't go to this extreme. It appears on the surface to be a random homicide, but people don't walk in off the street and do that." He turned and pointed toward the house. "A woman lives here. The perpetrator was after her. From what you say, he could not have known he would find a man. He didn't know the victim."

"Perp was either a faggot or crazy," Nichols said. "Maybe both."

Jeremiah shook his head in disagreement. "I don't know," he said.

He paused and stared across the lawn. "Major, the boy's death is not what this is about. The death was a statement of some sort." He looked at the major. "Help me out."

For a long moment Major Worthy did not answer. Then he said, "What does that tell you about the perpetrator?"

"Several things," Jeremiah said. "When you put it all together, it tells me the perpetrator was a pervert. Regular homosexual killers, as violent as they are, don't go to this extreme. When I see a victim treated this way, I believe we will see the perp again. People who do this don't stop with one victim. They have some sort of fire burning in their belly."

The major stood with bowed head, thinking.

"Tell you something else," Jeremiah said. "When a man kills someone, he reveals a great deal about his background and his motivations. The body was out in the open. It was not hidden. In fact, it was on display. Whoever did it wanted the body to be found. The body was uncovered. Not even a sheet over him. That tells me the perpetrator liked what he did; he was proud of it. He felt good about it. Whoever this guy is, he thinks he is smarter than we are. Either that, or what he is doing means so much to him that he has to humiliate the victim, even after death, by putting his body on display."

Major Worthy sighed. "You think it was racial? A random racial homicide?"

Jeremiah shook his head. "I doubt it. Most killers stay within their own racial groups."

The major thought for a moment. "What about the sexual angle?"

Buie paused. He had been hoping the major would not bring this up. "I won't know until I get the medical examiner's report," he said. "But I expect him to tell me that before the bedpost was used, the boy was raped."

The major winced. "And what does that tell you about the perpetrator?"

Nichols grunted, a sign he wanted to speak. As the major and Buie turned, he took his cigar from his mouth and said, "We see that, first thing we think of is the Greeks. They're bad about screwing people in the ass."

Major Worthy sighed. Homicide cops reduce everything to basic racial or ethnic questions. "So do the Arabs," he said in half anger and half derision.

Nichols stared. "No shit," he said. "They do that?"

"Sure they do," the major continued. "If there are no camels."

Nichols pondered this. To a homicide cop who has spent years in the dark end of the human behavioral spectrum, it is entirely possible that Arabs have carnal knowledge of camels. It was clear from Nichols's face that he was considering the mechanics of this.

The major waved his hand in a gesture of exasperation. He turned to Jeremiah.

"Okay. Get back to the violence. The extent of the violence. What else does that tell you?"

Jeremiah paused. He did not like the role the major was taking in the homicide investigation. But Buie had not asserted himself because, after all, the major's fiancée was the mother of the victim. And Buie knew, with the sixth sense of a longtime homicide cop, that the easiest way to get information was to go along with the major.

"Cutting off someone's head is a messy job," he said. "Unless you use a sharp and heavy implement—say a sword or an ax—it can take a long time. The vertebrae, muscles, gristle, make it almost impossible for an amateur to do with a knife."

He paused. "But that boy's head was sliced off as neatly as if a doctor had done it. Same with his genitals. The perp knew what he was doing. Maybe he was a professional. But, Major, why would a professional killer do that to a kid he never met? A professional doesn't mutilate and kill strangers."

"Doesn't decide on the spot to become a fudge-packer, either," Nichols said. "I told you the guy is either a faggot or crazy. I'd say both."

Major Worthy motioned for Jeremiah to continue.

But Jeremiah wanted answers. "Why was a professional killer in your fiancée's house, Major? What was in the papers you say he might have taken?"

The major looked across the lawn. "You think he was after my fiancée?"

"She lived here," Nichols said. He paused, then said, "You realize he'll be back."

Jeremiah cleared his throat. He paused a moment. "Major, in anticipation of that, we left a little ear."

A *little ear* is a small, passive, and easily hidden eavesdropping device. It operates for months on tiny batteries.

Major Worthy shook his head. "No way. Take it out." His tone brooked no argument.

Jeremiah nodded.

Nichols took a deep breath. He was so muscular and big-boned that when he took a deep breath, he looked for all the world like one of those enormous gas-inflated figures that are towed down the street in a parade. He tried again. "Major, if the guy is as good as Sergeant Buie says, he won't miss next time."

Major Worthy stared at the detective. "I'll take that responsibility," he said. "Take the ear out."

"Major, you didn't answer my questions earlier,"

Jeremiah said. "Why is a killer after your fiancée? What's in the papers?"

Major Worthy again looked across the lawn at his fiancée. Her eyes still registered the horror she had seen. Her face was tight with grief, and he could see silvery tracks of tears against her skin. Later, in private, she might collapse. But it would not happen in public. She was in control. She had not reacted as would most women who had discovered the mutilated body of a son. For a quick moment he felt an immense amount of pride in her.

Glory Gowon was Nigerian, the daughter of a prince and a member of Nigeria's true and traditional royalty. Her father was one of the Obas of the Yoruba, and she could trace her family back to the royal city of Ife. She was a poised and educated woman who, years earlier, had been married to the senior intelligence officer in the Nigerian army, a man who'd disappeared back in the eighties in the aftermath of a coup.

One of the few areas of conflict between the major and his fiancée, and the reason she had taken more than a year before agreeing to marry him, was her patronizing attitude toward Atlanta blacks. As a Nigerian, she considered them a disgrace to all black people. They lacked ambition, were devoid of culture, spoke in a virtually unintelligible parody of English, and were too quick to shout racism and to blame white people for every problem of mankind.

Vernon Worthy knew she was wrong. Atlanta was an urban magnet that drew young, educated blacks from all over the world. Here, particularly in government, they prospered as in no other American city. A greater percentage of black people was in the upper reaches of city and county government in Atlanta than in any other city in the country. In the police department alone, Atlanta had more black majors than New York, not to mention a black chief and three black deputy chiefs. The former chief, Eldrin Bell, had used the Red Dogs, his squad of head-cracking zealots, to vault into the mayor's office. More black people held jobs in middle and upper management in Atlanta than in any other major American city. And more black people in Atlanta drove Mercedes and Volvos and Saabs than in any other place Vernon Worthy had ever seen. In fact, Atlanta had more black millionaires than any city in the world.

Atlanta was a *black* city.

He looked at the two men staring at him and remembered Sergeant Buie's question. He looked at Nichols and said, "Detective, excuse us a moment."

Nichols looked at the major.

"Take a walk, Detective," Major Worthy said. "Go get that little ear."

The muscles in Nichols's jaw clenched. His chain of command was to Sergeant Buie and then to the captain in charge of homicide. Theoretically, even the chief of police could not give orders to homicide detectives at a homicide crime scene.

But this was Atlanta.

Nichols looked at Jeremiah. He nodded.

Major Worthy waited until Nichols was inside. He put a big hand on Jeremiah's shoulder. "We need to talk."

Jeremiah pulled back a half step, causing the major's hand to fall off his shoulder.

"Major, are you obstructing—?"

"Sissy, I'm asking you as an old friend. Come to my office and read the papers. It won't take an hour."

"Major, I want you to address me by my rank and name."

The major stared. His eyes were sad. Once he and Jeremiah had been close friends.

Jeremiah's eyebrows shot up as the major's statement sank in. "What papers?" he asked.

"Sergeant Buie, I sent a document to the chief a few days ago. He said he discussed it with the mayor, and they both agreed it was not worth investigating. He ordered me not to make a copy for the office but to return it to my fiancée and to forget it."

Again the major paused. "I made a copy."

The major turned and held out his hands toward Jeremiah. "That's what I want you to look at. Read it. Afterward, do as you like. It's your investigation. But read it first."

Jeremiah tried to hide his astonishment. A police major does not lie to the chief, not if he wants to keep his job. Jeremiah had occasionally withheld information about cases from his superiors; there was no reason to tell them everything. They were idiots. But he could not imagine the major deceiving the chief.

What could be in the document?

Jeremiah turned as if to look for Nichols.

"Just you," the major said. "Read it. It will help separate the sheep from the goats."

"When?"

Major Worthy nodded toward his fiancée. "I have to be with her for now. Three o'clock tomorrow."

"I'll be there." Jeremiah turned to go inside.

"Sergeant, what about the media people? They want to talk to homicide."

Jeremiah opened the door and looked over his shoulder. "Major, you been throwing your weight around my crime scene. You got all the answers. You talk to them."

7

Mid-October and Atlanta is steaming. Temperatures in the eighties, violent thunderstorms and tornadoes to the west, and the air is so filled with humidity that clothes stick to the body and tempers flare. Heat lightning flashes in the eastern quadrant. Existence is a matter of rushing from one air-conditioned building to another—that is, for those who can afford it. Many in Atlanta cannot.

Jeremiah Buie walked out the rear door of the Fulton County Medical Examiner's office and squinted up at the leaden sky. Outlined against it was a misshapen oak tree at the edge of the parking lot. The upper limbs had been chopped across the top to make way for electrical lines, and the lower limbs had been whacked away to give space to telephone lines. The result, made more grotesque by bare limbs and windblown paper caught in the branches, was a stark caricature, a mockery of a tree.

"Heads up," Dean Nichols said as he came through the door.

Jeremiah quickly looked to his right and then to his left. He had forgotten for a moment that the area around Grady Hospital is a no-man's land on the border of three warring gangs. The inner-city area is controlled by a gang of young blacks made up of the first generation of crack babies to reach their teens—full-grown psychopathic geek monsters who call themselves the King's Men. Their savage and indiscriminate violence is made more horrible by the quotes from Dr. Martin Luther King, Jr., that they recite to victims before killing them.

"Freedom has always been an expensive sort of thing."

Pow!

"In the nonviolent army, there is room for everyone who wants to join up."

Slash!

"You express a great deal of anxiety over our willingness to break laws. This is certainly a legitimate concern."

Thunk!

A few blocks south near the stadium is turf dominated by an aggressive Asian gang called the Ghost Shadows. These lads are pushing hard against downtown Atlanta. Also seeking to move into the turf are two Hispanic gangs: one, the sons of blue-collar migrants who call themselves Wet Necks, and the other—extremely violent—the Rod and Gun Club.

Strife between the groups is frequent and marked by exchanges of fire from automatic weapons. It is made more bitter by the resentment Atlanta blacks feel against Asians and Hispanics, who, almost overnight, it seemed, went from being insignificant minorities to powerful economic forces that pushed blacks out of jobs they felt were historically and rightfully theirs. A half-dozen innocent bystanders had been killed in the past month by stray bullets in gang fights. This part of Atlanta is in a virtual state of anarchy.

Despite the warring groups, the fenced parking lot behind the medical examiner's office is relatively safe. Gang members come here often enough to identify dead associates that this block is associated with death. Gangs skirt this block if possible.

To Jeremiah, the muggy, clammy outside air was better than the air inside the medical examiner's office. Being in a sauna, even if it is on the edge of a twenty-four-hour-a-day shooting gallery, is preferable to being inside the cold room—filled with death and chemicals and stainless steel tables and stacks or organs and vital parts that once made up human beings. And most of all, filled with the pervasive smell of decomposing human bodies, a smell that heavy doses of cleansing agents cannot overpower.

Jeremiah took a deep breath and slowly let it out as if to clear from his lungs the smell of the charnel house, where for the past two hours he had been looking at the gray-black disembodied remains of the homicide victim and listening to the medical examiner's dispassionate exegesis of the killing.

There had been none of the jocular banter that almost inevitably is part of the autopsy procedure. Not this time. The only thing approaching that was when the medical examiner pulled back the sheet to reveal the boy's severed head, his torso, and the shriveled penis and scrotum.

"Kid is like Gaul; he is divided into three parts," Detective Nichols said.

Jeremiah looked at him in surprise.

Nichols shrugged. "Hey, I'm more than the Good Humor man. I read."

Jeremiah looked up at the looming hulk of Grady Hospital, a sprawling, grimy ziggurat that had dominated the southeastern edge of Atlanta's skyline almost a half century and took another deep breath. He glanced to the right, where the parking lot emptied onto Coca-Cola Place. If any wandering gang members came along, they could enter the parking lot only through that gate.

"So what do you think the major will say this afternoon?" Nichols asked.

"I don't know. But it better be good." Jeremiah stared at the gray sky and scudding clouds. "Looks like Scotland," he mumbled.

"You been to Scotland?"

"No, but I read, too." He paused, still looking at the sky. "Perp did a job on that kid."

"You got that right," Nichols agreed. He chewed his cigar and looked up and down the street.

The two men were silent. They were remembering what the medical examiner had said.

Any of several injuries could have killed the boy. But the amount of blood sprayed in a wide semicircle around the room indicated the boy had been killed when his throat was cut from ear to ear. The beginning of the second cut—the medical examiner called it a "tail"—picked up almost exactly where the first cut ended. It continued through the neck and between the sixth and seventh vertebrae, thereby neatly removing the boy's head.

Had the severed genitalia been the only wound, the boy would have died from loss of blood. Had he been left without medical attention for an hour or so, the bedpost in his rectum would have killed him—certainly from the resulting hemorrhaging and possibly from a vagal response. Sometimes when the rectum is stretched beyond its normal size, the shock causes the vagus nerve to kick in and cause cardiac arrest. Patients being given barium enemas, a relatively common diagnostic procedure, have died from cardiac arrest caused by a vagal response.

Finally, the boy might have been killed by strangulation. Petechial hemorrhaging, red dots of blood found under the eyelids of strangulation victims, indicated he had been choked to the point of unconsciousness.

The choking caused engorgement of blood vessels in the head, somewhat like squeezing a garden hose, and the resulting hemorrhaging under the eyelids. The choking probably was done to control the boy while he was being raped.

A ligature mark was clearly apparent once the blood from the dismemberment had been washed away; "a circumferential furrow without upward tenting," the M.E. called it. The ligature mark, plus the fact his hyoid bone had not been broken, as it might have been had he been choked manually, showed he had been strangled with a cord or small rope. The lack of "upward tenting"—the ligature mark commonly found in hangings—indicated he had been choked from the rear.

Semen had been found in the rectum, leaving no doubt that the boy had been criminally assaulted. The semen had been collected on two swabs and put into a glass tube. An investigator from the M.E.'s office would take the swabs to the state crime lab for DNA typing. Usually it took anywhere from three to six months to get test results, but since the victim was known to a major in the Atlanta Police Department, this one would get special treatment; the results would be available in two weeks, maybe ten days.

Two sets of radial tears around the anus and the perineum had been found. Bowel lacerations were obvious. The smaller lacerations, probably caused by a penis, had been accompanied by significant hemorrhaging, indicating the rape had occurred when the boy was still alive. The examination showed no previous rectal perforations and no thickening of the mucosa on the lining of the rectum—the boy had not had rectal intercourse in the past. And he was HIV-negative.

The second and larger set of radial tears—those caused by the bedpost—were much more extensive. Although the bedpost had been jammed against the sacrum with considerable impact, bruising and lacerations there were not marked by hemorrhaging. This trauma occurred after death.

At first glance, a classic case of homosexual overkill. When homosexuals kill, they often are irrational and frenzied. A victim might be stabbed forty or fifty times in the same area.

But the boy's death went beyond those frenetic killings. The strangulation, dismemberment, severed penis placed in his mouth, the bedpost—and all to a victim whom the perpetrator could not have known—indicated something beyond a typical homosexual murder. This was a stranger-to-stranger killing. The intended victim was the mother.

No, Jeremiah was more than ever convinced his earlier assessment had been correct: the boy's death was not about death. The homicide was a billboard, a statement.

But about what?

And why?

One of the M.E.'s more interesting findings had not been noticed at the crime scene because it was covered with blood. A massive bruise covered the scapula region of the victim's right shoulder. The medical examiner had swabbed the wounds— the skin was broken in several places—in hopes of picking up traces of saliva which could be typed. But there had been too much blood. He could not pick up enough saliva.

The bruise, lighter in color than the victim's skin, was photographed. A small ruler with increments ticked off in centimeters was placed alongside the bruise. The pictures could later be reproduced on a one-to-one ratio.

The medical examiner was crisp and professional. He was a young man who appeared to be only a few years out of medical school, and he was meticulous as he took a wooden embroidery ring, applied a powerful glue to one edge, then placed the ring over the bruise and pressed it firmly against the skin. After several moments to allow the glue to set, he used a scalpel to cut around the outside of the wooden ring. Slowly he lifted the ring, pulling away a circle of skin with the bruise in the center. The skin could not shrink, for it was stretched over the ring like a drumhead. This evidence he carefully placed inside a plastic container of formalin and gave to Jeremiah.

"Papers are on the table," he said.

Jeremiah nodded and signed the paperwork acknowledging receipt of the skin sample and thereby maintaining the chain of custody.

"This may be a bite mark," the M.E. said. "Take it to a dentist to make sure."

Jeremiah nodded. He had mixed feelings about dentists and bite marks. Sometimes he thought these dentists belonged with the fringe lunatics who became involved in homicides. He remembered the Gwinnett County case back about 1990, in which four dentists gave four conflicting opinions about a bite mark. And then there was the Krause case in DeKalb County in 1991, when two dentists identified bruises on the victim's neck as bite marks and another two dentists said the marks were only bruises.

The big problem is that the few dentists interested in forensics are not objective; they are pro-prosecution. Years before, Jeremiah had learned that when a dentist says, "My testimony will send the bastard to the chair. We'll make him fry," that he better have additional—and better—evidence to take to court.

But if the M.E. thought this might be a bite mark,

Jeremiah had to follow up. "I haven't used a dentist in some time," he said. "Is there anybody you recommend?"

"Yeah, his card is tacked up over my desk upstairs."

Jeremiah nodded towards Nichols. "Call him and set it up. You talk to him."

"I know the drill," Nichols said around his cigar. He chuckled at his humor.

The M.E. watched as Nichols disappeared through the door of the cold room. "That guy will come in here with a tag on his toe one day," he said. "And I'm going to have to surgically remove that cigar from his mouth. Does he sleep with the damn thing?"

Jeremiah laughed. "It's the only thing he can get to go to bed with him."

Five minutes later Nichols returned. "He wouldn't talk to me. Said he dealt only with the senior officer on a case. Wants you to meet him for lunch." He chewed his cigar. "Son of a bitch has an ego the size of Disney World."

Jeremiah picked up the plastic container, nodded toward the M.E., and left through the rear door.

He and Nichols were standing in the parking lot behind the medical examiner's office. Time in the cold room had caused each to wrestle with the same dark image: that he might be killed on the Job and there would be an autopsy and his mortal remains would be sliced into neat piles of viscera and stacked on one of the steel tables alongside the empty shell of a body.

Nichols looked at his watch: five minutes after

eleven. "Sergeant, you're meeting that guy at eleven-thirty. You're gonna have to hurry to make it."

"Where am I meeting him?"

Jeremiah opened the door of his car and sat down. His upper body sloped backward at about forty-five degrees.

"You always drive from the backseat?"

Jeremiah muttered a curse. "This damn car. Tell me where I'm meeting the dentist."

"Downtown. That Chinese restaurant near Peachtree Center. Hsu's. Know where it is?"

Jeremiah's white eyebrows rose and his eyes sparkled in anticipation. "My favorite restaurant. The guy has taste." He turned on the ignition and shook his head in disgust when the car backfired, then began wheezing and sputtering.

"You coming?" Jeremiah asked.

"Don't eat Chinese food."

"Why?"

"I told you about that. The chinks kill cats and put them in the food. I'm afraid I'll order chicken and wind up eating a cat. I hate cats."

Jeremiah smiled. "Thank you for sharing that little personal revelation with me."

Nichols waved his cigar expansively. "Anytime, boss. By the way, in case you call, I'm getting a divorce and I'm stopping at a pawnshop before I go back to the office."

Jeremiah waited. He did not get the connection. "I'm sorry. I didn't know," he said.

"It happens," Dean said.

"Tell me about it," Jeremiah said sardonically.

Dean looked at his cigar. "I'm picking up a camera so I'll have something to do with my time. Besides, I'm not always happy with the shots the ID techs take. I'm going to start taking my own pictures at homicides."

Jeremiah nodded. "Take your time," he said. He started to drive away, then slammed on the brakes and leaned out the window. "Hey, how will I recognize this bozo?" he asked.

Nichols shrugged. "He'll be carrying a pair of pliers."

8

Jeremiah sauntered through the arched doorway of Hsu's and sniffed appreciatively at the spicy aromas from the kitchen. As he waited for the hostess, he looked around. The dining room was small and elegant: soft off-white wallpaper with highlights of muted iris. Atop each of the glossy rosewood tables was a small bouquet of fresh flowers. Precisely in the middle of each side of each table was a small white place mat.

Soft oriental music played in the background.

To Jeremiah's right, the first thing guests saw upon entering were three roly-poly Buddha-like statues. The first was a man holding a peach—the symbol of long life. Beside this was a statue of a man dressed in the ornate robes of a high government official—the symbol of success and power. The third statue was of a smiling man whose happy family represented good fortune.

Jeremiah rubbed the belly of the third statue.

Already the dining room was half full. Most of the tables were filled with groups of women. A few couples and several groups of businessmen in dark suits were scattered around the room. Jeremiah saw no man sitting alone.

"Hello, Jeremiah. One for lunch?"

Jeremiah looked to his right. Anna Hsu, who owned the restaurant, was walking toward him. She was a tall, slender woman whose straight black hair framed a face of startling beauty.

"I'm meeting someone," he said. "Don't guess he's here yet."

"What does he look like?" Anna asked.

Jeremiah paused. "I have no idea."

"What is his name?"

Jeremiah's eyebrows shot up as he suddenly realized that Nichols had not told him the dentist's name. "Anna, I don't know that, either." He paused. "He's a doctor," he said quickly.

"Ah, a doctor."

"Actually, a dentist."

Anna stared at Jeremiah. "You've been working too hard. Shall I seat you or would you like to wait in the bar?"

"The bar."

Jeremiah sat at the end of the bar and ordered scotch. Jura. A single malt scotch from an island off the west coast of Scotland where his family had once lived. The scotch was as robust as a highland malt but with a slightly peaty taste. He drank it as God intended single malt scotch to be drunk: no ice, but with a splash of water to bring out the bouquet.

He was very careful with the plastic container holding the piece of bruised flesh. As he looked around at the quiet elegance of the restaurant and listened to the soft music, he wished that the dentist had wanted to meet some other place. He sipped the scotch.

Moments later he saw a bearded figure in a long raincoat striding rapidly down the hall. The man appeared to be in his mid-forties, was slightly stooped, and was walking so fast the open raincoat flapped out behind him. Jeremiah stood up.

As the man passed the entrance to the bar, he glanced inside. His eyes locked inquisitively on Jeremiah. Without breaking stride he careened inside, held up two fingers of his left hand for Anna, and said, "Two for lunch," while at the same time he stuck out his right hand for Jeremiah.

"I'm Dr. William Green," he said in a loud voice. "My friends call me Pinky because when I was in dental school I bit my lab instructor's little finger. You must be Sergeant Buie."

"That I am," Jeremiah said, smiling at the rush of words. "Pinky Green. I like that." He paused. "Why'd you bite your instructor?"

Dr. Green motioned for Jeremiah to follow him toward the dining room. Jeremiah picked up his scotch with one hand, the plastic container with the other, and followed.

"He hurt me," the dentist said. Dr. Green stopped and leaned toward Jeremiah when he talked. He was very intense. "Name'll stick with me all my life."

"Why don't we go ahead and order—get that out of the way—then we can talk," he said over his shoulder as he turned and walked rapidly into the dining room.

Jeremiah nodded as Anna seated them near the

wall at a table for four. He placed the plastic container in the empty chair on his left and, from force of habit, looked around to see who was sitting near them. His emerald eyes sized up each diner. Across the aisle sat a table of four elderly women. Behind the dentist sat two businessmen.

The dentist wiggled, twisted about, and simultaneously shucked off both his raincoat and suit coat, leaving the suit coat inside the raincoat.

"Thank you for coming on such short notice, Dr. Green," Jeremiah said as he pulled out his chair. He spoke softly, hoping the doctor would do the same. Anna ran a classy restaurant.

Dr. Green motioned him to silence as he grabbed the arm of a passing waiter. To Jeremiah, he said, "I know Chinese food. I'll order if you don't mind." His voice remained loud.

"Fine." Jeremiah gave up. The guy had no volume control; he could speak only in a voice guaranteed to be heard in the next county.

The dentist placed two orders for hot and sour soup. He pursed his lips and held an upraised finger toward the waiter. "Mongolian beef for me and your famous shrimp with black bean sauce for my friend," he said.

He sat down, making sure his coat was arranged properly inside his raincoat. The man was constantly in motion. He wiggled his shoulders and pulled at his beard and fidgeted in his chair.

Jeremiah realized he would learn the most by simply allowing the dentist to talk. Pinky Green would feel constrained by answering direct questions. He was bursting with knowledge and wanted to share that knowledge. Judging by the volume of his voice, he wanted to share it with the world.

The dentist clasped his hands, looked down, then raised his eyes to the ceiling and began rubbing his hands together. The guy fairly hummed with tension; he was one of those people who, after about five minutes, induces extreme fatigue in all those about him.

He leaned forward, eyes locked on Jeremiah.

"Let's find a starting point, Sergeant Buie. I understand you are the person in charge of a homicide investigation."

"That's correct."

"Sergeant Buie, what do you know about forensic odontology?"

Jeremiah's white eyebrows arched upward. "Nothing, Dr. Green. You'll have to walk me through."

Dr. Green liked the answer. He steepled his fingers, took a deep breath, made a grimace of concentration, then leaned across the table so quickly that Jeremiah stiffened.

"Until the last year or so, forensic odontology was more art than science," Dr. Green said. "Sometimes it was difficult to determine if a bruise was nothing more than a bruise or if, in fact, it was a bite mark."

He looked up as a waiter delivered a pot of hot tea quickly followed by bowls of soup. Dr. Green poured two cups of tea, picked up a large white plastic spoon, leaned over the bowl, scooped deeply, and began ladling soup into his mouth.

After a moment he looked up. "Medical examiners thought very little of us. There was one case where a medical examiner used a rather dull implement to cut off a woman's breast. He sent the breast to a forensic odontologist, who said the breast had been bitten off."

He shrugged in distaste. "Medical examiners wrote that up in the journal of the American Academy of Forensic Sciences." It was clear he did not approve.

More soup. "That particular dentist was too anxious to please—too anxious to help the police."

Jeremiah nodded.

"Then we began using ultraviolet and infrared photography. Ultraviolet light has shorter wave lengths and therefore penetrates skin less than regular light."

More soup. Dr. Green pushed the bowl aside. "You know, I'm sure, that skin basically is dead tissue." From the tone of his comment, it was clear he did not believe Jeremiah knew this.

"The underlying fat has no blood cells. So when you look at a bruise you are not seeing skin or subcutaneous fat; you are looking at muscle. That's where blood collects. Blood collects in the muscle. Photographs of bruises, until the advent of ultraviolet photography, showed virtually no surface detail."

Jeremiah noticed a few glances from other diners were coming their way. Talk of a woman's breast being cut off had piqued the attention of the two businessmen sitting at the table behind the dentist. The four women across the aisle were in mild shock. They froze for a moment. Surely they had not heard what they thought they heard, not in this elegant Chinese restaurant.

But Pinky Green was oblivious to everything except his food and his lecture.

The waiter arrived carrying two plates on his right arm and two bowls of rice on the left. He parceled out the food. Dr. Green used chopsticks to fill his mouth with beef. He chewed three or four times, swallowed, then took a long drink of water—half the glass—followed by a loud slurp of tea. He stared at the ceiling as he used his tongue to chase wayward pieces of half-chewed beef around his mouth. He swallowed.

"Now, there are two basic types of bites," he said in a didactic voice. "Anger bites and passion bites. Anger bites can be anywhere on the body. A person who bites in anger—and this is most common among women—will bite whatever is available. Nose. Fingers. Face. Anything."

The chopsticks became a blur, hauling beef from the plate to the dentist's mouth. The remainder of the glass of water was downed and followed by more tea. Dr. Green waved his hand to attract the waiter's eye—the restaurant was becoming crowded—stabbed his finger toward the water glass, and continued.

"Passion bites are just what the name indicates: bites committed during passion. On women these bites are most often found on the breasts, buttocks, and genital areas. I've seen cases where the nipples were almost bitten off. On men: genitals and scro-tum."

The women at the adjacent table jumped as if they had been poked with cattle prods. They stared for a moment at their food, and then, as one, they turned toward Dr. Green.

Pinky Green remained oblivious.

"Now you have a very basic background in the principles of forensic odontology," he said. "What do you have for me? Tell me about this case." He leaned over and the chopsticks became a blur.

Quietly and concisely Jeremiah briefed Dr. Green on the homicide. The women at the adjacent table relaxed and continued with their meal.

"So what do you want me to look at?" Dr. Green said.

Jeremiah tilted his head toward his left. "It's here in this container. Perhaps after lunch we could sit in your car and—"

"Nonsense," the dentist said impatiently. He used his tongue to chase pieces of beef hiding around his gum lines, sucked on them appreciatively, then swallowed. He picked up a spring roll, took a large bite, wiped his fingers on the napkin, then held out both hands, palms up, moving his fingers rapidly as he motioned for Jeremiah to hand him the plastic container.

Jeremiah handed it over. Reverently the dentist opened it. He reached to the side, picked up a pair of unused chopsticks, and slowly pulled the embroidery ring from the container, holding it up as formalin dripped into the container. The biting smell of formaldehyde spread quickly in the dining room, causing diners to look at their plates and wrinkle their noses. The dentist exchanged the chopsticks for a napkin and held the embroidery ring high. He moved around in his chair, tilting the ring back and forth, seeking the best light.

Anna stared from across the room. Jeremiah would not meet her eyes.

Jeremiah ate slowly while Pinky Green—his food forgotten—stared at the drumhead of flesh from different angles, occasionally making sounds of satisfaction. He pulled a magnifying glass from his pocket and examined the bruise at close range. Then he leaned back in his chair, tilted the embroidery ring at different angles, all the while muttering and mumbling to himself. Finally, with the ring of bruised flesh held high overhead in his right hand, he looked at Jeremiah.

"Two questions you must ask in bite-mark identification," he began. "Number one: How unique is the dentition? Number two: How much detail is in the bite mark?"

"Dentition?"

"The teeth," Dr. Green said impatiently. He rolled his upper lip back and tapped a fingernail against his front teeth.

Jeremiah stared. Why the hell couldn't the guy just say teeth? Don't dentists speak English? He smiled and nodded.

"This is a bite mark. Definitely. No doubt about it. Absolutely none." Pinky Green pulled the embroidery ring closer. "It's rare to have what we call a 'cookie cutter imprint'—clear marks of both upper and lower teeth. That in itself speaks volumes to me." He paused.

"What does it say?" Jeremiah knew a cue when he heard one.

"It says that the perpetrator almost certainly was gay. In almost all anger bites, both people are moving about. The biter can't get a good grip. The same is true, although to a lesser degree, in passion bites. The reflex action on the part of the person being bitten causes the person to pull away."

The dentist held up his left hand, four fingers clasped together as in an upper jaw and the thumb curved under as in a lower jaw. He moved the thumb and fingers as if a mouth was closing.

"As the teeth come together," he said, "they usually scrape across the surface of the flesh, creating what we call drag marks. If one tooth is longer than the others, the resulting drag mark is more pronounced. If a tooth is shorter or missing, this shows as a gap in the drag mark."

Dr. Green waved the embroidery ring. "The drag marks are minimal here. Only a trace. That indicates the victim was not moving. He was submissive, perhaps even unconscious. And the bite mark is near the crown of the shoulder, a location where a gay man would bite during anal intercourse."

The dentist almost rose out of his chair in his intensity. He waved the embroidery ring. "Only in homosexual bite marks is this found," he said. "At the moment of orgasm the man leans over, takes a big bite"—the dentist snapped his jaws—"and holds on."

Jeremiah heard forks dropping at the table across the aisle. He wanted to turn to the women and apologize, but to do so might break the dentist's train of thought. And the dentist was on a roll.

Dr. Green pointed to the embroidery ring. "This is an almost perfect cookie-cutter imprint. I must have photographs."

"I'll get them for you."

"The person who owns this mouth has a parafunctional habit," Dr. Green said.

"A what?"

"A parafunctional habit that has marked his teeth. A tailor holds pins in his teeth; a man who smokes a pipe puts it in the same part of his mouth. Parafunctional habits."

Dr. Green again pointed to the embroidery ring. "This person has nicked and chipped the edges of several teeth. Small marks, barely visible here. But enough to indicate to an expert the presence of a parafunctional habit."

"What could it be?"

Dr. Green shrugged. "I have no idea."

Then the dentist, who clearly did not like to admit ignorance on any point of dentistry, leaned across the table, smiled conspiratorially, and for the first time spoke in a low voice. "The man you are looking for will be easy to identify," he said. Then he smiled and leaned back in the chair.

Jeremiah stared and waited for the dentist to explain.

Pinky Green enjoyed the reaction. He savored it for a long moment before leaning across the table again. "He has unique dentition."

"Okay." When would the little creep get to the point?

Dr. Green pushed the plates aside and placed the embroidery ring on the table. He pointed. All Jeremiah saw was a more or less circular bruise. But the doctor pointed to an area of lighter color—the bruised flesh—and with a satisfied tone said, "The incisal edge of tooth number eight, the upper right central incisor, is split or jagged; it has a rough edge."

He looked up at Jeremiah. Jeremiah nodded.

The dentist's smile increased. Again he leaned over and pointed at the mark inside the embroidery ring. "But even more significant, see this dark area. The teeth have bruised the skin on either side. And note this. Tooth number five—here behind the cuspid on the upper right—is the first pre-molar. It is out of the plane of occlusion."

"What does that mean?"

"It means the tooth either is missing or is broken off. That's why the flesh was not damaged here while it was damaged on either side."

"Can these imperfections—if that is the right word—be seen if someone is talking to this fellow?"

"Unless he has a very high smile line, no. His lips cover them."

"But if I find him and you examine his teeth, you are prepared to swear in a court of law that he is the person who made these marks?"

Dr. Green nodded. "I am. I'll put him in jail for you." He reached for the remainder of his spring roll.

Jeremiah sighed.

The four ladies at the next table stood up. They

held handkerchiefs over their noses. One turned toward Jeremiah and, with a thin, icy smile, said, "I hope you gentlemen enjoyed your lunch."

The dentist, mouth filled with spring roll, looked up and nodded. "Beef is good," he said.

Jeremiah returned the embroidery ring to the plastic container.

He was going to catch hell from Anna.

9

Jeremiah was ten minutes early when he walked into Major Worthy's office, nodded, and said, "Major, I'm ready to listen."

Jeremiah was tense. He was in a tough spot. He was investigating a homicide case and, by the department's standard operating procedures, was free to conduct the investigation without outside interference. But the department was rife with politics and race.

The major sensed Jeremiah's tenseness and tried to loosen up the meeting. He smiled, threw his hands wide, and said, "So. How are you, Sissy? You don't mind if I call you Sissy here in my office, do you?"

Jeremiah did not answer. It was Vernon Worthy who had given him that nickname. Back when the two of them had just graduated from the academy and Jeremiah was learning to play the bagpipes. That was when he first began to wear his kilt to Manuel's Tavern and hope that someone, anyone, would ask, "Are you a sissy?" The question had caused him to invite entire tables of men into the parking lot, where, had it not been for Vernon Worthy, he would have been beaten to a pulp more than once. Those had been the glory days—a white guy in a kilt and a black guy with an attitude—the two of them taking on all comers, both forgetting they were cops as they brawled in the parking lot.

Jeremiah shrugged. "I'm doing well, thank you, Major."

He was all business. Old times were gone. The two men had gone their separate ways years ago when Vernon Worthy became part of a handpicked group of black officers who rose rapidly through the ranks to become senior officers. Jeremiah had worked in larceny, narcotics, vice, on the federal task force, and in homicide. He had an outstanding record in each division. But he was still a sergeant. And he would retire a sergeant. Part of the reason was a fitness report Worthy had written on him years before when, as a young lieutenant, Worthy commanded narcotics. He wrote that Jeremiah was incapable of taking orders from superior officers. Worthy simply meant that Jeremiah was too independent to work within the framework of what is essentially a paramilitary organization. But the comment on the fitness report was interpreted by many black officers to mean Jeremiah would not take orders from a black superior officer. From that moment his chance of promotion had dwindled to zero.

"I hear about you from time to time," the major said.

Jeremiah's white eyebrows arched in quarter-inch question marks.

"Signal twenty-nine at your address the other morning."

Jeremiah shrugged. He'd forgotten the major slept with a radio by his bed. "Some people don't appreciate fine music," he said.

"I know that's right," Major Worthy said, looking over Jeremiah's head. He had his own opinion about bagpipes. Then he nodded and smiled. "I have to admit that 'Amazing Grace,' my favorite song, does sound good on the bagpipes."

Jeremiah nodded in agreement. "Once you've heard it on the pipes," he said, "it never sounds quite the same on any other instrument."

The major pulled open a desk drawer, slid his hand under a folder, and slowly placed it atop the desk. He pushed it toward Jeremiah. "Read this," he said. "You ain't gonna believe this shit."

"Then we talk, Major. You assist me in my investigation or I go over your head. If that doesn't work, I go public."

Major Worthy nodded in understanding. "Read it," he said. He wrinkled his nose. "What's that smell?"

Jeremiah held up his right hand. "Formalin. From the M.E.'s office."

Major Worthy winced. He tapped the report with his finger.

More than an hour later Jeremiah looked up in astonishment. He had been impatient and filled with skepticism when he began, wondering what sort of scam the major was trying to work. He skimmed the report. Then he went back over it slowly, reading and rereading various passages. Finally he leaned back in his chair and looked out the window.

Vernon Worthy's fitness report on Jeremiah had been correct. He had a basic flaw—a childish defiance toward those in authority. In addition to his belief in street-level law enforcement, in doing things his way, he simply could not accept supervision. From anyone. And in a big-city police department, such a flaw meant that he was constantly in trouble with his superiors.

While the officers above him were the closest targets of convenience, Jeremiah thought that taking on those who were socially or politically powerful was even better. Jeremiah would cheerfully work eighteen- and twenty-hour days on the off chance that he could arrest a wealthy businessman, a well-known politician, or a prominent Atlantan.

That was why he was so stirred by the report. If the report were true, he could tie yesterday's homicide to one of the best known and most politically powerful men in Georgia.

Jeremiah jumped from his chair and began pacing the floor in front of the major's desk. "This came from your fiancée?"

"Yes."

"Where did she get it?"

"Her former husband. He was killed during a coup. She smuggled it out of the country."

"Why is it here now? After all this time?"

"When she first came to the States, she went to New York. She showed it to the feds up there. CIA, FBI, DEA. She got the runaround. Nobody believed it. They thought it was the crazy ramblings of a bunch of us niggers."

There was no bitterness in the major's voice, only acceptance.

"So she came to Atlanta?"

Major Worthy shrugged. "It had nothing to do with this. She didn't like New York. She had a sister here. So she moved."

"What about the report?"

"She'd been burned by the reaction in New York. She gave up on it. I've known her for several years and it was not until last week she showed it to me."

"You showed it to anyone?"

"Of course," the major said impatiently. "I can't sit on something like this. I showed it to the chief and he took it to the mayor."

"Their reaction?"

Major Worthy paused. "They said it was a fantasy, that it was driven by politics and that it was not worth pursuing." The major raised his eyes and stared at the wall over Jeremiah's head. "Now that my fiancée's son has become a victim, it is clear they were wrong. Somebody thinks this is important. Important enough to kill an innocent young man."

He stared at Jeremiah. "They were wrong. And I'm going to get to the bottom of this."

Jeremiah nodded in understanding. But the major could not participate in this case. Superior officers did not become part of cases that involved family members. The process went from prosecution to persecution when that happened.

"Major, you know they won't let you get involved in this case. It's a matter for homicide."

The major shrugged.

Jeremiah resumed pacing the floor. "We all know about the Nigerians and Atlanta Airport," he said. "We've arrested dozens, maybe hundreds of them in the past ten years or so. If there ever was such a thing as a natural criminal class, it's the Nigerians. They invented most of the scams around today, everything from bogus credit cards to bank scams to phony oil leases. When I hear the word Nigerian, I think crook. We have arrested so many Nigerians at the airport that when Andy Young was mayor and trotting off to Lagos every other week, he made an official complaint to the president of Nigeria. Told him to stop sending us so many crooks."

Jeremiah stopped and shook his head. He rested a big hand atop the report. "But we thought they were dopers and con men. We never plugged it into any organized plan the way this report does."

Major Worthy smiled. "As long as the chief thinks it is Dead Sea fruit, you are going to have a difficult time investigating it."

"What does that mean?"

"He didn't say Dead Sea fruit, but that's what he meant. I told you. He said the report is speculative and that the allegations are not worth pursuing."

Jeremiah stood up. "Well, there's nothing speculative about this homicide. They can't say a homicide is not worth pursuing. And I'm pursuing it."

"You working it?" Major Worthy was surprised.

Sergeants are supervisors. Cases are worked by detectives. In addition, Buie believed that all homi-

cides are created equal, that the murder of a homeless person deserves the same care and attention as
the murder of a Buckhead socialite. That he gave
preference to a case, that he singled out a case to
work, spoke volumes.

Jeremiah shrugged. "Gowon was your fiancée's
son. Any case involving someone close to a zone
commander justifies the personal involvement of a
sergeant. Yeah, I'm working it."

Major Worthy stared at Jeremiah. "The chief
won't stop you from working a homicide," he said.
"But you know he will want to be kept informed."

Jeremiah nodded.

"And you'll have to send him all the paperwork."

Again Jeremiah nodded. "If it's not on paper, it
didn't happen" was one of the chief's favorite ex-
pressions. He liked to say that brainwork, foot-
work, and homework all were important, but that
the most important of all was paperwork.

"Major, you know that somebody in the chief's
office or the mayor's office leaked this. That's why
the perpetrator went to your fiancée's house.
There's no other explanation."

The major leaned across the desk and pointed a
forefinger at Jeremiah. "That's what I meant yesterday when I told you this was more than a homicide. The guy was after this report."

"He was after your fiancée."

"She's now under police protection."

"Twenty-four-hour?"

Major Worthy shook his head. "She won't allow
that. She's staying with me at night, but she wants

to be at her house during the day. Won't allow any officers there. I had a couple of detectives put on stakeout where she won't notice them. And a couple of SWAT guys are hidden in a van. Nobody can get past the SWAT guys, so she should be okay."

He shook his head. "Virginia–Highland is my relief pocket. She should be safe."

He toyed with a pencil on his desk. "I'm going to ask her to put that house up for sale. She will never be comfortable there. We sealed off her son's bedroom."

The two men were silent for a long moment. Then Jeremiah picked up the report and weighed it in his hand. "Major, we get the guy who committed the homicide and we got us . . . "

He stopped. His eyebrows climbed high in excitement. He continued. "We got us a plan by the Nigerians to—"

"The Muslims," Major Worthy interrupted. "That is more important than the fact they are Nigerians."

Jeremiah nodded. "You're right. We got us a plan by the Muslims to smuggle drugs from Nigeria through Atlanta in order to finance a fifteen-year plan to elect . . . "

"Frederick A. Carr," the major said slowly.

"To elect Frederick A. Carr, the former U.S. Attorney from Atlanta, as the next U.S. senator from Georgia, and—"

Major Worthy finished. "And then run for president of the United States."

10

Tony the Dreamer sat in his dining room and chewed on a lamb bone.

He felt a slight tinge of concern about what had suddenly taken place in Atlanta. Nothing he couldn't handle. But until the last few days, Operation Bilal had proceeded flawlessly. Now he had a minor problem.

Tony had to solve the problem. He had to put Operation Bilal back on track. He could do it. Even though the Americans now knew of Operation Bilal, they thought it concerned a man running for the U.S. Senate and then the presidency. They did not know the ultimate goal.

Tony was confident of outwitting the Americans; the Jews were a different matter. The longer they remained unaware of Operation Bilal, the better. Second, Frederick Carr was engaged in the final hectic days of a political campaign. If Tony could keep Carr in the background—if he could resolve this bothersome problem before Carr learned of it—all the better.

Tony deeply feared the man whom, even in private, he thought of as the Hidden Imam—not for physical reasons, because the man was not at all

physically prepossessing. But rather for religious
reasons. There was nothing in any other religion to
compare to the position held in Islam by Carr. He
alone, of all Muslim leaders who had tried for hundreds of years, had pulled together the warring
contentious factions of Islam. Various Egyptian
leaders had tried. Ayatollah Khomeni of Iran had
tried. Saddam Hussein of Iraq had tried. All had
failed. But Carr succeeded. Not since the Prophet
himself had there been a man of such power. He
had the power of life and death over a billion Muslims. Beyond him was no recourse and no appeal.

Tony involuntarily shivered. He knew that
among the few intelligence services aware of his
existence, he was referred to as Tony the Dreamer.
The Mossad or the CIA, he did not know which,
had given him that name because he killed people
with such lingering and diabolical cruelty that they
dreamed of death. But if the Hidden Imam even
suspected that all was not well in Atlanta, Tony
would suffer a fate more horrible than any of the
people he had killed.

Tony pushed aside the lamb and reached for a
plate containing a single pastry shaped like a doll.
It was filled with honey and, for Shiite Muslims,
symbolized those who had broken the Prophet's
chain of succession. Their blood, represented by the
honey, was symbolically shed each time a pastry
doll was sliced open.

Shites usually ate the honey-filled pastry only on
the eighteenth day of Dhu-al-Hijjaj, but Tony had
found a small Muslim store over on Martin Luther
King Drive that made the pastry and he ate them

frequently—not so much for the taste as for the ritual and symbolism. He enjoyed slicing the dolls open, then cutting them into small pieces.

Tony ate slowly, and when he finished he pushed aside the plate, stood up, and walked into the living room.

He looked out the window and was surprised to see that a group of young men had congregated across the street near the school. With their white tennis shoes and jeans, they all wore dark blue or pin-striped suit coats. The King's Men. It had to be. Their initiation rite had two parts: first, memorize at least three one-sentence quotations from the writings of Dr. Martin Luther King, Jr.; second, kill a man who was wearing a suit. The jacket of the suit then became a permanent part of the gang member's uniform, his colors.

The school detectives soon would run them off.

Tony shook his head at the curious ways of Americans. He ran his tongue over his broken tooth and sucked on it reflectively. He was in no danger from the police. He knew that an aging homicide sergeant had taken over the case, and he knew every piece of evidence that had been collected. The tight skin of his face creased in what was almost a smile when he thought of the evidence and what would happen to it.

His smile increased as he thought of the woman. He knew how he would kill her and he knew when it would happen.

Tony's eyes brightened as he licked his thin lips and rubbed and pulled at his groin.

It was Friday, the Day of Gathering, and he had

been to the noon prayers at Al Farook Masjid. He preferred the mosque on 14th Street because he could find anonymity among the fifteen thousand members and because so many of the members were Asians and Arabs rather than Atlanta blacks.

He continued to rub his groin. He had attended to his spiritual needs, now there were other needs. He looked about the austere apartment. He needed to get out, to go somewhere.

He looked out the window at the young men across the street. He was glad the school detectives had not arrived.

11

Jeremiah hung up the telephone and sighed in exasperation. Wacky dentist Pinky Green had called four times since their lunch two days ago. Jeremiah thought that sending him the infrared pictures of the bite mark would make him happy. But now the guy was coming up with a theory a minute. His latest brainstorm was that the person who had killed the boy might be from a Third World country. Dr. Green said people from Third World countries rarely visited dentists. That explained why a person would walk around with a broken tooth.

Jeremiah lost interest after the dentist reluctantly agreed the perpetrator might also be someone, anyone, who simply could not afford dental care.

Jeremiah rubbed his eyes and looked around the squad room. Dean Nichols was over in the corner. He had put aside his scrapbook of homicide victims to read the newspaper and was humming softly, some erratic, unrecognizable tune.

Grandpa was on the phone, probably talking to his psychiatrist. Grandpa was only thirty-six, but he had a fifty-year-old's face. The bartenders at Manuel's had begun calling him Grandpa several years before, then other cops picked up the nickname. Grandpa couldn't let anyone know how much the nickname pained him; his fellow cops would smell blood and bore in. So he developed a nervous laugh and a facial tic. After the Georgia Baptist nurses who hung out at Manuel's began calling him Grandpa, he became impotent. He talked to a shrink twice a week for a year. The shrink told him to stay away from Manuel's. But every time he thought he was strong enough, he would return. And every time someone would shout, "Hey, Grandpa," and he would slink back to the psychiatrist. He had visions of becoming, along with Steve Newberry and the Newberry Salute, part of cop lore in Atlanta. His future was not bright.

Then there was Jack Tracy, a cop who inevitably was called Dick Tracy until several years before, when he was shot in the groin. Now he was known as Dickless Tracy. He did not like the name.

The only other person in the squad room was Caren Diamond, a new detective sent over on orders from the major in charge of CID. Jeremiah's boss, the captain in charge of homicide, had nothing to say about the transfer—he hadn't even known of it until a major called and said the new detective was on the way to the office—which caused Jeremiah to believe that the orders came from one of the deputy chiefs. That's all he needed, a detective with political pull. Jeremiah had been trying for more than a year to bring on another detective. No luck. Now all at once Caren Diamond shows up. A female homicide cop, the only thing more laughable than a female motorcycle officer.

Caren was a big woman, not plump or horsey—simply a big woman. And elegant—nicely tailored clothes, big and obviously expensive costume jewelry. She did not look like a cop. She was thirty-five, younger than the other homicide cops. But there was a crisp, professional air about her.

The male homicide detectives, all of whom, like Jeremiah, thought female detective was an oxymoronic expression, would be impressed by her appearance. After all, homicide cops were the best-dressed police officers in the city.

Jeremiah sighed and returned to his paperwork. All his life, women had caused him nothing but grief. He did not think or speak ill of his former wife, yet in his heart of hearts, he remembered her as a prudish and judgmental woman with the personality of a stump—and a woman who in bed was almost as lively as a stump. Why had he married her? He had left her for another woman. Two years later that woman had left him. In his dark and bleak moments of Celtic despair he appreciated the symmetry of what had happened. But for protective reasons he had since adopted a ricochet theory of dealing with women. He ricocheted through their lives for a night, or several nights, and then careened off into the darkness.

And then this Caren Diamond is thrown into his office. He looked at the singing lines of her breasts, her wide hips, and sighed in despair.

She was not a woman that he, no matter how drunk, would call Nessie.

He returned to business. He would have liked to put Caren into the assaults squad for several months to see if she had good informants, if she wrote good reports, how she handled stress, if her intuition was good. That was the normal procedure for a new detective assigned to homicide. But he needed help too badly. The backlog of homicides was too great. Once she visited the cold room with Dean Nichols, she would be tossed out on her own.

Once every rookie cop had had to visit the cold room and observe an autopsy. But that had been stopped. Jeremiah, however, insisted that all new homicide cops follow the time-honored practice.

He smiled when he thought of what Nichols would do. Before the autopsy began, he would have Caren lean over the corpse, nose to nose and eyeball to eyeball. He would tell her that this was so she could get past the feelings people have regarding the dead. While she was leaning over the corpse, Nichols would put his hand on the cadaver's abdomen and press hard, causing the cadaver's lips to flutter open as the residual air in the lungs was forced out, and Caren's face would be blasted by the cold, fetid wheeze.

If she cried out in disgust and horror and jumped away from the table, Nichols would be happy for days. He might actually smile.

Jeremiah opened the case file on his desk. Christopher Gowon, Jr., the son of the major's fiancée, had been dead less than a week and already the file was an inch thick. He rubbed his eyes.

He was suffering from information overload. Hundreds of crime-scene details kept running helter-skelter through his brain. Those details must be sorted out. The DNA test from the semen was the best evidence. The M.E. was sending the semen to the crime lab within the next day or so.

There were several good footprints tracked in blood down the hall of the house. One of the unknown prints lifted from the scene had been that of the victim. Perhaps the other belonged to the perpetrator. But it could belong to anyone who had visited the house.

Then there was the bite mark. Pinky Green thought it had ecclesiastical weight, and he was coming up with an average of two theories a day for what had happened. Old Pinky had ideas he hadn't even thought of yet.

In addition to the evidence, and there was a great deal of physical evidence, there was a chance of popping the guy when he returned for the major's fiancée. He was certain to go after her.

To add an ominous and nagging note to the investigation, there was the leak of information about the Nigerian intelligence file. Someone from either the mayor's or chief's office was leaking information to the perpetrator; otherwise, he would not have known of the intelligence file. And the file was the only thing taken from the home of the major's fiancée.

Jeremiah made a mental note to guard all information about the progress of the case. That would be almost impossible. Withholding information about a homicide from a superior officer could get him fired.

Overshadowing everything else was the omnipresent frisson of excitement that came with knowing this investigation, if brought to a speedy conclusion, could affect the senatorial election, only three weeks away. He could knock off a senatorial contender. It would be a fitting case on which to retire.

It was not often that homicide investigations had such ramifications. But, hell, Nixon had been kicked out of office because of a bungled burglary. What was so incredible about a homicide keeping a senatorial candidate from being elected?

Jeremiah caught himself. He could not afford to think like that. He must treat this only as a homicide case. Once the homicide was solved, then whatever happened, happened.

He rubbed his eyes again. He looked at his watch. Almost noon. Friday. The following morning he was taking the major out to Stone Mountain for the annual Scottish Games. Hearing several hours of bagpipe music would clear his head and let the intuition and insight bubble to the surface. He and the major could talk.

It would do Worthy good to get out of uniform, get out of the house, and walk around the rolling meadows where the games were held. That was tomorrow. Right now he had to deal with Friday. Friday afternoon was still ahead of him. And worse, Friday night.

It was on Fridays that the most vivid memory of his life reoccurred. Not every Friday, thank God, but on more Fridays than he liked to think about.

Jeremiah licked his lips. He wanted a drink. He had never managed to shake the Friday memories. He loathed the freshness of them. He loathed the impact of them. After all this time, it was as yesterday. His Celtic streak caused him to think it was part of his heritage, that those blessed by being Scottish must also bear the burden. And part of that burden was the growling, snapping animals that came unbidden and unwelcome out of some distant mental fen to yawp of things unpleasant.

The memories lasted only seconds but contained volumes. It was a Friday night. He was fourteen, the oldest child, and his father, the police chief in a small north Georgian mountain town and a man with whom he had fought constantly, had been dead only two weeks. Jeremiah was the man of the house, partners with his mother in supervising his two younger sisters.

It was not late when he came home that night. But for the first time in his life, his mother was not up waiting. She always waited when he was out. She said she could not sleep while he was away. But that Friday night when he came home, she was nowhere in sight. Her bedroom door was closed.

Jeremiah's reverie was broken when Dean announced to the squad room, "This town is going down the toilet."

"What's the matter?" Caren asked.

Dean took his cigar from his mouth and used it to point at the newspaper. "Says here that a chain of drugstores is giving free tests for colon cancer and that last year more than twenty thousand people responded."

"So?" Caren was puzzled.

"Think about it," Dean said. "To have the test done, you got to send in a sample of crap. Each sample contain probably half an ounce of crap. If twenty thousand people send in samples, that's ten thousand ounces of crap. That's more than six hundred pounds of shit in the U.S. mail. Our mail system is clogged with shit. Literally. Think about it."

Caren stared at him. "I'd rather not." She looked at Jeremiah and rolled her eyes.

Jeremiah smiled.

He knew how to break this mood. The one absolute cure for the Friday memories was to have lunch with friends at the Drug Enforcement Administration. Visiting DEA could cause even someone who was in a suicidal depression to become euphoric. The Atlanta DEA office was a blend of the bizarre and the unbelievable mixed with a liberal dose of the incredible.

He picked up the telephone and dialed his friend Ron McBride. Ron was an Irishman, which was almost as good as being a Scotsman, who supervised DEA's asset-forfeiture group. In the group were two blind women, three deaf women, and an administrative officer who was thirty-five but thought she was twenty.

And then there were the equal-opportunity hires. Ron was doing such an outstanding job in seizing assets of drug dealers that he had to hire people whose sole job was entering financial data into DEA computers. DEA had contracted with the city to hire forty computer operators. The city sent over forty hires who had no law enforcement background. Most of them did not have a high school education. None of them had any idea of security, the sensitive nature of the information they loaded into the computers, or the need for accuracy in their work. All they had was an attitude.

Ron had asked for a transfer. Anywhere. It was refused.

Ron told Jeremiah that a half dozen or so DEA agents were taking Sally, the administrative officer, out to lunch that day to celebrate her most recent divorce and that he was welcome to join them.

Jeremiah had not been gone five minutes when Caren looked up from her desk. "When are we going to the medical examiner's office?" she asked Nichols.

"Gimme a few minutes," Nichols said idly. He looked up from his scrapbook. "We'll go down there and observe an autopsy. That'll put me in the mood for lunch. Maybe stew." He checked for a reaction. There was none.

"Then we can go out and arrest some homeless people." Still no reaction. Nichols returned to his scrapbook.

Caren waited a moment. Then she stood up, walked across the room, and began skimming through the case file Jeremiah had been reading.

12

Tony the Dreamer drove slowly through downtown Atlanta. His car doors were locked and he was alert, eyes wary of every car, every pedestrian. Downtown Atlanta, with the exception of CNN Center, which seemed to throb with some sort of cosmic energy, was an empty and desolate place; the rotten and parasite-infested core of the city. Years earlier, the banks, law firms, insurance companies, real estate offices, all had moved from Five Points, the fabled heart of downtown Atlanta, north to Midtown.

Downtown Atlanta was an urban nightmare, one that the befuddled dream merchants at the Atlanta chamber of commerce still refused to recognize. The chamber, in its unswerving dedication to central Atlanta, remained downtown. And now the hosanna singers and the drum beaters at the chamber thought it was natural that in this bright and shining city on the hill, as they preferred to think of Atlanta, they should have their cars parked by armed security guards while they raced for the safety of an elevator. They saw nothing unusual in working behind locked office doors manned by still more armed guards. It was normal not to be able to walk city streets at noon and to be forced either to bring lunch or to have lunch brought to the office. And it was just part of living in the city for all employees to leave together after work, to cluster defensively together in the lobby while armed guards brought down their cars from the parking decks, and then to have guards check the nearby traffic light so they could dash out of the garage and through the light without stopping.

Among the cities of the world, Atlanta was unique in the degree to which it was concerned with image—only with image.

Like a floozy whose fancy clothes conceal a body covered with chancres and whose permanent smile disguised a mind made dotty by paresis, Atlanta continued to flounce and flirt.

Like Nineveh of old, the rejoicing city on the hill that thought it was the only city, Atlanta preened and strutted and became more unmanageable than New York and more barren than Detroit.

The city ignored and denied its lost sheep while it eulogized its fat cats.

The primal underbelly of Atlanta, crime and racism, both of which were denied by City Hall and local businessmen, had continued to grow until they dominated the private fears of most citizens. Gang warfare, robberies, multiple homicides—many with racial overtones—rapes, and a cornucopia of random violence became the daily bread of Atlantans in the early 1990s.

At the same time, any casual visitor to the city would think he had dropped in on Valhalla; that the cup of this city was running over with brotherly love; that all citizens, black and white together, were marching arm in arm toward the promised land.

The city boasted of a future that would never be while denying a present that was all too obvious. The civic emblem of the city was a phoenix rising from the ashes, but it should have been a prostitute blowing a trumpet. Nothing could better capture the true nature of Atlanta than could a strumpet with a trumpet.

The city had always been that way. From the very beginning it had been a city where fuzzy myth took precedence over hard and gritty reality. That was why Operation Bilal was taking place in Atlanta. That was why Tony the Dreamer had come to Atlanta.

Hundreds of Nigerian students attended college at the Clark–Atlanta University complex. And Atlanta had a large community of Nigerian expatriates. So there was nothing unusual about young Nigerians coming through the Atlanta airport—nothing, that is, except for the heroin they had strapped to their bodies or in their luggage. That heroin had raised millions of dollars in the past fifteen years—millions that, once laundered, funded the political aspirations of Frederick A. Carr.

In the early years, it had been Tony's job to supervise the heroin-smuggling operation, to control the sometimes overweening ambition of young Nigerians. God, he hated the Nigerians. The most venal and avaricious people on earth. All they thought of was the money they provided for Operation Bilal; they forgot that without Frederick A.

Carr, without the Hidden Iman, they were nothing but black people with money.

Acting as an enforcer for the drug smuggling operation had gradually shifted to becoming a back-channel Mr. Fixit for Frederick A. Carr during his years in Atlanta as the U.S. Attorney. Every corporation or movement or organization with a large staff—and Operation Bilal was all of these—needs an in-house son of a bitch, an enforcer, someone to say the unpleasant and to do the unspeakable. That was Tony the Dreamer.

Atlanta was the perfect city for Operation Bilal. In the beginning there were those who thought New York should be the springboard from which Islam would launch its most ambitious plan. But the large Jewish population in that city had the potential to cause a major security problem. When Jesse Jackson, America's charismatic avatar of chronic unemployment, referred to New York as "Hymietown" in the mid-1980s, he codified an anti-Semitism among blacks that long had been suspected by American Jews. So Operation Bilal found in Atlanta a warm and cozy place of gestation. Atlanta is a black city and there is more anti-Semitism among blacks than among whites. And because an ever growing number of Atlanta blacks were turning to Islam and new mosques were being built every year, there was considerable sympathy and support for Arab causes.

And the ultimate Arab cause, the only lasting Arab cause, is the destruction of Israel.

Tony's lips—he had the thin, tightly pressed lips of a Baptist minister who is sleeping with the ugly woman on the back row of the choir—stretched in what almost was a smile.

He turned north on Peachtree Street. The people he sought should be somewhere in the next few blocks.

Tony slowed as he passed through the maze of buildings at Peachtree Center. This was the turf of the Rod and Gun Club. They were prime suspects in several drive-by shootings in which rocket-propelled grenades and stinger missiles had been used to blast the headquarters of opposing gangs. The members were the sons of marriages between Mexicans and Americans. They denounced their Mexican background and preferred to be known as Anglos.

But Tony was interested in more personal things about the gang members. If what he had heard about these macho young men was true, then . . . well, he would find out for himself. He made an illegal right turn onto Martin Luther King Jr. Drive, the street known throughout Atlanta simply as MLK, drove slowly for a block, then made an illegal left-hand turn to pass along the east side of Peachtree Center.

Nothing. He crossed Peachtree again, then turned south. Still nothing. He turned west onto Harris Street and there they were, wearing the red and orange silk jackets upon the backs of which were affixed in considerable size and detail the insignia of the Rod and Gun Club. They were pissing against the wall of the Merchandise Mart, and it was this, as much as their colors, that identified them to Tony.

Hispanic emigrés, particularly those from Mexico, had problems with two laws in Atlanta. First, they never understood a city ordnance that said liquor could not be consumed within a hundred feet of a liquor store. They bought liquor, opened the bottle as they walked out the door, and began drinking. Cops constantly were arresting them in the parking lot of liquor stores. Second, they did not understand the law against urination in public. Such a law was against human nature. If they had to urinate, they did. And it mattered not where they were when the urge struck. There seems to be little chance the Hispanic community would assimilate into American society as had dozens of other ethnic groups over the past several hundred years. They are determined to drink booze in the parking lot of liquor stores and then piss on the side of the nearest building.

Now two young men were standing on the sidewalk by the side entrance of the Merchandise Mart—an ideal location whence to watch the door of the Capital City Club. No doubt they were waiting to mug any member who departed without a security guard.

Tony slowed as he approached. He stared intently, trying to determine if what he had heard about the members of this gang was true. One of the boys turned toward Tony. He slowed until he had almost stopped. He drew closer. He stared.

He could not determine if what he had heard was true. But there was enough evidence to make the cause worth pursuing.

He checked the rearview mirror. Nothing. And

there was no one ahead of him on the block before Peachtree Street. He stopped, set the parking brake, and opened the door. He stepped outside and walked to the rear of the car, stepping carefully over the gate of a storm drain, and opened the trunk. He stared inside, apparently confused.

One of the gang members looked at Tony almost in disbelief, looked at his partner, and smirked. He was a beefy kid, obviously a weight lifter—full of himself, his youth, and his strength. He opened his jacket and swaggered toward the slender man who was staring into the trunk of his car.

Followed by his partner, whose face seemed set in flint, he stepped off the curb and moved close to Tony.

"Hey, man," he said. His thumbs were hooked into his belt. "You."

Tony looked up and for a moment the gang member was startled. He was looking into the blackest eyes he had ever seen, eyes that seemed almost on fire. Unconsciously he looked to the side to make sure his partner was beside him.

"Yes," Tony said. His voice was very soft.

"The fuck you doing here, man? You know where you at?"

"Yes."

The gang member pulled back and stared more closely at Tony's black hair and dark skin. "Man, you a brother?" he asked with disdain.

"Yes" came the soft answer.

The gang member was feeling more confident. He had four inches and about fifty pounds on this guy. He looked at his partner and nodded toward

Tony. "Hear this shit? 'Yes. Yes. Yes,'" he mocked.
"All he says is yes." He bent over until his nose
was almost touching Tony's nose. "Can't you say
anything but yes? This is Rod and Gun Club country, man. Fuck you doing here?"

The gang member's partner stepped closer. But
he was still two steps away.

Tony shrugged in apparent diffidence. "I'm making some calculations."

The first gang member pulled back a half inch.
His brow wrinkled. "Calcu—the fuck you talking
about?"

The second gang member stepped forward. Now
he was close enough.

Tony smiled. It was an icy smile that did not
reach his dark, burning eyes. "I'm calculating
whether or not both of you will fit into the trunk."

The two gang members looked at each other in
disbelief. The first was so surprised that he slipped
into Spanish. "*Se caga en mi,*" he said to his companion. Then he caught himself, turned to Tony
and said, "If we gonna fit? . . . Man, you don't
know—"

Simultaneously, the two young men reached for
the pistols in their belts. They were not fast enough.
They had barely begun moving when Tony struck.
His extended fingers jammed high and hard into
the V of ribs on both young men. He hit as though
he were trying to punch through to their spines. He
hit with such shock and force that the eyes of the
two boys bulged, and they sprang onto their tip-
toes as their arms arched wide. The trauma to their
hearts rendered them unconscious. They would not

regain their senses for thirty seconds, maybe a full minute.

Before they could collapse, Tony swung the first gang member over the edge of the trunk. He caught the second over his shoulder in a fireman's carry, pivoted, and flipped him into the trunk. Then he swung the legs of the first gang member around until they were inside. It had taken about six seconds.

"My calculations were correct," Tony said softly. "You fit very nicely."

He pulled the pistols from the belts of the two men. Semi-automatic weapons with extended double-stacked clips that held twenty-four rounds. A lot of firepower. That is, for those who like guns. Tony turned, stooped, and tossed the two pistols into the storm drain.

With scraps of towels from the trunk, he blindfolded the two young men. Then he pulled a length of rope from the side of the trunk and tied it tightly around their ankles and wrists.

He would have to hit them again before he could take them into his house. Maybe a couple of times to get their attention and convince them it would be useless to fight. That was okay.

He looked over his shoulder. No traffic. He leaned forward and reached for the first of the gang members. Finding what he sought, he stopped and his eyes widened in astonishment. The stories were true. Tony repeated the procedure with the other gang member and found the same thing.

Tony straightened up and closed the trunk. He was anxious to get home.

13

"The way to hold a man is to give him exactly what he wants," Sally said. She spoke with the firm certitude of one who has been drinking for several hours. "Give a man what he wants. Any time. All the time. Do that and you'll never get divorced."

Sally looked up and down the long table filled with DEA agents and secretaries, then nodded in approval of her own wisdom. Her thick, tousled blond hair fell around her face. She tossed her head in a practiced maneuver, throwing her hair over her shoulder and emerging with a dazzling, if slightly droopy, smile that swept the dining room of the Ritz Carlton-Buckhead. DEA agents did not often congregate in such hushed and imposing surroundings. But the purpose of the party was to celebrate Sally's third divorce, and such a gathering needs at least the trappings of class and decorum.

Sally swirled a finger through her glass of bourbon, stuck the finger in her mouth, and sucked away the liquid. She licked her lips.

"But, Sally, we're here celebrating your divorce," one of the DEA agents said. "Your marriage didn't work. Does that mean you didn't give your husband what he wanted?"

The agent smiled. Sally, even at her most decorous, was flashy and outspoken. From the beginning of the lunch, she had dominated the conversation with ribald jokes and off-color remarks. Filled with the lunacy of the newly divorced and the need to prove the failure was not hers, she quickly responded to the DEA agent's remark.

"My divorce had nothing to do with that," she said. Her eyes danced with confidence. She was holding back information that would destroy the other person's argument. The DEA agent had interviewed enough people to know the signs.

"Oh?" he said.

Down the table, Jeremiah and Ron McBride were talking quietly, trying to ignore the ever increasing locus of intensity around Sally.

Jeremiah told Ron about the homicide and the Nigerian intelligence file, about the leak of information that he suspected came from either the office of the chief or the mayor. He told Ron of the physical evidence from the homicide: the footprint in the blood, enough semen to use for DNA tests, a piece of skin with an excellent bite mark, and a slightly fuzzy fingerprint. The problem was finding the person who had left the evidence behind.

"Funny you should mention Nigeria," Ron said. "I had a buddy, a guy I went through the academy with, who was country attaché at the embassy in Lagos when that coup went down." Ron took a long drink of beer. "He got killed in the turmoil after the coup. Nobody ever knew what happened." He shrugged.

He thought for a moment. "Somebody out there

knows something," he said. "No matter how careful this guy was, no matter how good he is, he made a mistake. He has made or will make a mistake. Somebody out there knows who he is. Ninety percent of the people in jail are there because of their own mouths. They talk to a wife or girlfriend or somebody in a bar. Somebody out there knows this guy. You just gotta find him."

Jeremiah shrugged. "I'll do it this afternoon." He sipped his scotch.

Ron pulled his pipe from his pocket, pushed at the tobacco, then sucked idly on the pipe. He frowned in concentration. "You're positive the kid was killed by a stranger?"

Jeremiah nodded. "He had been in the country only for a few days. It had to be a stranger."

"Who had the most to gain by killing the kid? The woman was the target. She brought the report out of Africa; she knew the background and could cause whoever is behind this a lot of grief. Why would someone involved in this kill a kid who is not connected? And in such a brutal fashion?"

"You think it might have been somebody local?"

Ron shrugged. "I'm thinking out loud. I don't think they could hire a contract killer who would have branched out like that. My feeling is the killer is someone who is directly involved in this plan to elect a Muslin senator."

He shook his head. "Fucking Arabs."

"What do you mean?"

"First, not all Muslims are Arabs, but almost all Arabs are Muslims," Ron said. "Islamic literature is in Arabic. The Arabs are the center of Islam. But in the entire history of the world, the Arabs have never put together any sort of long-range plan like this. They are terrorists. They fight among themselves so much that they can agree only on immediate plans, such as terrorism."

Jeremiah was not sure he understood the cadenza about Arabs. He pressed ahead. "But why would someone involved in the plan take a chance like that? I'm gonna catch this guy and that's going to blow the whole thing out of the water."

"They obviously thought the risk of exposing the plan justified killing the woman."

"So if the killer is somebody involved, he almost certainly is a Muslim."

Ron nodded. He sucked on his unlighted pipe.

"Most Muslims are black?"

Again Ron nodded. "In Atlanta, yes. Willy likes to convert to Islam. But don't leave out the Arabs."

Ron had been an intelligence officer for a tank battalion in the 1991 Gulf War. And like many American soldiers who have fought foreign wars, he continued to hate the enemy long after the war was over. American soldiers came home from World War II hating Japanese and Germans; they came home from Korea hating Koreans and Chinese; they came home from Southeast Asia hating the Vietnamese. Ron came home from the Persian Gulf hating Arabs. All Arabs.

Ron studied his pipe. "I mention the Arabs again only because of the sexual angle. I know the general rule is that people most often kill within their own racial or ethnic group. But I don't think Willy could have committed the homicide you describe.

The element of vengeance makes me think it was an Arab. Arabs have turned vengeance into an art form. And the sexual angle adds to that."

Ron waved his pipe. "Let me tell you about Arabs," he said. "Arabs are men who live in the assholes of little boys and keep their eyes toward heaven. Sex is part of paradise. But Arab men don't want to wait until they get to paradise."

Ron stopped. A waiter stood across the table flicking an imperious finger toward the pipe.

"I'm not smoking it," Ron said.

The imperious finger waved again. The waiter pinched his nostrils with his thumb and forefinger, grimaced, and shook his head. He motioned for Ron to take the pipe outside. Ron returned the pipe to his pocket.

"This town's going to hell," he grumbled. "That faggy prick waves his finger at me again, I'm going to break it off and shove it up his ass."

He turned to resume his conversation with Jeremiah. But Sally's voice, rising in mock outrage, carried down the table and interrupted them.

"Oh!" she said. "What does 'Oh' mean?" Before the DEA agent could explain, she continued. "Listen to me. I did things for Donny that few other wives even know about. And if they did know, they wouldn't do." She laughed and waved her hand expansively. "Hell, you've seen the pictures."

Several DEA agents rolled their eyes. Everyone in the office, including secretaries and contract workers, had seen Sally's pictures. Even the blind secretaries had been told about the pictures. Sally liked to photograph herself and her former husband in various sexual acts and then pass the pictures around the office. She saw nothing unusual in this. She was proud of her body and the esoteric uses to which she put it.

Donny, her former husband, was a helicopter pilot for the city, and one of Sally's most famous pictures was a Polaroid he had shot while flying over downtown Atlanta. The helicopter was tilted in a steep turn. The pictures showed Sally's head in her husband's lap, and, over his wide-eyed expression, could be seen downtown Atlanta and the domed stadium.

"Great shot of the dome," Sally invariably said when she showed the picture. "But notice the blow job. The dome was packed for a football game that day. It was a bowl game. Eighty thousand people. I gave Donny a blowjob over eighty thousand people. Nobody has ever done that before." Then she would laugh and say, "He was blown away."

Jeremiah had tuned Sally out for a moment. He was thinking of what Ron had said about a possible Muslim suspect. "It fits," he said.

Ron agreed. "Just like the wops when they came to America around the turn of the century. Had nothing. Life was cheap. They turned to crime. Kill some son of a bitch as quick as they would look at him. Then they got legitimate. In the eighties and early nineties Willy replaced the Italians as the most violent. Mainly crack dealers. Geek monsters. Vicious. Kill you for five dollars. Then they began to clean up their act and try to get respectable. That's when the spics moved in. I thought they were the worst of all. They'll cut your ass from here

to next Tuesday. The meanest geek monster in
Carver Homes or Dixie Hills or East Lake Mead-
ows will stand up and say sir when a Cuban or
Mexican walks by. Hispanics are violent as hell."

"But Muslims are meaner?"

Ron looked across the dining room, where the
waiter was peering at him through a small window
in the door that led into the kitchen.

"I know they are," he said. "All the other groups,
the wops, Willy, the spics, they all wanted their
share of the pie, their part of the American dream.
Not the Muslims. They want the whole pie. And
then they want to throw it out the window. Look at
history. Every place they've ever gone they've im-
posed Islamic law. They don't want to assimilate.
They want to force everybody to assimilate with
them."

He nodded toward the waiter who still peered
through the window.

"I should have known better," he said in anger.
He pointed toward the waiter. "I thought at a
restaurant like this we could be above the fruited
plain. Wrong again. Before I die, I want to see two
things: a Atlanta restaurant with straight waiters
and a University of Georgia football team with
white running backs."

Jeremiah nodded. But he was not paying attention to the waiter. He sipped his scotch and thought
of what Ron had said.

"I was focusing on the wrong thing."

"Your perp is a wacky Muslim. Although that's
redundant," Ron said.

He looked around the dining room. An elderly

couple sat at an adjacent table. Across the room was a table of businessmen and another table of three couples. A waiter stood near the wall, where he folded napkins and stacked them on a table. No sign of the waiter on smoke patrol. Ron stuck his hand in his pocket and seized the comfort of his pipe. He reached for a bowl of fruit sitting on the table and slid it closer, then pulled his pipe from his pocket and hid it, clutched in his hand, behind the bowl of fruit.

Jeremiah shrugged. "I'm going to call the major. He's not supposed to work on this case, but he can help me. Tomorrow morning before we go to Stone Mountain, I'm going to canvass a couple of black neighborhoods and ask about young Muslims, a guy with a jagged tooth."

Ron was about to respond when Sally's voice rose high over the conversation. "I even did menage à trois for Donny." She looked around the table. "How many other wives would do that?"

The old man at the next table paused a moment, then continued eating. At the table of businessmen, two diners glanced toward the DEA table. The waiter against the wall continued folding napkins, expression unchanged.

"Don't forget deep throat," Sally said. She laughed and added almost bitterly. "Man's favorite pastime." She flounced her blond hair and stared at the DEA agent who had been baiting her. "Trouble with being good at that is it's all you men want. You forget there are other things to do."

The DEA agent, who used tradecraft even in casual conversations, neatly avoided the shot she lobbed across his bow by going on the offensive. "Sally, you must have staged some of those pictures you have," he said. "Otherwise, if you can do all you say, why would Donny divorce you?"

Sally's smile disappeared. "I divorced him." Her voice rose. "He didn't divorce me. I divorced him." She picked up her glass of bourbon and took a big swallow. "He was the most boring asshole I've ever seen. He could be in a twelve-car pileup where twenty people died and come home and make it sound like he was reading a phone book. He was DULL." She stuck out her tongue, pointed a finger toward her open mouth, and made a gagging sound of disgust.

"Well, maybe," said the agent.

Sally stared. "You listen to me," she said, enunciating each word loud and clear. "I can deep throat any man alive."

Ron shook his head. "Sally is about to go into orbit," he said. "Sit back and watch."

Jeremiah laughed. This was twice in recent days that he had gone to lunch with people who created a disturbance. Maybe there was something in the air that caused people to go bonkers.

Sally looked up and down the table. "All the way," she added.

"Donny was a helicopter pilot," said the young DEA agent. "That's not much of a frame of reference."

Another agent concurred by nodding his head. "Hell, a high school cheerleader can deep throat a helicopter pilot. It's not like it was a real man."

Even the blind secretaries laughed.

Sally half stood in her chair, raised an arm overhead, and repeated, "I said *any* man. I can deep
throat *any* man alive." She looked around. "I guar-
antee it."

"Prove it," challenged one of the younger agents.

"You wish," Sally laughed. She reached for her
glass of bourbon and tilted it back.

The DEA agents looked at each other and
shrugged.

Sally was losing her audience. "By God, I will
prove it," she said. She looked around and saw the
bowl of fruit in front of Ron. "Slide that bowl of
fruit down here, big boy," she said.

Ron moved his pipe under the table and with his
other hand pushed the bowl of fruit down the
table. Sally plucked a banana from the bowl and
held it high. "I can prove it with this," she said.

"What is it?" one of the blind secretaries asked.

"A banana," said one of the agents.

"How big is it?" the secretary said.

"Helicopter-pilot size," the agent said. "Not very
big."

Sally flounced her hair, tossed the banana onto
the table, and sat down. "Okay, Mr. Smarty," she
said. "You pick the banana. You get the biggest banana you can find and I'll deep throat it."

The businessmen across the room were staring
openly at Sally. One of them looked as if he wanted
to join the party. The old man at the next table was
dawdling over his food and cutting his eyes toward
Sally. The waiter against the wall was folding napkins, apparently oblivious to everything but his
work.

"Push that down here," the young agent said, motioning toward the bowl of fruit. He picked through it, then shrugged. "They're all helicopter-pilot size. Anybody could do what you're talking about with these things."

He looked up just as the imperious waiter, the one who did not like Ron's pipe, emerged from the kitchen. The agent motioned him over.

The waiter stopped a few feet from the table. He looked at his watch and raised his eyebrows. Eventually he spoke. "Yes?"

"You got any more bananas back there? Big ones?" the agent asked.

The waiter looked at the bowl of fruit. "Is anything wrong with our fruit?"

"There's too much of it," Ron growled. "Too many fruits."

The young agent held his hands about a foot apart. "What we want is an industrial-strength banana," he said. "The world's biggest banana. Go back there and find us one."

"I'm very sorry, sir, but those are all we have."

"Could you bring me another scotch?" Jeremiah asked. "And my friend here will have a beer."

The waiter sighed and disappeared.

Ron, impatient with the young agents, leaned forward. He pointed his finger to the young agent who had done most of the talking. "You go down to the Disco Kroger on Piedmont and get the biggest goddamn banana they got in the produce department." He turned to another. "You go down to Cub Foods and do the same." He pointed again. "You go north to the grocery store at Cherokee

Plaza and buy the biggest banana you see." He raked his glance over the three agents. "Use your blue lights. First one back gets a drink on me. The one with the biggest banana gets two drinks. If you are first back and you have the biggest banana, you get next Friday off. Now get outa here."

The agents left the table so fast that two of them knocked over their chairs. Thirty seconds later, the wail of sirens came from the driveway as three unmarked cars, blue lights flashing from the roofs, screeched from the driveway of the hotel, forced their way through the red light on Peachtree Road, and split in three different directions.

"Federal agents always use sirens and blue lights when they go grocery shopping?" Jeremiah asked, white eyebrows climbing in curiosity.

Sally leaned across the table. "Wouldn't you?" she asked.

Jeremiah studied her for a moment. "Now that you mention it . . . "

He looked up. One of the businessmen from across the room was standing by the table, his hand on Jeremiah's shoulder. Jeremiah looked up and shrugged the hand away.

The businessman, eyes on Sally, ignored him. Sally smiled.

"You fellows having a party?" the businessman asked.

"Yeah, a private party," Jeremiah growled.

"Sounds like you're having fun." The businessman could not take his eyes off Sally. She smiled again and tossed her hair.

"Sir, he told you this was a private party," Ron

said. His voice was hard. "Would you mind going back to your table?"

The businessman looked at Ron and laughed. "You fellows are not very hospitable, are you?" He turned back to Sally. "I bet you are a lot more hospitable."

He patted Jeremiah on the back.

Like most police officers, Jeremiah disliked being patted on the back by civilians. He stood up, pulled a switchblade from his belt, snicked open the blade, stuck it under the businessman's chin, and in a deadly whisper said, "Go away."

The businessman blanched, turned, and slowly walked away. He was followed by Sally's laughter.

Ron laughed. "I didn't know Atlanta police officers carried knives," he said.

"Good ones do," Jeremiah said.

It was no more than two or three minutes later that the businessman, bolstered by comments from his companions that no one would create a scene in the Ritz Carlton, returned to the table.

With no preamble he seized Jeremiah's shoulder and pulled hard, twisting Jeremiah around in the chair. "That little knife of yours doesn't scare me, buddy," he said. He turned and smiled at Sally.

Jeremiah bolted upright, pulled his big semi-automatic pistol from his belt, and with considerable force rammed it under the businessman's chin, forcing his eyes toward the ceiling.

"How about this little nine-millimeter, asshole?" he whispered.

A gasp of pain and horror came from the businessman. Without saying a word, he crabbed away—not toward his table, but toward the front door. He did not look back.

A few minutes later, everyone in the dining room looked up at the wail of converging sirens. The first car arrived with a screech of brakes. An agent jumped out clutching a banana and raced through the doors, pushed a bellhop aside, and turned left to run at full tilt through the bar and into the café. Before the guests could recover, two more cars squealed to a stop and men, also carrying bananas, jumped out, leaving their car doors open as they raced into the lobby.

Augustine, one of the older agents, who had gone to Cub Foods, arrived first and plopped a banana, an enormous banana, on the table in front of Sally, blew out his breath, and looked around the table in triumph.

"Guess I won," he said. He turned to Ron. "I called on the radio, got a phone patch, and called the store manager. Had him meet me at the curb. I barely slowed when I came through the parking lot. Gave him five bucks and was outa there. Told him it was federal business." He looked around the table. "Guess I won," he repeated.

Ron shook his head in disbelief. "You used the radio?" he said. "That moron we work for heard your siren over the radio."

DEA agents were under specific orders about using sirens. Usage had to be explained in writing.

Augustine shrugged. "What the hell is he gonna do? Transfer me to DEA?" He laughed, pointed to the banana, looked at Sally, and said, "Okay, little darling. Deep throat that."

At that moment the other two DEA agents raced into the café, both breathing hard, both holding up a banana. Augustine stepped forward, took their bananas, and put them on the table. His clearly was the winner.

"Yep, I won." He pushed the banana toward Sally.

Sally eyed the banana. "You don't think I can do it?" she said. Her green eyes challenged him.

By now the table of businessmen—their numbers fewer by one—had turned away from their table, hands folded neatly in their laps, faces expressionless, as they watched. The elderly man at the adjacent table kept sneaking sidelong glances while his wife urged him to finish his meal. The waiter against the wall was still folding napkins.

Sally picked up the banana.

"We can't see from down here," Augustine said. "Stand up."

Sally stood up. She weaved a bit as she smiled benevolently upon those staring at her. "I'll make it easy for you," she said. She turned, hiked up her skirt, and stepped onto her chair. She used a foot to push her drink aside, then stepped atop the table. Her hands slid down her hips and her finger pulled at her skirt, hiking it up her thighs.

Sally, who could make a four-star production out of walking to the water cooler, was in her glory. She was particularly proud of her legs, and the higher rose her skirt, the wider grew her smile.

The imperious waiter burst through the door to the kitchen. He was going to stop this nonsense.

Standing atop tables was not allowed at the Ritz Carlton.

Ron saw the waiter steaming in their direction, stood up, and moved around the table. He reached out and seized the waiter's arm. From inside his coat he pulled the wallet containing his badge. He flashed the badge, holding back his coat so the waiter could see his pistol.

"Back off, Tinker Bell," he growled. "This is federal business. You say one word and I'll put you in jail for interfering with federal officers. You got that?"

The waiter, eyes wide, backed up a step and nodded. "Yes, sir," he said, scurrying backward a few steps before turning and retiring to the kitchen. Ron grinned, pulled his pipe from his pocket, stuck it into his mouth, and waved for Sally to continue.

Sally stood with her legs apart so her skirt would remain hiked around her hips. She smiled, tossed her hair over her shoulder, and motioned for Augustine to hand her the winning banana.

She slowly peeled the banana, rolling her hips from side to side. One strip of peel pulled slowly down, then another, then another. She shifted the banana from her left hand to her right and dropped the peel onto the bowl of fruit.

"Big banana," Augustine said.

"I've seen bigger," Sally said.

Augustine blushed as the other agents laughed.

"How big is it?" one of the blind secretaries asked.

"Bigger than helicopter-pilot size," said one of the agents.

Sally suddenly had an idea. "Anyone have a camera?" she asked. This was an opportunity to add a new picture to her collection—one she could put on the bulletin board, maybe even fax to every DEA office in the country.

"Forget the camera," Augustine said. "We're all witnesses. If you want a picture, we'll talk to the APD artist in homicide and have him do a drawing. Buie can arrange that."

Sally looked at Jeremiah. "Can you do that?"

"Absolutely."

"I'll be in a painting," Sally said. She raised her eyes toward the ceiling. Then she returned to the business at hand. She flexed her knees and bent her back until her hips were thrust forward. Her left hand, fist clenched, was high in the air. Her head tilted back until her hair dangled freely. She turned the banana and pulled it downward until it touched her lips. After a brief pause she pushed the banana through her lips, deeper and deeper until it disappeared. She moved her right hand away. The banana could not be seen.

In what sounded like a prayer of gratitude, the old man at the next table slowly said, "Great God Almighty."

His wife sighed.

The businessmen burst into spontaneous applause.

Jeremiah shook his head. "Women who drink bourbon will do anything," he said.

Sally pulled the banana from her mouth and held it overhead. She turned and bowed toward both ends of the table, waved to the still applauding businessmen, then threw back her head and laughed. She stayed atop the table, skirt still pulled around her hips. "Jeremiah," she said. "Can you send the artist over to DEA later today while everyone's memory is fresh?"

Jeremiah's white eyebrows rose. He smiled. "Sally, this is not something one forgets."

"Oh, you're sweet," she said. "Would you like a copy of my painting?"

"I would be flattered."

"Will you put it in your office?"

"If you don't mind."

"I'd like that." She clasped her hands together. "Just think. A painting of me in homicide." She did a quick shuffle.

Jeremiah looked around the dining room in appreciation. The Friday afternoon blues were gone. He felt much better. He smiled at the expression on the old man at the next table. The businessmen still stared at Sally, and the waiter against the wall was still folding napkins. "You fellows work long hours," Jeremiah said to the waiter.

The waiter, eyes on Sally, shrugged. "Mister, I been off duty an hour."

14

About the time Jeremiah was ordering another drink at the Ritz Carlton, an investigator for the Fulton County Medical Examiner was entering the men's bathroom on the second floor of the M.E.'s office.

The investigator had been a homicide cop for twenty years before retiring and hiring on with the medical examiner's staff. The job was easy and the hours were regular. If a death was not a homicide—that is, if it was from natural causes—it belonged to the M.E.'s office rather than to homicide. Most of the cases were easy: old people who checked out after a heart attack or a stroke.

He never looked at their faces. Only civilians, who thought of bodies as people, looked at the faces. He did not even consider them people, just material to be transported to the morgue.

The investigator, a misnomer of a title, was burned out. All he looked forward to was putting in another four years. Then he would be vested with both the city and the county pension system. He would retire.

In the investigator's coat pocket was a cork-sealed glass tube containing gauze swabs. The swabs were heavy with semen taken from the rectum of a homicide victim. A sticker on the outside of the tube indicated that the homicide officer in charge of the case was a "SGT. J. BUIE."

The investigator entered the stall, took off his coat, and draped it from a hook on the back of the door, then lowered his pants and sat down. He stretched forward and adjusted his coat where he could easily reach the pocket. Then he unrolled a long section of toilet paper, folded it several times, and placed it across the top of his lowered pants. He began fondling himself. A moment later he was masturbating.

The investigator ejaculated on the folded toilet paper. Several moments later, when his breathing slowed, he carefully reached for his coat and removed the glass tube. The cork he placed on the floor. He fished into the coat pocket again and removed a small package containing fresh swabs. With a pencil he fished the sodden swabs out of the tube and dropped them between his legs into the toilet. He counted the swabs. There were two. He used two fresh swabs to soak up the semen on the toilet paper. These swabs he pushed into the glass tube, which was resealed with the cork. The tube was returned to his coat pocket.

The investigator cleaned himself, flushed the toilet, and stood up. As he pulled up his pants, he looked down to make sure no swabs remained in the toilet. He opened the door and shrugged on his coat. As he washed his hands, he stared into the mirror over the sink. He adjusted his heavily slicked-down hair, pulling the long strands across the bald spot. It did not work. The bald spot, shiny with hair tonic, gleamed under the fluorescent lights. The investigator sighed and dried his hands. As he left the bathroom he casually glanced at his watch.

After he transported the glass tube to the crime lab, he would have time for a couple of beers at Manuel's Tavern. He could afford to celebrate.

He had just made five thousand dollars.

15

Single-malt scotch, the liquid gold of Scotland, can cause a man to feel gratified, fortified, and transmogrified—maybe even sanctified. But by mid-afternoon Friday, Sergeant Jeremiah Buie had transcended these stages to become what he called "beatified," which is to say he was in a beatific mood, one in which he looked upon the world with gentle eyes and a forgiving heart. He had achieved a state of grace.

Going out with the DEA crowd had been a good idea. Generous amounts of Jura scotch had been a better idea. Now he could fend off the snarling black Celtic dogs that chose Fridays to gather in the dark recesses of his mind.

Thoroughly beatified, he planned to swing by the office for a minute and then go home, where he would have a few more drinks of Jura, the finest single-malt Scotch made, and—if the dogs got too close or growled too loudly—haul out the pipes.

His shoulders were back and his green eyes were dancing when he strode into the homicide offices. He stopped at the front desk and checked his inbox. No mail and no phone calls. Good.

Buie looked around the office. It was almost time

for the shift change, and most of the evening-watch detectives were in the office; several of them were milling around Caren Diamond's desk, grinning, scratching their balls, and trying to see down her sweater.

One detective, everyone called him Alpo, wasn't even trying to hide his lechery. Alpo got his name because every case he worked on turned into dog shit. At Manuel's Tavern the bartenders thought his name was Al Po. The younger bartenders called him "Mr. Po."

Alpo was one of the few homicide cops banished from the ring of camaraderie that tied the officers together. For one thing, he had the disgusting habit of dropping his false teeth into his coffee and sloshing them around with a pencil before returning them to his mouth and sucking coffee from the crevices.

Second, no black officer would be his partner because he carried a couple of steak knives inside his coat, cheap knives he had bought from a television advertisement. He liked to talk about how, if he were involved in a shootout with Willy, that he would throw down one of the steak knives and claim the shooting had been in self-defense.

Jeremiah didn't like Alpo and had twice refused to allow his transfer to the day watch. Jeremiah believed homicide cops were special. Anyone could stop a speeder or lock up a drunk. But only the best could solve a murder. Alpo was not one of the best.

Buie took a long look at Caren. Today she was wearing a black sweater with the top three buttons unbuttoned, a black leather mini-skirt, and black stockings. She wore a lot of jewelry—not simple jewelry, but triple-layer, fan-shaped rhinestone earrings, a heavy silver necklace with a pendant that was lost somewhere under her sweater, and three or four rings on each hand, a combination that on anyone else would look cheap and tarty. On her it looked exotic. Come to think of it, she was an exotic woman. Perhaps it was the green eye shadow she wore, eyeshade that emphasized her big dark eyes. Maybe it was the full, pouty lips. Or maybe it was her eclectic taste in clothes. The day before she had worn a floor-length cotton dress and the day before that a severe gray suit with a white high-necked Victorian blouse. She dressed up everyday, and everyday someone commented on her clothes. It was as if she had been indulged as a baby and dressed up in different outfits each day so relatives could nod and smile in appreciation and the practice had carried over into adulthood.

Whatever it was, Caren Diamond was a woman who did not mind standing out in a crowd. She wanted to stand out. It took a lot of poise, even chutzpa, to wear the clothes and accessories she wore, and not every woman could do it, just as not every man could wear an ascot.

Buie watched. Alpo, lechery virtually oozing from his pores, was leaning over Caren's desk telling a joke. She stared at him, listening to his palaver as if he were the only person in the world, and at the punch line she leaned back in her chair, clapped her hands in appreciation, and laughed— an exuberant, gutsy laugh.

But Buie noticed that her eyes were veiled, almost distant. And he realized she was a thousand miles away. Whatever she was thinking of, it was not Alpo. Unlike many bright women, she did not seek confrontations with men who were her intellectual inferiors.

As Caren leaned back, her eye caught his and she immediately stood up, waved aside the cluster of men around her desk, and walked across the room toward Jeremiah. Behind her, a half-dozen detectives held their breath and watched the leather skirt bunch and twist as it fought to contain the movements of her hips.

"Goodgodamightydamn," Alpo said, making no effort to lower his voice. "Her legs reach all the way up to her ass. We ought to make her the morale officer."

"Hello, boss," she said.

"Anything going on?" Behind Caren, the detectives stood as if mesmerized. Jeremiah nodded down the hall. "Let's go to my office," he said.

She smiled in appreciation, put her hand on his arm, and said, "Thanks."

That was something else Jeremiah had noticed about her. She was a toucher. When she talked to someone she often touched their arm or shoulder. The childlike innocence of the gesture caused her touch to be almost electric.

"Leave the door open," Jeremiah said as they entered his small office. He sat on the edge of his desk and waved toward a chair against the wall. "Sit down."

But Caren slowly closed the door, pausing to peer down the hall. And in that moment, the Friday long ago, the reason Fridays were dog days for Jeremiah, came flooding back with such strength that for a moment he was overwhelmed. He gasped at the memory.

The door to his mother's bedroom had been closed that Friday night. Thinking that, for the first time ever, she had gone to sleep while he was out, he tiptoed down the hall toward his bedroom. As he undressed, he looked out the rear window and saw a red car parked under a cedar tree near the back of the lot. It was clearly visible in the moonlight. He instantly recognized the car; he had seen it many times. It belonged to a couple who were his parents' closest friends. On Friday nights, as far back as he could remember, the two families had had dinner together, usually at a restaurant over the mountain in Dillard.

Jeremiah walked down the hall and knocked softly on his mother's closed bedroom door. He heard movement followed by rustles and mumbles and anxious whispers. Then, inexplicably, the small record player in his mother's room began playing, and he heard the rousing sounds of the old big band recording, "Stomping at the Savoy." Even today he hated that song.

After a while the bedroom door cracked and his mother peered through—just as Caren was doing—and in a peremptory tone said, "What is it?"

Why didn't she open the door and talk to him?

Almost embarrassed, he told her about the car. She said Mack, that was the family friend, was traveling and wanted to leave his car at the house.

What a flimsy lie she was telling. His mother was lying to him. Mack was in the bedroom.

He wanted to shout that Mack lived only two miles away and why didn't he leave the car at home with his wife? But he did not. Meekly he returned to his bedroom.

He was still awake when his mother, wearing only a light robe and holding Mack's hand, tiptoed through his bedroom toward the back door. It was almost dawn.

As his mother stood on the back porch waving, Jeremiah rose up in bed and saw Mack's red car, showing no lights, ease across the backyard and down the long driveway toward the road.

Several months later, while returning home at 3:00 A.M., Mack collided with a truck loaded with pigs. His body catapulted through the windshield of his car and through the wooden frame of the pig truck. His body was so mutilated by the pigs that no one ever knew if he had been killed by the crash or by the pigs. The local newspaper, a small weekly, published a story saying Mack had had a fatal accident while returning home from an out-of-town job. But Jeremiah suspected he had been at the house again.

As was the macabre fashion at the time, a small white cross was erected near the spot where he died. It was to remind other drivers that here a fatality had occurred, to be a careful driver.

Every time Jeremiah passed the spot, even years later when the cross had been removed, he felt a measure of satisfaction.

It was not until Jeremiah reached his late thirties

that he became aware of the underlying philosophy that controlled his dealings with other people: Everyone, soon or later, will betray you. He looked back and realized why his relations with women had been so transitory. He expected them to be unfaithful. Before that could happen, he usually ended a relationship. Or he deliberately created a scenario that left the woman no choice but to move on.

Do it to them before they do it to you.

Now he was fifty, and even though he could understand, in an intellectual sense, that it was fruitless to hold onto the past, he could not control the old emotions. He became angry every time he realized anew he still was influenced by that Friday night long ago.

Jeremiah snapped out of his reverie. Caren was speaking. She had closed the door, turned around, and was looking at him in a peculiar way.

"What is it?" she asked.

"I'm sorry," he said.

She paused. What caused the sergeant to go away like that?

"I wanted to say that I know you don't like women police officers, especially in homicide," she said. "I know you didn't want me here. Thanks for giving me a chance."

Jeremiah nodded. "You're smart and you're doing a good job." He looked at his watch. He was uncomfortable with Caren. "Well, I had no mail and no phone calls," he said. "I was going to call the major, but I can do that from home." His eyebrows arched. "While I'm drinking scotch," he added.

He paused and stared at her curiously. "What are you doing this evening?"

Caren looked at Jeremiah for a long moment. She smiled and shrugged. "It's Friday. I had planned to—"

"I forgot," he interrupted. "Your sabbath begins at sundown."

"Yes, but—"

"Those evening watch guys bother you?"

Caren's smile slowly disappeared. "I can handle it."

He reached into the desk, pulled out a key, and gave it to her. "This is the key to my office. Come in here if you want some privacy."

"Thank you." Slowly she reached for the key.

"I'll be at home. My beeper's on."

Caren nodded.

Jeremiah walked through the door toward the elevator. He pressed the button, entered, and went down.

He no longer felt beatified.

16

The young Mexican gang member, the beefy youth who was a weight lifter, looked up at Tony and shook his head. Even though he lay on the floor, hands and feet bound, the kid was defiant.

The second gang member, also bound, said nothing, but his eyes followed every move Tony made. He was waiting.

"I ain't one of them perverts," the beefy kid said, raising his head to glare at Tony. "Try that shit with me, man, and I'll break your fucking back."

Tony's tight lips stretched in a parody of a smile as he walked across the small living room of his house. He pulled the *jambiya* from under his shirt and held it, point down, toward the boy's face. His smile increased when he saw the quick flash of fear in the boy's eyes. Those who talked the most about their strength and toughness were the first to fold when they confronted true power.

Tony jabbed the curved knife toward the boy's face. As he expected, the boy closed his eyes and flinched. In that moment Tony reached down, seized the boy's left shoulder, and quickly pulled him over on his stomach. The gang member barely realized what had happened when Tony dropped, one knee striking hard in the boy's kidney and causing his body to arch in pain. As the boy's head rose off the floor, Tony reversed the *jambiya*. He slammed the pommel of the knife hard into the boy's temple. The boy's body relaxed and slumped to the floor.

Tony stood up, glanced once at the limp body at his feet, then smiled as he looked across the room. The second gang member stared as if transfixed.

"Am I going to have to do this to you?" Tony asked in his soft voice.

The gang member continued to stare. But in the black, burning pools of oil that were Tony's eyes, he saw nothing but his own mortality. His eyes dropped. Slowly he shook his head.

Tony smiled, picked up the *jambiya*, slid the point under the unconscious boy's collar, and walked the blade down his back, nearly parting the shirt. When he reached the belt, he pushed harder and the blade slid through the belt. He turned the blade slightly and ran it along the back of the boy's right leg. He did the same with the left leg. Except for the sleeves of the shirt bunched around the boy's elbows, the young man was nude. Tony stared for a long moment, admiring the muscles in the boy's back, the trim, hard buttocks, the oak-like legs.

He had to find out if the stories were true that he had heard about the gang members. He stuck his toe under the boy's hip and pushed until the limp body was face up. As the body rolled over, the right arm was flung wide and thudded against the floor.

Tony stared.

The stories were true.

* * *

A keening wind was tossing pieces of paper down Marietta Street as Tony drove into a parking lot across the street from the Omni Hotel. Dust-filled air muted the glow of streetlights as Tony looked around. No other cars were in the lot. The streets were empty. No pedestrians, not even conventioneers, would be crazy enough to be on the street in this part of town at this hour of the night. He reached over and removed the blindfold from the young man who sat next to him; the second gang member. The boy's head drooped. His hands were clasped together so tightly they trembled.

"Remember what I told you," Tony said. It was not a question.

The boy nodded. He would not look at Tony.

"Everything."

Again the boy nodded.

"Get out."

The boy slowly raised his head and looked at Tony, wondering if this were a trick, if he were about to be . . .

"Get out," Tony repeated.

Keeping his frightened eyes on Tony, as if he expected a horrible retribution, the gang member reached for the door handle with his right hand, opened it, and eased from the car. The sound of the wind increased. The boy wanted to move faster, to get away, but he was in such pain that he could hardly stand. And worse than the physical pain, far worse, was the humiliation in which he had been immersed for the past several hours. Humiliation and a fear he had not known was possible. He stared at the ground, wondering if the soft-spoken man was about to change his mind; wondering if there was some diabolical deception at work here; wondering if he was about to die.

"Remember what will happen to you," Tony said. "The same thing that happened to your friend."

The young man nodded and backed away a few steps before turning and slowly shuffling across the parking lot. Tony looked at his watch. After he disposed of the body in the backseat, he would take a bath and say his prayers.

Then he would go for the woman.

Tony drove north up the bold ridge of Peachtree Street and over the bridges of the downtown connector. The bridges were high and exposed to the full force of the wind that bludgeoned the city. Tony's car swayed and shuddered. The relentless wind brought back memories of another time, a long-ago time that gave birth to Operation Bilal.

The harmattan had been blowing for three weeks, blowing until day was like night and all existence was dreary. The dry, sand-filled wind from the Sahara had overcome even the equatorial humidity of Lagos, a city built on islands, and made the air so dry that throats were parched and tempers shortened. Some feared the wind had stolen their souls.

Still the harmattan blew. The seemingly omnipresent winds were made more dreadful by the fact they had arrived early this year. Usually the winds blew during the winter. This year they had begun in late summer.

Only a person filled with commitment and overflowing with religious zeal would ignore the enervating wind and venture onto the hazardous streets of Lagos.

Adamu Zahir was such a man. He was an assassin. And it was a measure both of his power and his self-confidence that he went about this night's work alone. At 4:20 on August 28, 1985, the morning after the coup, he stepped from a white sedan and strode purposefully down a dark residential street in Ikoyi, a residential area west of downtown Lagos. The smell of hibiscus hung heavy in the night air.

As Adamu Zahir walked, he fingered the rosary in his pocket; it had ninety-nine beads, one for each of the names of God. He murmured the *shahada*, the irreducible minimum of Islamic belief: "There is no God but God and Muhammad is the Prophet of God."

Although many men knew his reputation, the name Adamu Zahir was known to few. To agents of the Mossad and CIA, the young Arab with the eyes of a raptor was known only as Tony the Dreamer. He had a tight-skinned, narrow face and a cruel mouth. His eyes burned with intensity and were brightened by intelligence. And for one so young— he was in his early twenties—he had a command presence that was startling.

The Mossad and CIA would have paid a fortune for his picture, for his real name, for background information. What little they knew of him was sketchy secondhand information. Their files described him with such generalities as "messianic," "highly intelligent," "remorseless," and "skilled murderer."

The Mossad and CIA always described foreign

assassins as "murderers." They used more palatable euphemisms for those within their own ranks who performed the same function.

The overall picture of Tony the Dreamer, shadowy though it was, was of a dedicated and experienced agent, an extremely dangerous man. Western intelligence agencies knew his growing reputation as an assassin, but there were two things they did not know about the man they called Tony the Dreamer.

They did not know he was a sexual psychopath.

And they did not know that within the orderly and highly structured world of the Shiite Muslims, he was considered a defender of the faith, Islam's retributive sword of justice. He was a burning symbol of the movement to resurrect the narrow construction of the unspoken sixth pillar of Islam: "striving in the way of God," what some called the jihad, or waging war in the name of Allah.

Men of such power unconsciously displayed their authority. The assassin walked with the confidence and poise of a man who possessed the power of life and death.

He was faintly amused that even the military, which had ruled Nigeria for so long, was wary of the man he sought, the man who until the previous day had been chief of intelligence for the Nigerian military and the second most powerful man in the government. It would not be long before that man begged for the opportunity to tell his deepest secrets. On Victoria Island, in the basement of an obscure building near the harbor, that man, as had so many before him in the last few hours, soon would become a keening vegetable.

Tony the Dreamer smiled. It was a tight smile that did not extend to his eyes. He was an Arab, an Iraqi with a face that was lean with sculpted high cheekbones and eyes that seemed almost aflame in their intensity. His was a face from the desert, the face of a wandering bandit, of a man who was God-struck and half mad.

Not twenty-four hours had passed since Tony the Dreamer, over the wishes of men who were much older, had insisted that the time for the coup had come. An infidel army officer had learned of the most ambitious plan in all of Islam, and under no conditions must that secret be allowed to pass to the West. Years had gone into the planning of Operation Bilal. Once it was launched, the operation would take fifteen years to come to fruition. It would be consummated, appropriately enough, in the first year of the new millennium, in the year 2000. It would come in the autumn, the time of the year when, in the West, many people unconsciously slow down and begin to get their lives in order for the cold and bleak days of winter.

The plan must be protected at all costs.

The coup, which would start the clock on Operation Bilal, must proceed.

Now.

And so it did. The coup was not textbook perfect. A coup, in its proper sense, is both quick and bloodless. But the Muslims who overthrew the Christian government were not interested in such niceties. This coup had been only quick. The sword of Islam had shed much blood during the past few hours. The new Muslim government was in control and even more blood would flow. That was the thing about blood: once it was seen and smelled by men clad in the armor of a righteous cause, by true believers, the lust could not easily be satisfied. There had to be more. Always more.

Tony the Dreamer paused at the gate of the government-owned mansion that was the official residence for the chief of intelligence. He thought it amusing that the former government had given the home to a man who, as the coup demonstrated, was so woefully inadequate in his job. Had that man done his job properly, it could well have been Tony the Dreamer who tonight was being sought.

The uniformed guards of the former occupant had been replaced with guards who wore civilian clothes: loose-flowing robes in whose folds various weapons were hidden. Only in the West was military proficiency equated with crisp uniforms and erect posture. But these men, unlike Western soldiers, did not think of combat in terms of survival; for them, dying in war guaranteed entry into paradise. "Paradise lies before you and hell behind," they were told before battle. Their skill in combat combined with their willingness to die made them among the best soldiers in the world.

The guards quickly unlocked the heavy gate and would have pulled it open, but Tony gripped the bars so tightly that the ropy muscles of his arms trembled. The guards looked at Tony and then at each other. They were uneasy. The young Arab at the gate was said to be a nephew of the Sultan of Sokoto. The sultan also bore the title Sarkin Musulmi, or King of the Muslims. It was rumored that the young man at the gate also held one of the most exalted titles in Islam: Companion of the Right Hand.

Among Muslims, for whom eminence in Islam superseded all other achievement, he was one of the most feared men on earth.

The guards stepped back. Tony's eyes assaulted the mansion. A flicker of hatred crossed his face. Then he released the bars and nodded. The wary guards opened the gate and Tony stepped through. He paused. The corner of his mouth twitched in eagerness.

"*Allah akbar*," he whispered.

He strode swiftly toward the house.

As he walked, again he noticed the heavy, sweet smell of hibiscus.

The harmattan continued to blow.

Outside a new day was breaking. But in the basement of a building on Victoria Island, inside a room known as the Oasis—a room where it was always night—a naked black man was stretched across a stainless steel table. Taut chains locked him in a crucifix position. His eyes were shut and his breathing was ragged and shallow; his skin was drenched with blood and perspiration. The man's arms and legs had been pulled until the joints separated.

"We are not yet through, my friend" came the soft voice of his interrogator. Across the room, Tony the Dreamer stood up from the chair where he had been resting. He wiped his brow and took a deep breath. The air inside the Oasis was close, filled with the odor of urine and fecal matter; of horror and of despair and death.

Tony wore no shirt and he perspired almost as freely as the man on the table. He was bone weary. Rivulets of perspiration streaked his face and ran down his chest and arms. Tony's fatigue did not come because of the man on the table; he was nothing. He had told all he knew within several hours, and then, as did all visitors to the Oasis, begged to tell more. No, Tony was tired because he had spent much of the past forty-eight hours in the Oasis. So many people had become his guests after the coup. As Tony stared at the body of the man on the table, his fatigue vanished and was replaced with anticipation.

Tony walked across the room and stood near the table, careful not to get too close, for the stained cement floor under the table sloped into a clogged drain, and the slope was slippery with blood.

Tony the Dreamer reached for the large alligator clips hanging on the side of the table. The clips were attached to rubber-covered wires, and they sparked and hissed when Tony clanged them together. He smiled when the man on the table opened his eyes. Good. The man obviously remembered his first drink in the Oasis, the same offering all visitors received—a few eternal minutes with one of the alligator clips attached to his big toe and the other to his penis.

"Well, Colonel. You are awake," Tony said with a tight smile. He replaced the clips in their containers and smiled benignly.

"Told . . . everything," croaked the man on the table. He was a soldier and had seen enough of death to know he was dying. The wiry young man standing over him had inflicted pain that he had not known was possible to experience, terror he had not known existed, and humiliation from which it was not possible to recover. His fear of Tony was greater than his fear of death.

Tony's glance was almost affectionate. "Yes. Everything. Now I must tell you something."

He pressed a thick button under the table, and the door to his left opened. Four men, all wearing the loose-fitting garments favored by most Muslims in Lagos, marched into the room and surrounded the table. Their eyes were wary as they looked at Tony. They wanted to anticipate his wishes and carry them out as rapidly as possible. Tony flicked his head toward the man on the table. The men quickly unlocked the chains that held the colonel's limbs outstretched, then rolled his limp body over until he was facedown. Three of the chains were removed, coiled, and placed on hooks under the table. The fourth chain was looped around the man's waist and run through an overhead pulley, the bitter end dangling. Tony nodded. The four men strode rapidly from the room.

Tony picked up the chain and pulled. Muscles bunched and coiled on his chest and arms. Perspiration streamed down his chest. The man on the table grunted as the chain bit into his waist and hoisted him into the air. He was bent from the waist, and his knees and elbows dragged limply across the blood and sweat that covered the table.

"You failed, Colonel Gowon," Tony said. His voice was soft, even when he emphasized the word *colonel*. "You underestimated us. You failed to anticipate the coup. You failed to prevent me from learning what you discovered about our plans. You failed to protect your family." He paused. "The ranking intelligence officer of the Christian government, and you cannot even protect your family." He paused again. "The Americans also will fail. It is the will of Allah."

The man hanging from the chain said nothing. His life's blood had oozed down the sloping floor and pooled over the drain.

Tony the Dreamer raised his voice. There were things the man on the table must understand. "Colonel Gowon, your wife will give me the documents. The Americans will not know our plans until it is too late. Operation Bilal is safe."

The colonel did not respond. Tony slapped him hard, rocking the man's head and causing blood and spittle to fly through the air in a fine mist.

Tony stepped away from the table and reached for a cigar lying on a window ledge. He lit the cigar and grimaced in disgust at the smell of the tobacco. He puffed hard, not inhaling, until the end of the cigar was red and smoldering. He unbuckled his black cotton trousers, stepped out of them, and tossed them atop the chair. With little visible effort he sprang atop the table. His head was tilted to avoid the smoke from the cigar in his mouth. With one hand he held onto the chain suspending the man. He kicked the man's legs apart until they dangled over the edges of the table, then leaned forward, maneuvering. He held onto the chain with both hands and jerked the man's body toward him while, at the same moment, he lunged forward. The man whimpered—not at the pain, since his nervous system, in a sympathetic reaction several hours earlier, had stopped sending pain messages;

instead the man whimpered in this final degradation. Tony lunged repeatedly, his breath escaping in loud grunts. He leaned over the man as if protecting him, his lithe, muscular body wrapped around the man underneath.

Outside, the keening of the harmattan increased. The murderous innocence of the wind from the desert pounded Lagos, overwhelming the city and driving people to the edge of despair.

Tony the Dreamer pulled hard on the chain, groaned, and flung the cigar across the room. He drooped over the man for a long moment. Then he sighed and unfolded himself, backed away, and stepped down from the table.

Tony walked to the other end of the table. On a small shelf under the front of the table was his *jambiya*. With his left hand Tony the Dreamer seized the man's hair and pulled his head up until the two were face to face. The man's eyes were glazed; he could not see through the death fog that surrounded him.

"Your wife is next," shouted Tony. "Your wife is next." The *jambiya*, in a swift backhand motion, opened the man's throat from ear to ear. Tony pushed the man's head down, causing the sudden gout of blood to pour onto the table and then the sloping floor underneath the table. The pressure of the additional blood overwhelmed the blocked drain, and after a few gurgles, the pool of blood emptied and disappeared into the dark drains under the Oasis.

The harmattan continued to blow.

* * *

Glory Gowon's eyes widened in anger and disbelief as she stared at the flickering television set. She leaned closer. "No. No," she whispered urgently.

The television announcer, who had both the dour expression and garb of a Muslim cleric, barely was able to contain his pleasure at what he was reading. Certitude and self-righteousness were in his voice and demeanor. The man's message was rendered almost surrealistic by the plainness of the set: a bare wooden desk—actually, it was a small table—set against the backdrop of a white wall. It was the austere room as much as the man's demeanor that frightened Glory Gowon. The Muslims seemed to eschew even the most simple conveniences. She stared, mesmerized, at the announcer.

"I shall read the names of the traitors again," the announcer said. "Those executed as enemies of the government."

"No," Glory said as she watched. "He is not a traitor." The names were preceded by their rank; all of those killed had been members of the military, and in a deliberate affront the announcer first listed the names of enlisted men, corporals and sergeants, before those of officers.

Glory Gowon, hand to her throat, leaned forward. The announcer was calling the names of majors. He paused and looked into the camera. "Lieutenant Colonel Christopher Gowon," he said. The man's eyes glistened and it was clear he took personal pleasure in reading the name of the well-known colonel. Then, almost as an afterthought, he read the name of the former president of Nigeria.

"Oh, my God, they killed the president," Glory Gowon cried. "No. No. No. Not Chris. Not the president. What are they doing? What are they doing?" She shook her head in horror as she stared at the television set.

Glory Gowon was a Yoruba, tall and slender, whose black skin, in a certain light, revealed a pale red sheen. Her hair was pulled back tightly from her face and woven into a knot high on the back of her head. The dress she wore, a loose garment of an expensive black and gold fabric, told that she was not simply the wife of another government official; she was a woman of breeding, of style, of substance. Almost angrily she wiped the tears from her face and looked rapidly around the room. Chris was no traitor. He had been murdered, because of his job, his loyalty to the president, and his closeness with American agents in the U.S. Embassy.

The Muslims, even before they had used their positions throughout the government as the springboard for the coup, had been virulent in their hatred of Americans. They had constantly pressured the president to denounce the Americans and to sharply curtail the activities of embassy personnel, particularly the meddlesome agents of the Drug Enforcement Administration.

The telephone rang. Glory stood up. The phone rang again. She reached for it, then pulled back. What if it was one of the Muslims checking to make sure she was home? The phone rang, a strident, demanding sound. She picked up the receiver.

"Glory. Pete. You see the TV?"

"Oh, Pete," she cried in relief as she recognized the voice of the Drug Enforcement Administration agent who was one of her husband's closest friends. She sobbed. "They killed him."

The DEA agent was tense. The telephone line to Colonel Gowon's house almost certainly was tapped. But he had no alternative. He had to talk. He had to get a message to Glory. No problem. He was a former marine whose indefatigable zeal and intensity caused him to be called Duracell. He could do anything.

"Glory, listen closely," Pete said. "You've got to get out. They're on the way to pick you up. One of our guys saw them. Get out now. Don't bother packing. Just go."

Pete paused. Time to go for it. He took a deep breath. "Glory, do you remember what Christopher showed you right after you moved into the house, the thing you laughed about?"

Glory wrinkled her fine brow in concentration. She bit her lip. What was Pete talking about?

He prodded her. "The thing he said was there because of his job?"

"No. No. I don't remember."

Pete was growing desperate. He would have to be more specific. "You laughed and said you would plant mushrooms there."

She paused as realization dawned upon her. "Oh, yes, the—"

"Okay, okay," Pete interrupted. "You got it. Go there now. Don't pack. Just go. I'll be waiting. You understand?"

"I think so." She paused. "Pete, I'm scared. Please be there."

"Glory, before you hang up, one more thing. Christopher's papers. The investigation he was working on. Are those papers in his briefcase?"

Glory looked around the room. "No. I don't see it. It's not here."

"This is important. Very important. Those are papers he was going to give me. We think the Muslims found out and that's what precipitated the coup. Do you know where the briefcase is? Did he have it when he was arrested?"

"I don't know. I don't know." Glory turned and twisted as she looked about the room and tried to peer out the front windows. She clutched the telephone with both hands.

Pete sighed. "Okay. Don't worry. Just get on the horse and get out of Dodge. Go to the place we discussed. Run."

"Wait!" Glory paused. Something tugged at her memory. Time to get on the horse, Pete said. Horse. Horse. She suddenly remembered. Bilal was the horse upon which Mohammad was said to have ascended into heaven. Operation Bilal was the name of the investigation Christopher had been working on. She bit her lip in concentration. What had he told her about the documents? Her eyes roamed the room.

"Pete, I remember. The papers are—"

"No!" Pete shouted, "Don't tell me. If you know where they are, get the papers. Get the papers and run. Now."

"Please be there."

"I'll be there. Go. Now."

"Is that exactly what was said? All that was said?" asked Tony the Dreamer.

"Yes," said the man on the other end of the telephone conversation.

"Nothing else?"

"Nothing. We taped the conversation and re-played it twice before we called you. It is just as I relayed it to you."

Tony hung up. The Americans knew of Operation Bilal. He felt a quick flash of anger. The Americans again. Infidels, Jews, a ragtag collection of unbelievers, and they were aware of Islam's most sacred plans. From the conversation between the American and Colonel Gowon's wife—he smiled and corrected himself—Colonel Gowon's widow, the DEA agent knew of the documents. But he did not have them. Now the reports and files and analyses that Colonel Christopher Gowon had prepared were in the possession of his widow, and she was running to meet the American. But where? A place connected with Colonel Gowon's job as chief of intelligence for the Nigerian military, a place she thought was funny. A place where she said she would grow mushrooms.

Tony's mouth tightened in concentration. It had to be a place of darkness. A place of darkness and it was connected to his job. The house was provided by the government, one of the perks of the job. The post of intelligence officer had always been danger-ous and precarious. Since independence, there had been a half-dozen coups and probably three dozen attempted coups. After each successful coup, the intelligence officer of the overthrown government had been one of the first killed by the new adminis-tration. The director of military intelligence and the president were considered equally dangerous.

Now the colonel's widow possessed the docu-ments that were the reason for the coup—documents that, whatever the price, must be recovered. She was going to a place that she laughed at, a dark place, a place connected to her husband's job. Connected. Connected.

Tony smiled. A tunnel? That was it. Of course. It had to be a tunnel. For years there had been talk of tunnels leading from both the home of the chief of intelligence and from the president's official residence. The woman was escaping through a tunnel, probably from a basement room, to . . . to where? The exit could not be far away, not when much of Lagos was built on islands made of garbage and refuse. The water table was only a foot or so from the surface. The tunnel had to be a large waterproof pipe and it could not run far, probably no more than a block. And it would have to come out at another house owned by the government, either the government or by Colonel Gowon. But wait. He searched his memory for details of Colonel Gowon's file. He had read about the Gowon woman, but had not paid it much attention. Women were secondary creatures. He remembered that she was wealthy, so the house probably was in her name. Where would she and the American go if they reached the end of the tunnel? Obviously, to the U.S. Embassy. The embassy was on Victoria Island across the bridge from Ikoyi. A little more than a mile. At the embassy she would be given sanctuary while the Americans examined the documents. They would be in an embassy car, easy to identify. The young DEA agent would try to hide behind the sanctity of what the agents called "dip plates," which told all of Lagos this was an official embassy car.

Tony snorted. In the aftermath of the coup, he had instructed his men not to recognize diplomatic license plates, at least not for a few days. By the time embassy officials complained, it would be too late. Any mishap would be considered part of the turmoil surrounding a change in government.

He picked up the telephone. Tony smiled as he remembered an item from the file of Pete Williams, the DEA agent attached to the American embassy. It was ironic, but the agent was from Atlanta, Georgia, the city that was to play a pivotal role in Operation Bilal.

He spoke quickly into the telephone.

"Who the hell are you?" Pete asked as Tony the Dreamer stepped from his car. Tony did not answer. He nodded at the men holding Pete's arms. They released him but did not move away.

"Where is the woman?" Tony asked.

"What woman?"

"Do not play games with me, Mr. Williams. Your conversation with Colonel Gowon's widow is known to me." He looked at one of the men standing at Pete's side. "The woman was not with him?"

"No. This infidel was in the car alone. The whore was not with him."

"The documents? Were there no documents?"

The man shook his head. He was almost as frightened as the other Muslims. But he had not become an officer by allowing his fear to show. "There were no documents," he said.

Tony turned back to Pete.

"There is no time for this. Where are the papers?"

Pete was surprised at the urbanity and poise of

the young man. Not only was his English flawless, it was devoid of any accent. He was a most formidable man, and doubtless a high-ranking intelligence official in the new government.

"I bet I can whip your ass," Pete said. "You camel-fucking eater of pig shit."

Pete wondered how long he could delay the young Muslim. He needed a few more minutes. By then Glory and her escort, an embassy official, would be safe, racing in a private car through western Lagos and down the four-lane highway toward Benin, where Glory would be put aboard an Air Afrique jet bound for London. She had the documents and had agreed to discuss them with government officials in America. She had to be given more time.

Pete waved at the four Muslim guards who were holding AK-47s pointed at him. "Tell these sand niggers to put their guns down, and you and me can have it out. You and me. When I whip your ass, I walk. You win and . . . '' Pete grinned and shrugged; the very idea of this puppy winning was ludicrous.

"Mr. Williams, do not play these childish American games. You are not at your Disney World. I ask you once more, where is the briefcase?"

"You are illegally detaining an official of the American embassy," Pete said. He smiled at the young man. "And I can still whip your ass."

"Answer me," Tony said. "Answer me and your death will be quick and relatively painless. But if you continue to toy with me, I assure you that your death will be neither quick nor painless."

Pete grinned. He opened his fly and urinated toward Tony. It was an insult of almost unimaginable proportions, especially coming from an American. The young Muslim reacted as Pete had anticipated; his back stiffened and his breath was exhaled in a rush of indignation. But he quickly regained control.

"Very well, Mr. Williams. It shall be as you wish. You and me? That, I believe, is how you put it."

Pete grinned. He would have this kid for lunch. He motioned toward the Muslims surrounding him. "And what about these boys in their pajamas? They gonna stand clear while I clean your clock?"

"Mr. Williams, let us put things in perspective. Within the next half hour we shall have the woman and we shall have the documents. Soon afterward, my men will take turns with your wife and even with your young son. How old is he? Five? The perfect age for some of my men."

Pete crouched and pumped his left foot out in a movement that had it connected, would have broken Tony's knee. But the young Muslim, with no apparent effort, dipped and swayed, causing Pete's foot to miss by an inch.

"You, on the other hand, are about to die," Tony continued. "And your death will prove nothing except that you Americans have an endless propensity for demonstrating on an individual basis what your country manifests on the world stage: that you are nothing but talk, that you cannot back up your braggadocio and your bluster with action."

Tony paused. "You may carry that thought with you to the place you call heaven." Suddenly a curved knife appeared in his hand, and even Pete Williams, who had been a cop for fifteen years and had seen more than his share of street fights, had not seen where the knife was hidden. Before Pete's instincts could take over, the glistening blade flicked out and raked a long, shallow gash across his ribs. He winced, backed up a step, and clasped his hands to the wound. In that frozen second the outside edge of Tony's shoe struck the inside of Pete's right knee, not hard enough to break the kneecap, but enough to cause great pain. Pete fell to the ground but arose quickly, leaning over and holding his knee.

"That, I believe, is what you were attempting," Tony said with a tight smile. "It's commonly referred to as a side kick." He began circling the DEA agent.

Pete, stooped in pain, limped and hopped as he tried to continue facing the young Muslim. He held his arms high, the backs of his hands facing Tony, and repeatedly flicked his fingers toward his face. "Come on, asshole. Show me what you got."

He must prolong this as long as possible. Glory would soon be safe. The documents, which Christopher Gowon had said were of crucial importance, would be on the way to America.

Tony turned as if to smile in disbelief at one of his men. Then, without looking at Pete, again swung the curved knife in a wide circle, this time leaving a deep wound across Pete's stomach, spilling the agent's intestines.

Pete staggered in shock. He looked at the ropes of greenish gray trying to leap from his stomach. The odd thought crossed his mind that there was not as much blood as he expected, only a tinge of pink. He reached down and slowly and deliberately and methodically tried to push the intestines back into his stomach. Then he saw a gush of blood and realized that somewhere deep in his stomach an artery had been severed.

He was dying.

He looked at Tony. "Fuck you," he said, and clasped his hands over his wound as he slumped to his knees.

Tony realized he had gone too far with the agent. He had not meant to kill the man, not yet. He wanted only to frighten him enough to tell what he knew. Now the man was dying. And Tony knew from the look in the agent's eyes that in the time remaining, he would not talk. He nodded. Two of the Muslim guards seized Pete's arms and threw him to the pavement.

"You should not have become involved, Mr. Williams. You should not have become involved."

Pete Williams did not hear him.

17

Major Vernon Worthy stopped and shook his head in dismay when he saw the car being driven by Jeremiah. He opened the door and sat down, his knees jammed high in the air. He turned to speak to Jeremiah, who looked as if he were in the backseat, but Jeremiah spoke first: "Why are you wearing a uniform? I thought you were going to wear civvies and go out to the games with me."

"No, changed my mind. I told Glory I'd be home before noon."

He shook his head and grew solemn. "I'm worried about her. Got a feeling."

"You still have surveillance out there?"

"Yeah." The major paused. "I'm sure she'll be okay. Virginia–Highland is one of the safest areas of the city. It's my relief pocket."

The major turned toward Jeremiah and stared at him for a moment. "You wearing that dress to Vine City?" he asked.

Jeremiah's white eyebrows squeezed together. "Major, you and I had this same conversation twenty years ago. This is the kilt. It has a history going back hundreds of years. It is a tartan of Clan Donald, the oldest and most noble of all the Scottish clans. More specifically, it is the ancient hunting tartan of the Lord of the Isles. It is all that and more, but it is not a dress."

"Looked like a dress twenty years ago. Still looks like a dress," the major said. "If you're going out as a police officer, you should dress like a police officer. Why the hell you wearing that thing?"

The major laughed. He was silent for a moment. Then, almost as if he were afraid of being rebuffed, he said, "Remember how I used to kid you about your kilt? Back in the old days?" He paused. "Back when we were friends?"

Jeremiah stared straight ahead.

The major laughed. "Jesus Christ. I was a black kid from Barnesville, Georgia. I'd never seen a kilt. I thought it was some strange thing white men did that I didn't know about."

"I remember," Jeremiah said. He swung the car through the parking lot of City Hall East and turned left on Ponce de Leon. "I told you before: I'm going out to the games at Stone Mountain once we do this canvass. You going?"

"I don't know. Glory wants me to. She said it would give her a day by herself. But I don't know." He laughed. "I don't care about white men running around in dresses." He rubbed his hand across his mouth and shook his head in bewilderment. "Why you English guys hang onto that stuff?"

Jeremiah jammed on the brakes so hard that the major rocked forward against his knees. He grunted in discomfort. Behind them, brakes squealed as a car swerved to the side to avoid a rear-end collision.

"Major, your people came from Africa," Jeremiah said. "What tribe?"

Major Worthy looked at Jeremiah in surprise. He glanced over his shoulder at the cars stopped behind them and then back at Jeremiah. "What are you talking about?"

"What tribe?"

Major Worthy stared at Jeremiah. "I think they were Hausa. Let's go."

Jeremiah did not move. "What if I said you were a Zulu?"

The major laughed and shook his head. "Wrong tribe. Wrong country."

Behind them, a horn blew.

"Aah-haaaa!" Jeremiah said triumphantly. "Same with me. Wrong tribe. Wrong country. Major, my people are from Scotland. I hate the fucking English. They are an incestuous lot of fish-faced king worshipers."

"Move the car," shouted a driver as he slowly rolled past the police car.

"What's the difference?" the major asked.

"What's the difference between the Zulu and the Hausa?"

"Move the car, Buie."

Jeremiah grunted and accelerated rapidly. He turned left on Peachtree, then right on North Avenue. Ahead was Georgia Tech and beyond, a few blocks west, was Vine City. As the car crossed over I-85 and approached Georgia Tech, Jeremiah turned to the major, "The blood is strong, Major. The blood is strong. For me and for you."

Major Worthy did not answer.

"At least your chiefs looked after you," Jeremiah said. "They did their jobs. They didn't betray you."

The major turned and looked over his shoulder at Jeremiah. After a long moment he said, "You don't know what the hell you're talking about."

Jeremiah shrugged. "The clan chiefs ran us off the land in Scotland. Brought in the Great Cheviot and pushed us out. That was the beginning of our diaspora. Our chiefs replaced us with the Great Cheviot."

The major's brow was wrinkled. "What is a Great Cheviot?"

Jeremiah pressed the accelerator harder. The Coca-Cola headquarters, a fenced enclave surrounded by armed guards, was on the left.

"A sheep. A bloody sheep. Our chiefs replaced us with sheep. You chiefs didn't do that."

The major shook his head. "Buie, our chiefs sold us into slavery."

As Jeremiah turned left and approached Vine City, he glanced at the major. He laughed. "I thought we did that."

"All you white guys did was drive the boats. You couldn't roam around inside Africa. It was our chiefs who rounded us up and took us to the coast and sold us to the slave traders."

Jeremiah slowed and looked for a place to park.

He grinned. "Guess that proves we gotta watch out for the chiefs," he said.

"We sat by the rivers of Babylon and wept when we recalled the joys of Zion," Worthy said softly.

"What?"

"Never mind. Pull over here. I want to get this over with and go home."

Jeremiah pulled over and was about to stop when, up ahead by the corner, he saw her. She was standing near the sidewalk in the shade of a pecan tree, standing in the classic posture of a prostitute with her breasts thrust forward like the bowsprit on a clipper ship and her cantilevered butt thrust out behind. In Atlanta, such butts are called "Coca-Cola butts" because soft drinks can be stacked on the shelf-like protuberance.

The prostitute was a big woman wearing black knee-length boots, black hose, a black mini-skirt about the size of a handkerchief, and a low-cut black blouse. All of this was topped by a towering haystack of a black wig.

She was ready.

Jeremiah grinned, drove up alongside the woman, and pressed the accelerator, causing the engine to race. The woman looked over her shoulder and smiled. Her lips parted like a freshly opened can of tomatoes. The grin froze when she saw Major Worthy's uniform.

"Roll down the window," Jeremiah said. "Roll down the window."

"Buie, what are you doing?" The major slowly rolled down the window and glanced idly at the woman.

"The back window," Jeremiah said urgently. "The back window. I can't see out the front window."

The major sighed, reached over his shoulder, and rolled down the rear window.

Jeremiah leaned over, a rakish grin on his face. "Hey, baby," he said. "How much?"

She looked at him in astonishment. "Hello, Officer," she trilled, emphasizing the "officer."

"Hey, baby, we in homicide. All we interested in is dead people. Come on. How much?"

The major shook his head. "For God's sake, Buie."

The woman laughed. She vamped Jeremiah over her shoulder, pushed up her hair, and said, "You think I'm crazy enough to quote a price to the police?"

"Mama, you looking fine." Jeremiah laughed. "Sure do wish I could afford to spend some time with you."

"You crazy," she said, grinning and rolling her eyes. "Get your white ass out of here. You hurting my business."

Major Worthy reached over his shoulder and rolled up the window. He pointed straight ahead. "I couldn't say it any better. Get your white ass out of here."

Jeremiah laughed and eased away from the curb. He stuck his hand out the window and waved at the prostitute. "God, I love being a policeman," he said.

The major looked at him. "Where'd you learn to talk that shit? You been hanging out with the brothers?"

"Major, you forget, I used to work vice."

Jeremiah drove another block before he eased to the curb and stopped. "How do you want to do this?" he asked.

The major sighed. "If you dressed like a police officer instead of wearing a dress, you could go with me. These folks are not going to talk to a white guy in a dress. Just back me up."

"You want me to stay in the car."

The major opened the door. "I want you to stay in the car," he said. He walked down the sidewalk.

Jeremiah watched him for a moment. Then he leaned forward, trying to see out the right front window. "You hear what I said earlier?"

The major looked over his shoulder. He could not see Buie. "About what?"

"About chiefs."

"What about them?"

"We got to watch out for chiefs."

Major Worthy continued walking.

18

When Atlanta's domed stadium was built, real estate speculators tried to move in and buy the small rickety frame houses in the adjacent black ghetto of Vine City. They wanted to turn the property into parking lots and concessions that catered to those attending sporting events at the dome. Some property along North Avenue, the street facing the stadium, had been sold, but a block away, Vine City was still Vine City; only a few short blocks from the World Congress Center and the heart of downtown, yet one of the poorest and meanest areas of the city.

The people of Vine City, like the people of Lightning and Summerhill and Pittsburgh and Peoplestown and Mechanicsville and Buttermilk Bottom and Bedford Pine and Dixie Hills and Carver Homes and all the other black ghettoes of Atlanta, were poor and frustrated and without hope. For them, nothing would ever change. Violence was the only spice in their lives.

The major sighed, wiped perspiration from his brow, and waved for Jeremiah to pick him up. The major slid into the front seat. "I have cast my bread upon the waters," he said with a weary sigh. "Let's make one more stop up on the corner, and then I can go home and you can go hang out with the white guys in dresses," he said.

"Kilts, Major. Kilts."

"Yeah, yeah. Turn left here and pull over." Jeremiah stopped outside a grocery store on the corner of Magnolia and Vine, the very heart of Vine City. The grocery store, in reality a front for one of the biggest numbers parlors in Atlanta, was owned by a man known as Shaky.

Shaky, in his youth, had been one of the most talented flim-flam artists in America. He could talk anyone out of anything. Now he had throat cancer and wore a scarf to cover the gaping hole in his neck. When he spoke, it was with a high staccato rattle.

A group of young men stared malevolently. "You stay in the car," the major said. "These guys will have you for lunch if they see you in a dress."

"Kilt, Major. I wear the kilt."

The major ignored him. He stepped from the car and rose to his full height as he stared impassively at the gang of young men. Their eyes widened with reluctant respect. The major ignored their hostile silence and moved confidently among them, smiling, chatting, shaking hands. Then he stopped and said, "I want to know everybody's name." He pointed at the young man on the far left. There was no answer.

"What's your name, son?"

Finally, reluctantly, came the answer: "Box Head."

The major pointed to the next man, the one leaning against the grocery store. "Cool."

At each answer the major turned to the next. Even though he smiled, his pointing finger, the set of his shoulders, his air of command, let these young men know he was all business. Their responses came slowly.

"Cool's Brother."

"Fish Sandwich."

"Nozzle."

"Pretty Boy."

"Neck Bone."

"Shade Tree."

The major nodded. He paused for a moment and did not speak. Unlike many educated blacks who have achieved a measure of prominence, he was not embarrassed that these teenagers used street names rather than their real names. Street names gave them individuality and respect, two things denied by the world.

Oftentimes young black men are known only by these street names, even among their closest friends. These names are so important that until a few years earlier a nickname file had been kept by the intelligence unit of the police department. The file listed street names and cross-checked it with the person's real name, address, and associates. But black police administrators were embarrassed by the nickname file and ordered it discontinued.

The major turned to one of the young men. "Why do they call you Neck Bone?" he asked.

Neck Bone grimaced and looked away. "Man, what you talking about?" When he turned, the reason for his street name was clear. His neck was pencil-thin. Although his head was of normal size, because it rested upon such a slender column, it appeared unnaturally large. His neck appeared no larger than a man's wrist.

"Don't guess you'll ever get ring around the collar," the major said with a laugh. He put his hand affectionately on the boy's shoulder.

Neck Bone shrugged. He had heard all the jokes.

The major told the young men he was looking for a Muslim who could be a Nigerian but more likely was an Arab. He was passing out his business card and did not notice how the young men glanced at Fish Sandwich.

The major smiled and slapped the young men on the back and shook their hands. The young men smiled. Their hostility diminished. It was hard for them to be hostile toward a brother who was successful, jovial, confident, and who had a white man driving him around.

"You men see somebody like this, call me," the major said. "I want to talk to him."

Major Worthy waved and opened the car door. Fish Sandwich stood up, looked at the major's card, and then at the major. "Hey, man. Mr. Worthy."

The major looked up, "Yeah."

Fish Sandwich looked at Jeremiah. "Wherefor you get that chauffeur, man? That's some kinda uniform."

The major laughed. So did Cool and Cool's Brother. Neck Bone spun around in a circle and snapped his fingers. Nozzle and Box Head stared.

Fish Sandwich moved closer. "If I come down there and want to be a policeman, can I get a white man in a dress to drive me around?"

Major Worthy laughed. "I know that's right," he said.

Fish Sandwich looked at Jeremiah. "Hey, whitey, what you got under that dress?"

"It's a kilt."

The distinction was lost on Fish Sandwich. "I thought you was a woman," he said. "But I ain't never seen no white woman as ugly as you is."

Jeremiah reached for the door handle. The major grabbed his arm. "Let it go," he said.

The exchange had not escaped Fish Sandwich's attention. He pointed to Jeremiah and said, "Dude, you better keep your white ass in that car. You just drive the brother." He looked around, pleased with the admiration he was getting from the guys he hung with.

"And since you wearing that dress, don't sit too close to him," he said.

"I'm gonna kick his little ass," Jeremiah said through gritted teeth.

Major Worthy laughed and flicked his finger forward. "Let's go, Buie."

A moment later, as Jeremiah turned right onto North Avenue, Major Worthy turned toward him and said, "Tell you what, Sissy. Since I looked after you in Vine City, you owe me one. You look after me at Stone Mountain."

Jeremiah grinned in excitement. "You want to go to the games?"

"When there are a bunch of white men wearing dresses, I'd prefer you not talk of games."

"Major, it's —"

"I know, the . . ."

"Kilt," they said simultaneously.

19

One Saturday in late October, two homicides were committed in Atlanta.

The first body was found about mid-morning in the azalea bushes outside the Temple on Peachtree Road. The body was that of a young Hispanic male who had been dumped there about seven or eight hours earlier. His right temporal region showed the cause of death—a blow to the head with a blunt instrument. Rigor mortis had set in and the body was beginning to emit an odor that rapidly would grow in strength. Oxygen-depleted blood had settled in the lower back, giving it a maroon or plum-colored cast—"lividity on the dependent side," the M.E. would call it. The shoulder blades and buttocks, where the body pressed against the ground, were pale and bloodless. A few fly eggs had been deposited around the victim's eyes. Flies were buzzing about the body.

But the most amazing thing was the erection pointing into the air.

When Caren Diamond and Dean Nichols arrived, he was beside himself. He had accompanied her to the crime scene in order to introduce her to the uniform guys. It was her investigation. And after a few minutes she would be on her own.

"Did you read it?" a cop asked with a laugh.

"Read what?" Nichols said.

"The tattoo on his pecker? This guy has writing tattooed on his pecker."

Dean Nichols took his cigar from his mouth and looked at the cop. "You telling me he's got a tattooed pecker?"

The cop nodded and laughed. He was trying to embarrass Caren, but her expression never changed as her eyes roamed about the crime scene.

"You guys didn't move anything, did you?" she asked.

"Sure as hell didn't move him," the cop said, nodding toward the body. "Figured homicide would want to do that." He laughed again. "If you want to move him, pick him up by his handle."

"What does it say?" Nichols asked.

"Says, 'Love Keeps Me High,'" the cop said. "And you don't need a magnifying glass to read it."

Nichols stared at the body. "Son of a bitch has a hard-on a cat can't scratch." He moved closer, bent over, and stared. Over his shoulder he said to Caren, "Sometimes gas can cause an erection after twenty-four hours or so. And the M.E. says if a man dies with an erection, sometimes a semi-erection is maintained."

"Judging by the lack of odor and the small number of fly eggs in his eyes, he's not been here long enough for gas to cause that," Caren said.

Nichols turned at stared at her. Young homicide

detectives were not supposed to have opinions. They just gathered evidence. But she was right.

"And that ain't exactly a semi-erection," he said, pointing with his cigar. He shook his head in awe. "That thing's harder than Chinese arithmetic."

He unslung his new camera from his shoulder. "I got to go. I'm on call. Might be some homeless people out there I can arrest. But I got to get a picture of this for my scrapbook. Can't trust the ID techs on something like this."

He moved around taking pictures while Caren sketched the crime scene.

"Hey, Diamond," he said. "You go to the Temple, don't you?"

She looked at him. "Sometimes. Why?"

"They got a bathroom in there?"

She pointed toward a gray-haired man near the front door. "That's the rabbi. He'll show you."

Nichols slung his camera over his shoulder, gave the body a final glance, and as he walked away, said, "First time I ever saw flies using a man's pecker like it was the deck on an aircraft carrier."

The second homicide was discovered late Saturday afternoon.

The body was that of a woman in her late thirties or early forties, a slender woman who had been remarkably beautiful in life. Her dismembered body was found in the shower of her home at 1110 Rosedale Drive. The shower was free of blood, indicating that the perpetrator had let the water run over the body until the blood disappeared down the drain. The body was sprawled across the wide shower stall, feet up on the tiled ledge into which the white shower curtain hung. The head sat upright in the opposite corner, staring with lifeless eyes at its own body.

After the ID techs photographed the crime scene, detective Dean Nichols stepped into the shower stall and, on his hands and knees, stared at the severed head. He noticed a slight stain on the woman's lip and used a pencil to open her mouth. He held his handkerchief ready. His suspicions were confirmed when he looked into her mouth. Quickly he tilted her head to the rear. He sighed and looked at the uniform cop peering over his shoulder.

"Guy got himself a blow job after he killed her," he said.

"At least she couldn't bite," the cop said.

Nichols stood up. He looked at a small puddle of blood on the floor near the shower. The imprint of a shoe could be seen in it, the only blood found at the crime scene.

"I've seen that shoe before," he said. "Make damn sure nobody steps in it."

"The ID techs got pictures and made a cast," the cop said. "They said it was a good one."

"We got us a cereal killer here," Nichols mumbled.

The eyes of the cop widened. It had been many years since Wayne Williams had been implicated in some of the deaths in a case where more than a dozen black children had been killed in Atlanta, but even now the very mention of a serial killer caused seismic tremors in the police department.

"A serial killer?" the cop said.

"Cereal. Like breakfast food. This puppy always kills in the early morning hours. About breakfast time."

The cop stared at Nichols.

"Is the major still out there?" Nichols asked.

The cop nodded. "I understand he knew the victim."

"You might say that. My boss will want to handle this one personally. I'm sure the perp is the same guy who killed her son a few days ago."

Nichols looked at his watch. "The sergeant dropped the major off here about an hour ago. He doesn't have his radio on, no answer on the beeper. We left a message on his machine. He should be here any time. He'll want to spend some time alone in here with the body."

"That the Sissy?"

"Don't let him hear you say that."

Nichols sighed and looked around the shower stall. "What's the major doing now?" he asked.

"Last time I checked, he was talking with the surveillance detectives."

Nichols snorted. "Detectives, my ass. It's back to uniform and a foot patrol on the morning watch for those puppies."

He looked at the cop. "You mind stepping outside for a minute? I need to use the bathroom."

20

Near the end of runway 32 at DeKalb–Peachtree Airport in northeast Atlanta is a landfill. The entrance for cars is on Buford Highway a few hundred yards north of the original El Toro restaurant. Birds by the thousands are attracted to the landfill. They have caused the crash of at least one small jet by flying into the air intakes, but the county is unable to get rid of the birds and will not close the landfill. On weekends it is particularly popular as local residents line up to dump everything from old furniture to garden implements to toxic chemicals to boxes and cans containing God only knows what.

On the afternoon in late October, the small parking area around the landfill was filled with cars. The unending heat had caused materials in the landfill to fester and steam and emit odors that drew even more birds, most of them starlings, than usual. They filled the air overhead and parked in long, jerking, nervous flocks around a bulldozer that snarled and growled as it covered up fresh materials brought to the dump.

A slender man in loose cotton clothing was hardly noticed as he parked his car and stepped outside. He watched the bulldozer for a moment, then reached into the rear seat of the small car and pulled forth a large shopping bag. He walked toward the bulldozer, waited, and then as the driver was beginning to be concerned about his proximity, casually tossed the bag in front of the big blade. The driver glared and motioned for the man to move away. Civilians always wanted to play tag with the big blade.

The bag disappeared almost immediately, thrust and jumbled into the ragged mixture before the blade, then buried under the dirt that oozed and smoked and steamed and gave forth an aroma most malodorous.

The man, it was Tony the Dreamer, waited a moment. Overhead the birds fluttered and chattered impatiently as they waited, poised for a swift fruitful plunge.

Tony stared fixated at the bulldozer blade. The bulldozer rumbled back and forth, rearranging and burying and packing the flotsam of thousands. No one would ever find the tennis shoes. He had sliced the soles, then dipped them in gasoline and burned them until only shapeless hunks of charred rubber remained. Those hunks he wrapped in old clothes, packed them into a bag, and then tossed the bag into the landfill.

Tony smiled. The physical evidence collected by the old police sergeant was rapidly disappearing. He sucked reflectively on his broken tooth. On Monday the tooth would be replaced, and the old detective would be devoid of yet another piece of evidence. He dreaded the thought of going to a dentist, but it had to be done. He must clean up the problems in Atlanta.

"Hot, ain't it?" said a large man, sweat-soaked shirt flapping around his hips and perspiration beading on his face as he walked by carrying two boxes toward the landfill.

Tony did not answer. His brow was smooth and cool, and his clothes were crisp and clean. He did not think it was hot. He smiled as he thought of Atlantans and their ideas of what constituted bad weather. In the winter, or what passed for winter, anything more than a heavy frost on the streets and Atlantans reacted as if struck by an arctic blizzard. In the summer, if temperatures rose above the mid-seventies, they complained of the heat.

Tony smiled. He turned his gaze toward the sky and watched the anxious birds. Their flapping reminded him of how the woman had reacted this morning when he walked into her kitchen.

She recognized him. Instantly. It had been more than a decade since he had come to her house in Lagos and took her husband away, but she recognized him. In that frozen split second of horror, she backed up, raised her hands as if to ward him off, and began shaking her head in denial. Like any professional assassin, he expected that moment of horror, when her synapses did not connect and when she could not speak. He expected the moment and he took advantage of it by quickly moving toward her. He thrust his left hand forward, the space between the thumb and forefinger pressing against her larynx so she could not speak, and closed his hand tightly around her throat. He smiled at her wide, horror-filled eyes and her fluttering and squawking.

After a moment her struggle grew weaker and her eyelids began closing. He held her a moment longer, then slowly released her and watched her slide to the floor.

He stepped back. He had plenty of time. He had easily slipped past the two detectives who had staked out the house. They sat in a car a half block away watching the front door. And the SWAT team members he had pulled away by the simple expedient of offering a five-thousand dollar donation to a militant organization of young homosexual men and suggesting that they stage a demonstration at 8:00 A.M. Saturday.

Tony smiled as he remembered how he had entered the house and accosted the woman.

After he had choked her into unconsciousness, he reached down and used the woman's belt to tie her hands behind her back. He picked up a dish towel from the counter and stuffed it into her mouth. He wanted her conscious when he went to work. Moving as calmly as if he lived in the house, Tony turned and walked out of the kitchen. It had been dark when he was here before.

He crossed the hall and tried to open the bedroom door where he had found the boy a few nights earlier, but the door was locked. He was careful not to leave any fingerprints on the doorknob. Already the police had a partial print that they thought was his. Tony did not know whose print they had collected; it was not his.

He turned. At the end of the hall was the woman's bedroom. He entered and smiled when he saw the African art carefully placed on shelves or hung in rows on the white walls. He had tossed much of it to the floor the other night when he was looking for the hidden documents.

He had not realized the previous visit that the art was so extensive.

His smile was not in appreciation of the clay and terra cotta heads from the ancient Nok culture, or the intricate masks and wood carvings of the Yoruba, or even for the bronzes of Ife. He smiled because the report of Operation Bilal had been hidden inside one of the masks.

The thought of objects on the wall being referred to as art caused Tony to squeeze his mouth tightly in distaste. Like most Arabs, he professed to have no racial animosity toward blacks. He could quote the forty-ninth sura of the Koran, as could many Arabs who sought to prove their love for all mankind:

> *O, mankind! We created you from a single soul, male and female, and made you into nations and tribes, so that you may come to know one another. Truly, the most honored of you in God's sight is the greatest of you in piety.*

But Tony did not feel the words of this sura. He was derisive and patronizing of blacks and of any product of black Africa that purported to be art.

He had spent years at al-Azhar, the great Koranic university in Cairo, where he had been taught that Islamic culture was the greatest in the history of mankind. He had discussed with other Arab students how the artists of Islam had created thousands of monuments, among which were the Taj Mahal and the Alhambra, while the blacks of

Africa were building mud huts. Arabs were anointing their bodies with aromatic oils while the blacks of Africa were bathing in the urine of animals. Arabs worshiped their bodies while the blacks of Africa were using crude instruments to stretch their lips, elongate their necks, and tattoo their flesh.

As for literature, the rich intricacy of the Arabic language and the lavish intermingling of poetry and prose created an intellectual and aesthetic pleasure unique in all the world. The writings of Islam were not simply to gratify the ear or excite the imagination; through these writings ran the almost single-minded theme of man's relationship with God. And those who did not speak Arabic could never plumb these rich and salubrious depths. It was work that truly defied translation. Looking at even the best-intentioned efforts to translate Arab literature enabled anyone who understood Arabic to understand why the word *translator* often is synonymous with *traitor*.

Tony grew more and more angry. What literature had been created by black Africans? He snorted at the thought. Africans had no poetry, only a rhythmic prose and tribal chants filled with imagery. African literature stressed the immediate and concrete aspects of life—the here and now—just as its people continued to do in their lives. And there was nothing to approach the linguistic richness found in the Arabic. South of the Sahara—if one counted the dialects and secret languages—were some three thousand separate tongues—a Babel of nothingness. When Africans sought a synthesis between Africa and Europe or Africa and America, they lost most of what was purely African and further bastardized their meager literary heritage.

Finally, and to Tony perhaps the most important distinction of all, Atlanta blacks, who boasted of their African heritage, were eaters of pig meat. They ate pig meat in every form and every permutation known, and that alone was enough to cast them into the realm of outer darkness.

Tony reached out and knocked a priceless terra cotta mask to the floor. It cracked. He ground his heel into the crack, causing the mask to shatter.

He turned. Across the room a closet door was open. Clothes, muted and sophisticated clothes, were on the hangers. Two cardboard boxes were on the floor. He stooped and pulled one of the boxes forward. Inside he saw nothing but old, musty magazines. He picked up the topmost one and recognized it as *Newswatch*, a Nigerian magazine modeled after America's *Time* magazine. The magazine was dated October 1985, the month that Dele Giwa, the magazine's editor, had been killed by a parcel bomb. Tony's eyes brightened. Dele Giwa had been one of those pestilential journalists, a so-called crusader who modeled himself after Fleet Street or American reporters.

That's why he had been killed.

Tony thumbed through the magazines. All were from the mid-1980s, and many of them were issues that focused on the August 1985 coup that had brought a Muslim government to power in Lagos.

Tony tossed the magazines back into the box. The woman doubtless kept the magazines because her husband had died in the aftermath of the coup.

Tony had killed him.

He had also sent the parcel bomb that killed Dele Giwa.

Tony stood up. If the woman was so concerned with the coup that had brought a new government to power and launched Operation Bilal, she should have been killed years before. He would correct that oversight.

But first he would amuse himself.

The fluttering of the birds shook Tony out of his reverie. He shivered with delight, then looked at the people around the landfill. No one was looking at him. They were concerned only with tossing away the signs of their excesses, usually things that were old. In America everything that was old was rejected: houses, office buildings, clothes, cars, everything, even old people, especially old people. Nothing was valued unless it had the shine and gloss of the new.

In Islam, it was precisely the opposite. In fact, the *mutaw-wifs*, those nattering men who made up the Committee for Encouraging Virtue and Discovering Vice, often said, "Nothing that is new is good." Although their statement applied more to the social than to the material, the point was valid.

Thinking of the *mutlaw-wifs* caused Tony to look at his watch. He turned and walked briskly toward his car. He must hurry.

Soon it would be time for prayers.

21

It was shortly after 8:00 A.M. Sunday when two young Hispanic men sauntered into a convenience store on Peachtree Street. A Red Dog in the back room peered through a small one-way mirror. He tensed when he saw that the two men wore orange and red jackets, the colors of the Rod and Gun Club. One of them turned to look down an aisle, and the Red Dog saw the club emblem on the rear of the jacket.

The two young men pulled large semi-automatic 9mm pistols from their belts. One clubbed the manager into unconsciousness and set about riffling the cash register while the other stuffed miscellaneous merchandise, mostly junk food, under his jacket.

The gang members did not see a boy of perhaps thirteen or fourteen who was dawdling at the magazine rack near the rear of the store. The kid was frightened by the robbery but even more of what the black-garbed, shotgun-toting Red Dog did. The boy hid behind the magazine rack, and it was not until the store filled with uniformed cops that he was found and brought forth.

A homicide detective talked to the boy as the medical examiner came out of the store. The M.E.

pulled off his rubber gloves and tossed them aside. He nodded toward the sergeant.

"You stay right here, son," the detective said to the boy. "Nobody's going to hurt you. I'll be right back." The detective stood up and walked toward the M.E.

The young doctor nodded toward the carnage inside the convenience store. As with most victims of severe trauma, the young men had their clothes ripped from their bodies by emergency medical technicians. Their naked bodies were being photographed and had not yet been covered by a sheet.

"First time I've ever seen that," the young doctor said.

"What?"

"Erections sustained after death."

The homicide detective glanced through the open door. "They were kids," he said as if in explanation.

"Yeah, kids cut in half with shotgun blasts. How the hell can they have an erection when neither one has enough blood inside him to have a blood test done? And each has a tattoo on his penis."

The homicide detective stared at the M.E. for a moment. "Did it say 'Love Keeps Me High?' "

"How did you know?"

"We had one yesterday," the detective said. "I heard our new detective, Caren Diamond, talking about it."

The M.E. continued staring at the store. "I'm anxious to get what's left of these guys downtown. I want to check them out."

The homicide detective nodded. "Well, if you

discover some secret of eternal youth, let me know."

"You got it." The M.E. motioned for one of the young patrolmen. "When the body snatchers get here, tell them I said to rush this one," he said. "I want these guys downtown stat."

The guy nodded. "Yes sir."

The homicide detective smiled at the young boy who had been a witness. "Be right with you, son," he said. He stared at the store, replaying in his mind the Red Dog's statement of what had happened. The statement, in almost formal courtroom language, told how at 8:04 A.M. on the morning of October 22, while on stakeout duty at a convenience store in the eighteen hundred block of Peachtree Street, two Hispanic males entered. The aforementioned Hispanic males approached the manager, pulled two semi-automatic pistols from their belts, knocked the manager to the floor, and began taking money from the cash register. At that point, according to the statement, the Red Dog stepped from his place of concealment, identified himself as an Atlanta police officer, and called upon the two men to drop their weapons. Perpetrator Number One swung his weapon toward the Red Dog, who, in fear for his life and in self-defense, discharged his police-issued shotgun. Perpetrator Number Two swung his weapon toward the Red Dog, who, again in self-defense and in fear for his life, again discharged his police-issued weapon. He approached the two perpetrators. Both were dead.

The homicide detective smiled at the boy who had been a witness. "Okay, son," he said. "Now tell me what happened in there. Take it slow and don't worry about anything."

They boy looked around fearfully. The Red Dog was nowhere in sight. The boy looked at his shoes, pursed his lips in concentration, and then, with great, rounded eyes, turned to the detective.

"Like I told the policeman inside, man. I was in there looking at some magazines when these two dudes come inside, man. They pulled these big nines and one of 'em whacked the dude at the register up side the head. Frammed him good. They started digging out the money, man. 'Bout that time this dude in black clothes jumped out of the back room waving a shotgun. He say, 'Pull!' *Bam*! The first dude he hit the floor. The policeman, he swing his gun around and he say, 'Pull.' *Bam*! The second dude, he hit the floor."

The boy paused, shrugged, and said, "That's it."

The homicide detective stared at the boy. "You sure that's the way it happened?"

The boy nodded. "Man, them Dogs be bad," he said. "They be bad."

22

Sunday morning Vernon Worthy sat on the edge of his bed, a loaded pistol by his side and an open Bible on his lap, and tried to read. But his thoughts kept drifting to Glory, to her son, and to the unspeakable humiliation involved in their deaths. He looked at the page but saw only Glory's severed head in the corner of the shower stall.

He tried to remember a Bible verse that had helped him in the past, but could recall only how he and Glory had planned to be married, how they had looked ahead at the days of their years and had seen only happiness.

He closed his eyes to pray but could think only of the funeral that afternoon. Glory had no family in America. After a brief funeral service, her body would be shipped back to Nigeria to her family there, for burial. That was what she wanted.

He should have listened to Jeremiah and Dean about planting the "little ear" in Glory's house. She might be alive today if he had allowed the audio surveillance.

Vernon Worthy shook his head. A tear worked and strained away from his eye and slowly dropped down his cheek.

For almost fifty years he had avoided marriage. His work was everything. All he ever wanted was to be a cop. That enabled him to prove something to himself: that even though he came from Barnesville, a small town about an hour's drive and a hundred years south of Atlanta, that he, as a black man, could compete and excel in a white man's world.

As a boy, Vernon Worthy had attended a segregated school that used out-of-date books handed down from students at the school attended by whites. He played fullback on the school football team; one that played only against other black schools.

His only contact with white kids was at a field on the edge of town, a field near the cemetery where the paths crossed for black and white students as they walked home from their separate schools. For most of his high school years he wondered how it would be to go head to head with white ball players, with the guys who always had new equipment and new uniforms. Then one day at the field near the cemetery, after the white kids saw one of the black kids tossing a football into the air, an impromptu game arose. Neither side wore helmets or pads or cleats. It was bare-knuckle football, where only basic skills of running and blocking and tackling counted.

In that impromptu game Vernon Worthy realized for the first time that being white did not automatically mean being superior. He ran through them and over them as if they weren't there. He made four touchdowns. But what he remembered most was the fear in the eyes of the defenders when he charged them.

White guys, the guys with the new school books and new football uniforms, were afraid of him.

He was a better man than they.

He went to Morehouse College in Atlanta on a football scholarship, majored in criminal justice, and then served a hitch in the army as a provost officer. At army schools he found himself in classes with young officers who had attended the finest universities in America, and the Barnesville memories, the painful memories of out-of-date books and secondhand football equipment, came rushing back. Those guys from Princeton had never heard of Morehouse College. They did not know what it meant to be a Morehouse man. They thought it was a toy school in Atlanta where blacks went just so they could say they had been to college.

But he studied long into the nights, and in every class was graduated in the top one percent of students. To realize that with perseverance and application he could achieve more than white guys—to realize that not only was he intellectually as good, but in fact was intellectually superior to many white guys—was the greatest awakening of his life.

And out of that awakening came a serenity and self-confidence that could not be shaken.

After the army he joined the Atlanta police department and became an exemplary young police officer. Then Maynard Jackson, a garrulous bumbler who believed he had slept under the Shroud of Turin, became Atlanta's first black mayor. Jackson set about balancing the scales, redressing age-old grievances of black people, and Vernon Worthy was picked as part of a group of black officers who were jumped two and three ranks. He had mixed feelings about his promotions. They were the right thing for the wrong reason. Ability mattered more than color. He remembered the football field in Barnesville and he remembered the army classrooms, and he knew he could have been promoted on his own merit. He had the fire in his belly and he had the ability. He could become a deputy chief, maybe even chief. And he could do it on his own ability, in competition with whites. He did not need or want preferential treatment.

Other officers, even young white officers, recognized his leadership. He knew that the day he overheard two of them talking, and they referred to him by rank and name rather than as Willy, the collective name they applied to all black people.

Then, several years ago, he had realized he would rise no higher than major. It was not white men who were holding him back but his fellow blacks. In a city where most black elected officials were light-skinned—some could pass for white—and in a police department where the top administrators were light-skinned, he was simply too black. His skin was too dark. In the unspoken caste system among blacks, where those with the lightest skin and softest hair were at the top, he was an embarrassment.

In a black society where one of the most stinging criticisms against those who sought to join the white world was that they were "not black enough," he was too black. Sure, he was educated.

Sure, he was articulate. Sure, he was demonstrably one of the finest police officers on the force.

But he was too black.

Vernon Worthy, being Vernon Worthy, swallowed his pill. He did his job. He pressed on. Retirement was only a few years away. Almost certainly he would receive lucrative offers for security jobs in private industry.

His greatest hope was in Glory, in their soon-to-be marriage. He saw a new life ahead.

Now that, too, was gone.

The chief had relieved him of duty for several weeks. No one could be expected to work after his fiancée and her son had been killed within the space of days, especially not if he had found the bodies. And he certainly could not participate in the investigation.

Vernon Worthy looked up from the Bible and sighed. He closed it, placed the pistol in his belt, and stood up. With hands held limply by his sides, he began pacing.

The man who had killed Glory and her son was still out there.

Obviously the killer was after anyone who knew of Operation Bilal. That meant he would be coming for Vernon Worthy.

And for Jeremiah Buie.

Major Worthy picked up the telephone by the bed and dialed a number. Odd that now, after all these years, when he was in the twilight of his career as a police officer, he was thrust into close proximity with the man who had been his closest friend in the beginning of his career.

As he waited, his hand strayed unconsciously to the pistol in his belt. He looked around the room.

"Homicide, Sergeant Buie."

"Buie, Vernon Worthy. Can you come to my house?"

"Major, it's Sunday morning. How'd you know I was at the office?"

The major chuckled. "Sissy, you're just like me. You got nothing except the Job. I figured you went home last night, put on your dress, and got drunk. But unless you got too drunk and overslept, I knew you'd be at work. If you're not at work, you're home. Easy."

"It's not a dress, Major. I wear—"

"Yeah, yeah, I know. The kilt."

"So what can I do for you?"

"Anything going on with your guys? My radio's off."

"Yeah, few minutes ago one of the Dogs shot a couple of would-be robbers at a convenience store on Peachtree. We're on it."

"Good," the major said. Then, in an abrupt change of subject, he continued, "Sissy, we got to do something. This son of a bitch is always one step ahead of us."

"I am doing something. I'm at work."

"Come by here. Let's go over everything we got and think this thing out. We got to do something."

"Major, I'll be there in ten."

"See you then."

Jeremiah was putting on his coat when the telephone rang.

"Homicide. Sergeant Buie."

"What are you doing about that homicide involving the female?" said the voice on the telephone. There was no introduction. "Worthy's fiancée. What are you doing?"

"Who the hell is this?" Jeremiah asked.

"The mayor."

"Oh, Mr. Mayor, I didn't catch the voice." Jeremiah paused.

Mayor Eldrin Bell was famous for these peremptory calls. When he had been chief of police, any homicide officer involved in a case where the victim was a female could expect a call from him. Bell always had had a particular interest in homicide involving females. As he was a divorced man, and a man who took every opportunity to give his private telephone number to attractive young women, it was widely assumed that he looked upon the death of any female as a depletion of possible targets.

Jeremiah quickly briefed the mayor on the case.

"Keep me informed of any developments," the mayor said. He hung up without a good-bye.

Jeremiah hung up the phone and looked around the squad room. Sunday morning is the slowest time of the week in homicide, a respite after what is always a busy Saturday. A small staff is present, and they would rather be somewhere else. Couple of guys out investigating the multiple shooting on Peachtree. Everybody else out there hanging around. The chief, couple of deputy chiefs, and a half-dozen majors probably were there. When a

Red Dog blows away two people, a shower of brass falls on the crime scene.

No one else in the squad room except Dean Nichols and Caren Diamond. Nichols was toying with his new camera, and Caren was at her desk against the wall.

"Hey, Nichols," Jeremiah said. "How's the divorce coming?"

Dean looked up and nodded. "I found a lawyer who is going to do it for twenty-five dollars if I serve the papers. I'm doing that tomorrow or the next day. I can't wait to see the expression on her face."

Jeremiah was puzzled. "I thought she was filing."

Dean returned to his scrapbook. "She was supposed to. But she changed her mind. So I'm doing it."

Caren looked at Dean as if he were some sort of untouchable lab specimen.

Jeremiah sighed. He watched Dean thumb slowly through the scrapbook. "Nichols, you don't put every homicide in there, do you?" he asked.

Nichols sliced his eyes up in a quizzical fashion. "If you're thinking of the major's fiancée and her son, no. They're not in the book."

"Make sure they don't get in there."

"Don't need 'em. Got a lot going on. The shooting this morning will yield a couple of good ones. Got me some good ones yesterday. Diamond's case. Body of a young Hispanic male. Buck naked in the azalea bushes in front of the Temple. Had an erection that looked like a flag pole."

"After death? How'd he do that?"

"Damned if I know." Nichols spun around in his chair and looked at Caren. "Did you call the M.E. and find out that boy's secret? Whatever it is, I might want to patent it."

"Not yet," Caren said. "I've been busy. I'll do it in a few minutes."

Jeremiah walked toward the elevator. "I'm going to see Major Worthy," he said over his shoulder. "You can reach me at his house. Don't let anyone else know where I am."

Nichols watched as Jeremiah punched the elevator button. "Hey, boss," he said loudly.

"Yeah?"

Dean patted his camera. "Don't wind up in my scrapbook."

"Don't worry." Jeremiah smiled. "The perp is running dead."

23

Tony was not running. But he was walking fast. Very fast. He wanted to cross the grocery store parking lot before any cops in the adjacent parking lot at City Hall East saw him.

He was successful. Once he was halfway across the city parking lot he slowed. As he was angling toward the front door he saw a tall, muscular white-haired man, obviously a cop, leave the building. The man crawled into a battered-looking city car that wheezed and grunted and shuddered as he drove away.

Tony entered the front door and nodded at the security guard. The bored guard saw just another uniformed patrolman; hundreds of them came and went at all hours of the day.

What Tony was about to do held no fear for him. He knew that cops are easily intimidated by people in authority. They are a paramilitary group with a rigid command system. Anyone with a confident air, anyone who looks as if he belongs, anyone who is well dressed with just the right touch of impatience, can have cops falling all over themselves saying "yes sir" and "no sir" and being more than willing to please. Tony wore the uniform of a cop. He had a naturally cocky air.

He pressed the button for the elevator. He had been well briefed on the procedure he must follow and what he must say.

At the third floor, he stepped off the elevator, turned right, and entered the offices of the homicide squad. Behind a waist-high barrier was the squad room. Two people were there. In the back a woman bent over her desk. Sitting up front was a stocky guy who was toying with a camera.

With the unconsciously cold stare of a homicide detective, Dean Nichols looked up. He saw a cop wearing sunglasses and a hat. A real cowboy.

"Can I help you?"

"Yeah," Tony said impatiently. "I'm from the M.E.'s office. He sent me to pick up evidence in a homicide case. Skin with a bite mark on it. It's in a plastic container of formalin."

Nichols stared. The M.E.'s office had a staff of investigators. Why was a uniform patrolman representing the M.E.? He stared at the officer's name tag. "T. SOPORIF" it said. He reached for the telephone to call the M.E.'s office and verify that patrolman T. Soporif had been sent to pick up evidence.

"All the investigators are busy, and I get pulled in to be an errand boy," Tony said impatiently. "Yes sir, join the police department and haul skin around. You guys are weird."

Dean took his hand from the telephone and smiled. "Some people think so," he said. "I think we're all perfectly normal myself."

"Yeah, well, the M.E. said you guys had that evidence long enough, and he needs to make some more photographs. If you'll let me sign for it, I'll get outa here."

Tony looked around the squad room, as if being in the presence of homicide officers made him queasy. "It's like being in a morgue," he said. "You guys are undertakers."

Caren Diamond turned around and stared straight into the sunglasses of Tony the Dreamer. She felt an instant dislike for the cop. She did not know why. Her animosity was shared by Tony. He looked at her and his Arab blood sang out in alarm. He knew, somehow he knew, that she was Jewish— Jewish and trouble. He sensed it. And he wanted to do what he had to do and get out. No more toying with the guy up front. Just do it and leave.

Nichols pulled a cigar from his pocket, stuck it into his mouth, rolled it around a few times, and said, "You mean you don't want to transfer to homicide? This is where the big boys play."

With one hand he was toying with his camera. This was a good time to try the timer. He turned the camera so it was facing Tony, pressed the timer down, stood up, and walked toward the waist-high barrier.

Tony was staring at Caren and did not notice. He shook his head. "No, just gimme the stuff and I'll get it over there and get back on my beat." He looked at his watch.

Dean walked toward a locked door in the corner. Behind it was the vault that contained evidence from homicide cases. "We got it in the vault," he said. "Want to come in? See our souvenirs? Guns, bloody knives, blood-encrusted rope. Bloody clubs. We got it all. One-stop shopping here."

"I'll wait here," Tony said.

The Jewish woman in the back of the room was staring.

What did she know?

After a minute, Dean came from the vault holding a small plastic container. He placed it on his desk, then passed a printed form to Tony.

"Sign here," he said.

As Tony glanced at the form, Dean turned, advanced the film in his camera, again pressed the timer switch, and stepped to the side.

"Can't break the chain," Tony said as he signed. He picked up the plastic container and turned to go.

Dean pulled the cigar from his mouth. He smiled. "Officer, would you like to see my scrapbook? I got some really good pictures. Show you what it's like working in homicide."

"No, thanks. I have things to do." He smiled a tight smile, waved an imperious finger, and was gone.

Caren walked to Nichols's desk. Through the open door she could see the cop waiting impatiently for the elevator. He looked at her and turned back toward the elevator.

"Who was that?" she asked.

"A harness bull running errands for the M.E.'s office." Nichols picked up his camera and smiled. "I got that puppy's picture. If it's in the frame and if the exposure is right."

"What did he want?"

"Who?"

"The uniform who just left."

Dean shrugged. "Came to pick up that bite mark. The M.E. wants it." He looked up from his camera. "Did you ever call over there and ask about the pictures they took of the spic kid with the hard-on?"

"No, but I will." She stared at the closed elevator doors. "And I'll ask them about that officer. He bothers me."

She turned toward her desk. "I'll do it now."

Tony smiled as he drove out of the grocery store parking lot. As he turned right onto North Avenue, he glanced down at the container on the seat beside him. Another piece of evidence from the boy's homicide investigation was about to disappear.

Tony was bound for the corner lot near his house, the empty lot where every weekend the irascible man known as Old Black Joe cooked barbecue and brunswick stew and chitterlings. The smell of the cooking was the most horrible odor Tony ever had known. Especially that of the chitterlings cooked in lard. It would take all the discipline he could muster, but he would go there. He would stand in the heat from the pit, in the odiferous clouds of pig-laden steam that bounced back from the flimsy tin roof of the shelter over the pots, and when the old man's attention was diverted, he would drop the piece of skin inside one of the pots. It would be cooked in lard and consumed by an eater of pig meat.

People who ate pig meat deserved whatever they got.

And when the heat of the lard curled the bite mark into a tight wrinkle, the last piece of evidence would have disappeared. Pictures of the bite mark could not be introduced as evidence when the piece of skin itself was the highest and best evidence.

Tony was pleased at how well he was cleaning up the situation in Atlanta. Tomorrow he had an appointment to repair his broken tooth. Then, even if the police tried to use their pictures of the bite mark, they could not link him to the deaths of the boy and the mother.

Tony laughed. A short staccato laugh.

He turned left on Boulevard, paying close attention to a parked telephone-maintenance truck. American law enforcement had an uncommon predilection for choosing telephone trucks as surveillance vehicles. It was a favorite ruse, one they never seemed to grow weary of using. But this one seemed real: the truck blocked one lane of traffic, a utility hole cover was near the rear tire, and two men were asleep in the front seat.

Tony drove a few blocks, then turned right into a parking lot at Georgia Baptist Hospital and continued to the second level, where, in a dim corner, he parked and quickly took off the patrolman's uniform and donned civilian clothes.

As he left the lot, the attendant looked at the parking ticket in bewilderment. This guy had been inside three minutes.

"I changed my mind," Tony said. "Decided not to visit my uncle. Hospitals make me nervous."

The attendant nodded. "One dollar."

He pocketed the dollar as Tony drove out of the lot.

"Dumb son of a bitch," the attendant muttered as he watched Tony's car. "You didn't stay long enough to have to pay."

Tony drove toward downtown, his thoughts on the homicide investigation. He did not worry about physical evidence in the woman's case. He had deliberately left a footprint because he wanted the police to know that the same person had killed both mother and son. Now the shoe had been burned beyond recognition and buried where it would never be found. The footprints on which the police placed so much importance would lead only to a dead end.

He knew that several pubic hairs had been found in the woman's mouth. But they were only pieces of hair; no roots were attached and that meant DNA sampling was useless. A few fibers had been found on the floor where he had laid his clothing. But the cheap cotton shirt and trousers he had worn that day were sold in stores over America; millions had been manufactured. But even if his came from a lot that, for whatever reason, was distinct in some fashion, even if the clothes were traced to the store where they were sold, it would be another dead end for the cops.

He had burned the clothing.

The police had nothing.

He had Operation Bilal and the plans of Frederick A. Carr.

The only problem was that the police knew of

Operation Bilal. He had been told the only copy of the report was the one he found hidden in the woman's house. But he had been around too long to believe such a thing. The information in the report was too sensational for a cop to sit on it simply because his boss told him to do so.

The black major surely understood the significance of the report. A man did not make major without having some intelligence. And the woman would have told the major enough to make sure he pursued the case.

Tony never considered that the sheer implausibility of Operation Bilal had been its greatest protection, that the homicide was the real reason the cops were pursuing the case. The homicide had broken the veil of implausibility.

He told himself instead that cops were a suspicious lot; they would lie to anyone and everyone to advance a case. He could not afford to take a chance. The police major surely had a copy of the report. That meant the old homicide detective had read it.

But what to do about it?

The homicide investigation soon would come to an abrupt halt. It would, as the Americans said, "run out of steam" because there was no evidence. The big question was whether or not the two cops, the major and sergeant, could parlay what they knew of Operation Bilal into an investigation. His friend in the police department had said it would not happen.

But his friend was an idiot.

The major had been relieved of duty. And the

black officers who ran the department paid little attention to the old sergeant who was investigating the two homicides.

But Tony was very conscious of time. The weight of days lay heavily upon him. The election was only days away and every poll predicted victory for Frederick A. Carr.

Tony's friend in the police department advised him to lay low, not even to consider killing the major and sergeant.

The death of the mother and her son could be absorbed in the plethora of homicides taking place in Atlanta. Even though Glory Gowon had been the fiancée of a police major, she was a Nigerian. And the death of a Nigerian did not receive the highest priority from the police department. Her son, who had been in Atlanta only a few days, was of even less significance.

But the death of a police major and a police sergeant would open up a new and different universe, according to Tony's friend.

Tony listened to his friend. When he insisted on knowing Tony's plans, Tony was noncommittal. He did not believe the deaths of the two police officers would be of greater significance than any other deaths.

He was thinking of the future. Even after the Hidden Imam was elected senator, the two cops could go to the American media with their story.

Tony could not allow that to happen. It was his job to see that such a thing never took place. Too much was at risk. Too much money had been spent over too many years. A couple of obscure local policemen could not be allowed to put Operation Bilal at risk.

He must kill them.

First the major.

Then the old sergeant.

Tony crossed the viaduct behind CNN and glanced at the domed stadium. Ahead was the Clark–Atlanta University complex and the empty lot where the old man was cooking barbecue.

24

Caren Diamond hung up the telephone and spun around in her chair. Her eyes were wide. "The M.E. didn't send anyone over here to pick up evidence," she said.

Dean Nichols stared blankly.

Caren squeezed her lips together and shook her head in anger. "I *knew* there was something about that guy."

"You mean the officer who picked up the bite mark?" Dean said.

Caren nodded impatiently. She stood up and looked out the window over the parking lot. Nothing. There was no sign of the man who picked up the evidence. No cars were moving. No people were in sight. The guy was gone. She did not even know if he was in a police car or a private car.

"Yeah, yeah," she said impatiently. "The M.E. didn't send him over."

"Who did?"

"Good question."

Caren walked rapidly across the room and sat down at a computer terminal. The homicide-squad computer, which was tied into the city's mainframe, had access to everything from utility records

to auto tag files to the names of those in the city jail.
It also contained city employment rolls.

Seconds later Caren spun around, stood up, and
said, "No one on the rolls by that name. Is this a
joke? Whoever the guy is, he's not a police officer."

She walked towards Dean, seized his arm, and
repeated, "He's not a police officer."

"Then what the hell's he going to do with a piece
of skin from a dead man? A bite mark? He some
kinda pervert?"

Caren stood, feet apart, legs straining against her
skirt, eyes narrowed in concentration. "He's not a
police officer."

"Why do you keep saying that?"

"A cop would know we have pictures of the bite
mark. That piece of skin can never be admitted into
evidence. Too inflammatory. The court would
never allow it, just as the court would never allow
a body to be wheeled into court and introduced
into evidence."

She clenched her fist for emphasis. "It's the pictures that are important. The pictures and the testimony of the dentist. We've got, what? three sets of
pictures? Why would someone want the bite
mark?"

"If somebody takes evidence, it's to fuck up a
case," Dean said. "Obviously he wanted to burn
our homicide case. And you're right. A cop would
know the rules of evidence better than that."

Dean smiled, rolled the cigar around in his
mouth, and threw out his right hand in an expan-
sive gesture. "Speaking of pictures, I got pictures."
He grinned. He looked at the camera. His smile

slowly faded. "That is, if I had it in focus and if the timer works and if the exposure was right and if he was in the frame and if his face wasn't in the shadow of his hat."

He tapped the camera with his hand. "Maybe I don't have pictures. I'll develop this today."

Caren did not hear him. She was mentally moving the case along, trying to determine the possible impact of what had happened. A crucial piece of evidence in a case involving a police major had been taken from the homicide office.

Dean realized what she was doing and chewed thoughtfully on his cigar. He nodded in approval. "I like how you're always asking questions, always poking around," he said. "That's a good habit at work."

She looked over her shoulder. "But not at home?"

"You got that right." Dean pulled the cigar from his mouth and stared at the soggy end where he had clenched the cigar in his teeth. "Go back to your earlier question," he said. "Why would somebody steal evidence when we have pictures of that evidence? Take it one step further. Keep going."

"Keep going where?"

"What happens if a defense attorney discovers we don't have the bite mark? We don't have the highest and best evidence. What happens if he knows that all we have are pictures and a pro-prosecution dentist?"

Caren nodded in understanding. She sighed. "Shaky. At best we would be on very shaky ground."

Nichols stuck the cigar in his mouth and looked at the ceiling. "Right. The bite mark itself could never be admitted. But if it's missing, we got problems. Big time. The defense attorney can raise enough questions to poison the jury. The guy who took the bite mark is either damn smart or damn lucky."

His voice changed to a mocking tone. "Ladies and gentlemen of the jury, it seems the police have *lost* the evidence. *Lost* it. If they lost the most crucial piece of evidence, if they were that careless, what other mistakes have they made? What else have they lost? What sort of credibility can you, the jury, place in the police when they *lose* the most crucial piece of evidence in a case?"

Caren paced the floor. Her jewelry jangled as she walked. Her cheeks were flushed with anger. "He just walked in here and asked for it," she said tightly. "In the police station. He walked into homicide and asked for a crucial piece of evidence. And we gave it to him."

She tossed her hands toward the ceiling. "He made me look like an idiot."

Dean stared at her. "He made *you* look like an idiot? I gave him the evidence."

"Yes, but I was there," Caren said. "I was part of it. It was my fault."

Dean waved expansively. "Hey," he said, "you want to feel guilty? Be my guest. But this thing went by the book. A uniformed officer comes in and says he's transporting evidence to the medical examiner. Happens all the time. Nothing's gonna roll downhill on this one."

Caren bit her lip. She was trembling. But when she spoke, her voice was icy. "I *knew* something was wrong with that guy. I sensed it when he looked at me. And I didn't do anything. I didn't say anything."

She spun and paced back and forth for a moment, arms folded and locked, brow wrinkled. She stopped and looked at Dean.

"What are you going to do?"

Dean picked up a piece of tobacco from his lip, flicked it away, and reached for the telephone. "I'm going to call Sergeant Buie."

"Before you do, you might want to hear what else the M.E. told me."

Dean paused. "Oh, about the temple monument?"

"And the two gang members killed at the convenience store."

"Well?"

"Guy at the temple had a bite mark in the scapula region of his right shoulder."

Dean's eyes widened.

Careen looked at him. "And they all, the one at the temple and the two at the convenience store, they all had penile implants."

Dean laughed. "They what?"

"They all had penile implants."

"You mean eighteen and nineteen-year-old boys had inflatable peckers?"

"More or less."

"What do you mean, 'more or less'?"

"They were permanently inflated. There was no mechanism to deflate them."

"The M.E. told you that?"

Caren nodded. "He's sending over the paperwork with more details, but essentially that's what he said. They had permanent erections."

Dean grinned and shook his head.

"That's not all," Caren said.

"Take me to the promised land."

"They were tattooed."

"The gang members? Or the members of the members?" Dean chuckled.

"Each of the gang members had a tattoo on his penis."

"So did the temple monument."

"Why do you call him the temple monument?"

Dean shrugged. "He was out in the bushes in front of the temple. I figured he was a JAP toy."

Caren shook her head. "Don't ever change."

"I won't."

Caren sighed. "All of them were the same. The convenience store robbers had the same tattoo as the body at the temple." She paused. "It must have something to do with being a gang member, part of the Rod and Gun Club."

"Wait a minute," Dean said. "You telling me they each had the same thing tattooed on their peckers?"

"Penis is the term you are groping for."

"I ain't groping for anything." Dean paused. "How many members in the Rod and Gun club?"

Caren shrugged. "I have no idea. I can call Intelligence."

Dean studied his cigar. Then he cut his eyes toward Caren. "You think they are all erect members?"

She sighed. "Enough already. The real question is, why would teenage boys do that?" She paused and stared speculatively at Dean. "Detective Nichols, you do remember what it was like to be that age? Did you then have any reason for such an operation?"

Dean glowered at her. "What do you mean, *then*? I didn't have any reason for an operation like that then and I don't have any reason for an operation like that now and I won't have any reason for an operation like that when they lower me into my grave. In fact, I'll probably have to have a special lid on my casket. I'll be just like those guys."

"Yeah, yeah, yeah. But why would a teenage boy, especially a Hispanic boy who comes from a culture with such a macho tradition, have this operation?"

"Why don't you check it out? I got to call the sergeant." Dean reached for the telephone and pressed the buttons. He laughed. "This case is getting to be a real handful. The sergeant might want to come over and get a hold of things."

A moment later he paused and said, "Major, this is Detective Nichols. Could I speak to the sergeant?" Pause. He rolled his cigar around, then looked at the ceiling.

"Sergeant. This is Nichols. Something's up."

25

Jeremiah slowed as he approached the Georgia Dome. He turned left off Northside Drive and into Vine City. As he approached the corner of Vine and Magnolia, he slowed, causing the old gray car to begin loping and chugging and burping. The young men on the corner heard the car, then recognized him. They sneered in derision.

"Hey, man, you still wearing that dress?" shouted Fish Sandwich.

The other young men hooted and clapped.

Jeremiah slammed on the brakes. It was Monday morning and he had wanted to start the week off right. He wanted to forget the funeral the day before. He wanted to forget the growing anger he felt. He had come down here prepared to be a nice guy, to hang out and schmooze and then pass out the pictures. But now the majesty of the law had been offended. He wasn't going to take this crap from street corner hoodlums. It was time for a come-to-Jesus meeting.

The young men eyed him warily as he leaped from the car and strode rapidly onto the sidewalk.

"Against the wall," Jeremiah ordered. He pointed to the brick wall of the grocery store, the one that housed one of the biggest numbers operations in Atlanta.

Cool shook his head in disbelief.

Cool's brother looked away.

Box Head and Nozzle ignored Jeremiah.

Fish Sandwich stood up, arms bowed out to the side like the wings of an irate rooster. "Man," he said indignantly, "I ain't believing this shit. Why you be hasslin' the brothers?"

"Up against the wall," Jeremiah repeated. He used his command voice, his hard voice. The young men, slowly and with much sighing and mumbling, stood up, turned around, and put their hands on the wall. They knew the procedure.

Jeremiah went down the line, patting each one down. "I be hassling the brothers," he said, "because the brothers know something they ain't telling. They know the man who killed two people, two black people, and they haven't done anything about it. Therefore the brothers be a bunch of fuck-ups. That's why I be hassling the brothers."

Fish Sandwich looked over his shoulder. "What you care about black folk getting killed?"

"I care if polka-dot people get killed. I even care if white people get killed. Unless you understand that, you don't understand shit. And the only way to deal with you is to treat you like criminals. Which is what you are. Withholding evidence is a criminal offense."

"Man, we don't know shit," Fish Sandwich said.

"That is the truest statement you will make all day."

Fish Sandwich tried to twist away as Jeremiah frisked him. Jeremiah seized him by the belt and jerked hard, pulling Fish Sandwich off balance. In that moment Jeremiah quickly frisked under his arms and around his waist. He paused for a second as his hand found, closed around, and extracted a knife from Fish Sandwich's belt.

"Well, well, well. What have we here?"

Fish Sandwich looked over his shoulder. "Man, you living dangerous."

Jeremiah's white eyebrows racheted upward. He stuck the knife in his belt. "Oh, how is that?" he asked in a solicitous tone.

Fish Sandwich pulled away from the wall and thumped himself on the chest. He was indignant. "You be on our streets. Nobody comes to Vine City 'less we say so."

"Is that right?" Jeremiah's smile was so benign that Fish Sandwich felt no doubt about pressing on.

"That's right," he said. "Not even the King's Men or them other pussies come over here 'less we say so."

He shrugged his shoulders. "We let you come down here the other day 'cause you with a brother." He stepped closer to a still smiling Jeremiah. "But you a dumb old man to come over here all by yourself," he said. His mouth tightened. "We gonna whip your white ass and then kick what's left of you back to your side of town."

The next thing Fish Sandwich knew, he had been spun around, had his face shoved into the wall, and was doing a realistic imitation of how to eat bricks.

"You gonna whip my white ass just like I'm going to piss all the way to Savannah," Jeremiah said through gritted teeth. He shoved Fish Sandwich's face harder into the wall. "The problem with you is that you don't know when to shut up," he said. "Saturday you thought it was funny that I wore a dress." He pushed the back of Fish Sandwich's head.

"Oooowwww."

Blood, a bright and vivid red in the morning sunshine, leaped from the edge of Fish Sandwich's mouth and began to ooze down the bricks.

"Now you're threatening a police officer. You were right, you don't know shit. For your information, the proper name is kilt. I wear the kilt. I do not wear a dress." He pushed again.

"Oooowww."

"Say it. Say kilt."

"That's what you gonna be, man. Kilt."

Jeremiah pushed again. "What's your name, asshole? Are you Fish Sandwich?"

Fish Sandwich rolled his eyes. He was surprised the white cop remembered his name. His silence was an answer.

"Wanna change your name? Wanna be Shit Sandwich? Where you stay at, Fish Sandwich?"

"In the 'hood, man. Down on Magnolia."

Jeremiah looked at the six young men spread-eagled against the wall. "Anyone of you so much as twitch and I'll teach you about ass kicking. Then I'll see that you spend six months in jail for resisting arrest. You got that?"

He was answered by a sullen silence.

"I said, do you got that?" He shouted loudly enough that heads were poking out of doors up and down the street.

Cool and Cool's Brother and Box Head and Nozzle nodded and mumbled.

"I know that's right," Neck Bone said.

Jeremiah jerked Fish Sandwich by the arm and pulled him a few steps away.

"Want to go for a ride?"

"Fuck no, I ain't going for no ride with no white cop." Fish Sandwich looked at Jeremiah's battered police car. He snorted. "Especially not in that piece of shit."

Jeremiah leaned closer to Fish Sandwich. "I'll put your ass in the front seat and ride around the block a couple of dozen times, then take you up by the MARTA station where some of your fellow assholes hang out. I'll laugh a lot and reach over now and then and pat you on the back. We might even drive down MLK over to the corner where Old Black Joe sells barbecue and buy us some barbecue. Eat it in the car where everybody can see us. What'd you think of that?"

"I ain't believing this shit."

"I like the idea." Jeremiah spoke through gritted teeth. "We go for a ride and then I come back and put you out and I pass you a twenty and I thank you for the information and I laugh and I say you're a good man. What do you think of that?"

"I'd have to fight half the motherfuckers in Vine City." Fish Sandwich began to look doubtful.

"That's in the first five minutes. Then you gonna have to fight all the others. They'll think you're a snitch, and everybody will want some of you."

Now Fish Sandwich was beginning to understand the majesty of the law. The clicking of the wheels in his head was almost audible. "What you want?"

"In a minute I'm gonna have a pow-wow with you and the guys you hang with. I'm gonna show you a picture and I'm gonna give you a card with my name and phone number on it. I don't care what the others do, but you're gonna hit the bricks for me. You're gonna help me find somebody. You're gonna put out the word and then you're gonna call me and tell me where to find this guy. That's what I want."

"I ain't giving up no brother."

"Who said he was a brother?"

Fish Sandwich snorted. "You don't come to Vine City looking for white folk."

"Could be a brother. Could be an Arab. Not sure. As for giving him up, you either do it and we keep it a secret just between us, or I'll put the word on the street that you're my snitch. I'll pick you up and ride you around every day. What's it gonna be?"

The wheels were grinding. "I ain't calling no white cop." Fish Sandwich paused. "I might call Mr. Worthy."

"That's fine. You call Mr. Worthy. We work together."

"How'd he fuck up?"

Jeremiah laughed. He pulled the young man away from the wall. Fish Sandwich flicked a forefinger through the blood on his chin but did not wipe it off. He wanted the others to see it; he wanted them to know this white cop had pushed his face into a wall.

Jeremiah turned and approached the friends of

Fish Sandwich. "Okay, ladies, turn around," he ordered. "We're about to have a summit conference."

The young men slowly turned around, impassive faces toward Jeremiah, and waited. He pulled a sheaf of pictures from his pocket and began passing them out.

"Who this?" Cool asked.

"Looks like a brother to me," Cool's Brother said.

"Light-skinned dude," Box Head ventured.

"This is the man Major Worthy told you about the other day," Jeremiah said. "Now we got pictures. We want to talk to him about two homicides. About the death of Major Worthy's fiancée and the death of his fiancée's son."

Fish Sandwich's eyes widened. "Man, you didn't tell us Mr. Worthy's lady was snuffed."

Box Head waved the picture. "This be the dude what offed 'em?"

"We don't know. We just want to talk." He paused. "Anybody recognize him?"

The heads of five men moved as one, shaking slowly from side to side.

"Anybody ever seen this guy? He might have a broken front tooth."

The heads continued to shake.

"Anybody ever think they've seen somebody who looks like this?"

The heads shook.

Jeremiah passed out his card. "You all have Major Worthy's card. I'd like you to have mine. Call me if you see this guy."

"Where we supposed to see him?" Cool's Brother asked.

"We think he's a Muslim. So you might see him

around one of the mosques. He might hang out with other Muslims. Muslim stores. Muslim restaurants. On the street. Anywhere."

Cool and Box Head involuntarily turned toward Fish Sandwich. They quickly looked away. But Jeremiah had seen the glances.

"You a Muslim?" he asked. "You can't be a Muslim. Not with a name like Fish Sandwich."

"I been to the mosque a few times," Fish Sandwich said defensively. "Me and my girlfriend. The imam said I could change my name to an Arab name." He grimaced. He had said more than he should have.

"Which mosque?"

Fish Sandwich did not answer.

"Al Farook over on Fourteenth Street? That's the closest. Or do you go to Masjid al Muminun down on Capital Avenue?"

Again Fish Sandwich was surprised. How did this old white guy know the names of two local mosques?

"Al Farook Masjid," he mumbled.

"What's your girlfriend's name?"

"None of your business, man. "

"Come on, Fish Sandwich. You're not ashamed of her, are you? You ought to be proud to tell me her name." He turned to the other young men. "Aren't you gentlemen proud of your ladies? Of course you are."

"Formica."

"Formica? Formica what?"

"Formica Dinette."

"Formica Dinette? Is that her street name? What's her real name?"

"That is her real name, man. Formica Dinette. She ain't got no street name. She a lady."

Jeremiah paused. "Fish Sandwich and Formica Dinette. You two go together."

Fish Sandwich nodded. "That's what everybody says."

"I'm sure she will be changing to an Arab name also."

"I ain't talking to no white cop about no Arab names."

"Fish—since we're friends, you don't mind if I call you Fish, do you?—you might not believe this, but I hope you become a member of the mosque. It'll get your ass off the street."

Fish Sandwich shrugged. The old white cop had pissed him off and he had said too much. Now his jaws tightened and he looked away. He would not speak again.

Jeremiah nodded. He clasped his hands together and turned to the five young men. "Ladies, I've enjoyed our little chat. I hope we can get together again soon. And I expect to hear from one of you about this man we're looking for."

He turned and walked toward his car.

As he opened the door, one of the young men, he did not know which, began mumbling. Jeremiah could not hear the words, but he understood the tone.

He was wasting time asking these guys for help.

26

"Keep it quiet about getting the DNA results," Jeremiah said. He looked across his desk at Dean Nichols and Caren Diamond. "We've had too many leaks ."

"Any idea yet about who's doing it?" Caren asked. Today she was wearing black: a high-necked black blouse, a wide black belt, and a black full skirt that reached to the tops of her black shoes. Many women would have looked dowdy or funereal in a shapeless all-black outfit. Not Diamond. She wore large gold earrings, a heavy gold necklace, and enough gold rings and gold bracelets to open a jewelry store. She was breathtaking.

Jeremiah was not immune. He sighed and shrugged. "Has to be a cop. A ranking cop. Either that or somebody in the mayor's office."

"You working on it," Nichols said. It was not a question.

"I'm working on it."

"Back to the DNA," Diamond said. "All we need is a suspect so we can take a blood test and go for a DNA match."

Jeremiah nodded. "We got plenty of physical evidence, enough to put the perp away forever. But you're right. We need a suspect."

He looked at Nichols. "The phony cop, T. Soporif—by the way, there's no such name in the city directory, phone book, or any computer data base—is our best bet so far. We've all passed out the composite all over town, so we just have to wait. That picture has been our biggest break. It enabled the artist to make an excellent composite. So, Nichols, you keep your camera and take pictures of anything you want."

Nichols pulled out a cigar, licked it, and said, "I keep telling you I'm more than the Good Humor man." He paused. "By the way, anything happen on my giving that puppy the bite mark?"

Jeremiah shook his head. "That's over," he said. "If I had been here, I probably would have done the same thing. Don't worry about it."

Dean nodded.

"Okay, let's quickly run over what we have, and then let's hit the bricks," Jeremiah said. "We gotta find this guy. It's only a couple of weeks until the election. I'll entertain any ideas you have about flushing this guy." He nodded toward Caren. "Diamond, tell us what we have and what we need."

Caren nodded confidently. "We have footprints from both crime scenes. The same shoe. It appears to be a tennis shoe. We're trying to match the pattern to a brand. We'll determine the exact size, check every outlet in town, and if they were bought with a credit card, we got him there."

She pursed her lips for a moment, then continued. "Bite marks. The actual evidence there, as you know, is missing. We might have problems in court because of that; we might not. We still have the photographs and we still have the expert testimony of Dr. Green. The good doctor thinks the bite mark on the boy and the bite mark on the gang member are the same; he's not sure, but he's working on it."

"He *thinks* they are the same," Nichols said sarcastically.

"The width of the arch is the same in both cases—about four inches—very wide. Dr. Green says only two percent of the population has an arch that wide. And there are similarities in the actual bite."

Nichols rolled his cigar around in his mouth. "Two percent. Let's see, the population of the Atlanta region is about three and a half million. Two percent is what? seventy thousand? Seventy thousand people in the Atlanta area have an arch like that. That will go great with a jury."

Jeremiah nodded in agreement. "We have to follow it. Granted, I wouldn't base the case on it even if the sample had not been taken. All it takes is for one or two other dentists to disagree and the bite-mark evidence is out the window. But keep on it."

He nodded toward Caren. "Okay, we got DNA and footprints. We can get a conviction on either one. We got bite marks. Shaky. But we might need it. We have a composite of a possible suspect. Keep going."

"Beyond the physical evidence, we have some intriguing similarities in M.O. The knife. The perpetrator knows how to use a knife. He is a professional. I'm checking the computer for comparable cases to see what conclusions, if any, we might draw."

"What are you looking for?" Nichols asked.

"Everything. Type of crime in which knives were used. Racial and ethnic makeup of perpetrators in those crimes. Types of edged weapons used. Nature of injuries. Number of deaths. Everything. I'm looking for a thread."

"Willy uses knives," Dean said. "Willy and the spics. That's about it."

Caren and Jeremiah turned to look at Dean.

"Do you remember that business about being politically correct?" Jeremiah asked Caren. "Popped up a few years ago?"

Caren nodded. "I was in graduate school at Emory. Being PC was quite the thing among my professors."

"Would you say our colleague here, Detective Nichols, is being politically correct in his speech?"

Caren laughed.

Nichols shrugged. "I remember that politically correct shit. Lasted about six months, maybe a year. Another liberal trend. Just like swallowing goldfish and playing with hoola hoops."

"There you have it," Jeremiah said. "The philosopher among us."

"Make fun if you want, but the reason that stuff doesn't last is because there's nothing to it. Liberals don't believe it, but most people have walking-around sense. Most people figure these things out."

Jeremiah held up a hand to stop Nichols. He wanted to get the meeting back on track. But Nichols was not through.

"Let me tell you one other thing," he said. "Then I'll shut up about this. Liberals are usually young. Ever notice that? It's part of growing up to go through a liberal phase. Like having zits on your face. Young people discover liberalism the way they discover masturbation—and it makes them just as crazy. How many old liberals you know? There's nothing sadder than an old liberal. They're usually fat, and they wear clothes twenty years too young for them. Either that or they got AIDS."

Nichols waved his cigar. "If every person in America could be a police officer for one week, there wouldn't be any liberals."

Jeremiah nodded. "You are more than the Good Humor man." He turned toward Caren. "Diamond, please continue."

"The incident with the Hispanic gang members seems out of character for our suspect. If Dr. Green is correct and the same person made the bite marks, then I have to ask why. The Rod and Gun Club members, as far as we know, have nothing to do with this Nigerian plan."

Jeremiah interrupted. "Major Worthy says, and I think he's right, we should think of this as a Muslim plan, not a Nigerian plan."

"Okay," Caren continued. "What do Hispanic gang members have to do with this Muslim plan? It's out of character."

"Fudge packers are fudge packers," Nichols said.

He waved his cigar and continued. "It's easy. Those guys have penile implants. They walk around with permanent erections. Our boy is a fudge packer. He—"

"Oh, stop it," Caren said impatiently.

"Wait a minute," Jeremiah said. "This guy is a sexual psychopath. Look what he did to the boy and his mother. He's extremely violent. It's clear he's out of control. Look at the gang member. Didn't the M.E. say he was raped?"

Caren nodded. "He sustained major trauma in that area."

Dean laughed. "Major trauma in that area," he mocked. "What you mean is that three pickup trucks and a motorcycle could be parked in his asshole. Can't you say asshole?"

She paused. "Sometimes I am tempted."

"This guy is unpredictable," Jeremiah said. "Many killers have sexual problems, but not every one is a psychopath. Nichols, maybe you have something. Maybe the connection is not the Muslim plan but the sexual aspect."

He leaned across the desk. "Aren't the Red Dogs conducting sweeps for gang members?"

Nichols nodded.

"I'll ask the captain to call the major who's in charge of the Dogs. Any Rod and Gun Club people they pick up, we'll have them brought here for interviews."

"What about the health department?" Caren asked.

The two men looked at her. They did not understand.

"If the connection is sexual," she explained, "someone may have passed along some sort of STD at one time or another. The Fulton County Health Department has the records."

"Diamond, now I know why you're here," Jeremiah said in admiration. "Okay, go over there and see what they got. Pull in any gang member who has been treated for any sexually transmitted disease."

"There's one other thing." Caren said in what was almost a reluctant tone of voice.

Jeremiah waited.

"You said you did not get a computer hit with the name T. Soporif. I'd like to give the name to some people I know and see what they can do."

"I had DEA check it out in the federal computers," Jeremiah said.

Caren did not say anything. She stared at Jeremiah. Waiting.

His eyebrows lowered a fraction. "Are they in law enforcement?"

She hesitated a moment. "Yes."

"A government agency?"

"Yes."

"Okay, do it. Now, both of you get out of here and go knock on doors. Find this guy."

Caren hurried from the room so quickly that both Jeremiah and Dean stared after her.

She walked swiftly toward the elevator. She was afraid Jeremiah might ask her more questions about her friends. When she told Jeremiah they were with a government agency, she had not said which government.

27

Richard Alpha Martin Head, chief of police for the city of Atlanta, always signed letters and memos with his full name. But throughout the police department he was known simply as Dick Head. His nickname came not so much from his real name as it did for the nonsensical business jargon that both impressed and befuddled his fellow city hall bureaucrats. His everyday language was virtually unintelligible. His thinking process was a quagmire, a dank and murky fen from which no simple light-giving sentence could emerge.

The chief, while not bright, had a quick native intelligence, a feral sort of intellect that enabled him to prosper in a bureaucratic environment.

As a cop, Dick Head was not prepossessing. He was small, five feet ten, and he weighed only a hundred and sixty pounds. He made up for his lack of size by wearing a custom-designed uniform. It was the most non-regulation uniform any ranking officer had worn since Eldrin Bell was chief, the sort of uniform worn by the chief of state in a small, insecure Third World country, and one that would have been summarily stripped from anyone else in the department. The coat had padded shoul-

ders and enough gold braid and trim to make a
cheerleader envious. A gold fourragère was draped
over the left shoulder. Two gold stripes trimmed
the outside of the razor-creased trousers. A wide
black belt of the softest leather squeezed the chief's
waist and was held by a sunburst belt buckle, also
of gold.

Chief Head had come up through traffic and administrative services and had never been a beat
cop. When Eldrin Bell was chief, Dick Head had
been promoted to major and then to one of the
three deputy chief positions. Bell picked Head because he hated confrontations, was not strong
enough to be a threat, and would do whatever Bell
said. When Bell resigned as chief to run for mayor,
he suggested to the incumbent mayor that Richard
Alpha Martin Head be named the interim chief.
And then when Bell was elected mayor, he made
Head the chief. Head's assistants handled most
day-to-day operation of the department; he considered himself to be what he called a rabbit leader,
the man out in front of everyone else, but in truth,
he made decisions only when he was threatened.
When it came to survival, he would do what he
had to do.

He was involved in a homicide investigation, os-
tensibly because it involved the family of a police
major, but in reality because it involved Operation
Bilal, a little deal that had made him almost a million dollars—a deal that, as he thought of it, he had
opportunistically identified as the outline template
that would sink him into a frequency.

About the only thing Head had ever done on his

own was become involved with the Nigerians and the Arab he knew as Tony. He was in before he realized it. The relationship had begun years before, back when Head was a major. Both Tony and the Nigerians had strongly suggested they had a lot to do with his being promoted to chief. If the money they had paid him over the years, and continued to pay him, was any indication of their resources, then they very well might have bought the job for him. Looking at it from the standpoint of Tony and the Nigerians, Head considered their plan an excellent piece of management-system integration.

Today Dick Head sat on the edge of his desk in his large office on the top floor of City Hall East, carefully adjusted his trousers so they would not wrinkle, and looked to the west, up Ponce de Leon toward Peachtree, and pondered his dilemma. He was facing major structural issues, and it was time to become proactive.

Tony was running amok. Individuating too strongly. Stealing evidence in an ongoing homicide investigation had been the final straw. Tony insisted the chief obtain a uniform and tell him how to conduct himself, and against his better judgment, Head had acquiesced. He hated confrontations. But now it was time for reframing. He had tried to talk to Tony about rules of evidence and the best evidence rule and how the American jurisprudence system worked. But the arrogant bastard had insisted that if he stole the piece of skin containing the bite mark, the last bit of physical evidence against him would be gone. He had gone to a dentist and had a broken tooth replaced and a rough tooth bonded. The tennis shoes had been burned and then hurled in a dump. The DNA sample upon which homicide placed so much importance was worthless.

Head considered Tony to have a major shortfall in the area of interpersonal skills; he was the most condescending bastard Head had ever seen, though he would never tell Tony that. Tony hated blacks; he made no secret of it. He ridiculed the Nigerians and he ridiculed black Atlantans.

What miffed the chief was that his skin color was lighter than that of Tony's. And he had better hair than Tony—very fine, it was. He even had green eyes. Yet Tony patronized him and talked to him as if he were ten years old.

Look at the business of stealing the bite-mark evidence. It was only when Sergeant Buie filed a report about the incident that Head knew Tony had worn a name tag saying "*T. Soporif.*" That was stupid.

Now Sergeant Buie was investigating a possible connection between Tony and the death of the young Hispanic gang member. Head, in a state of high dudgeon, called Tony, who denied any involvement in the homicide. Head knew he was lying because the body had been tossed in the bushes at the temple. Tony disliked blacks, but he hated Jews with a passion that transcended logic. Dumping the body at the temple was how Tony actualized his contempt.

Sergeant Buie was another matter. The chief realized he might have underestimated the sergeant. Buie knew there was a leak of information regarding two homicides, and if the man could do any sort of theming at all, he would realize the leak had to be in the chief's office.

But Buie was nearing retirement. A threat to his pension would be the therapy focus basis to cause him to stay with the program.

The chief flicked a piece of lint from his sleeve. He would worry about Buie later.

The more immediate and more serious problem was Tony.

Head considered his options. He had known Frederick Carr since Carr's U.S. Attorney days in Atlanta. He had not talked to Carr since Carr had become a senatorial candidate, because somehow he knew that Operation Bilal's macro strategic plan linking dictated that he stay away from the candidate. But Carr was his only resource. Tony was out of control. Tony had placed Operation Bilal in considerable danger, and Head did not know how to incentivate the man to buy on to a formatting opportunity. Head was afraid of Tony. The Arab had the most frightening eyes he had ever seen. And he was absolutely inplacable. He killed when there was no need to kill.

Head watched the traffic on Ponce de Leon and realized what he should do. His thoughts drifted. He had to make a decision about Tony.

After all, he was the rabbit out front.

He was the prototypical rabbit leader.

28

The Georgia Power meter reader sauntered along St. Paul Avenue, a short street off the northwest corner of Grant Park. St. Paul is an old but gentrified street of large remodeled homes in what once was seen as an area of urban pioneers—a part of Atlanta where young professionals could turn a crime-ridden ghetto into a middle-class neighborhood. It is conveniently located only a couple of miles southeast of downtown Atlanta and contains both a renovated zoo and the Cyclorama, the world-famous Civil War diorama.

For a while it appeared Grant Park might become yuppified. But in the early 1990s it began sliding back into the slough from which it temporarily had escaped, and now it is once again an area of daytime burglaries and nighttime terrors.

The meter reader carried a small computer terminal. It weighed about a pound and could contain an address, the meter reading, and, for backup purposes, an identifying number for each meter.

Georgia Power had adopted electronic meter reading in much of Atlanta. A mobile unit was driven up and down neighborhood streets while onboard computers picked up signals from each meter. But Grant Park had not been switched over to the electronic system. Here a meter reader still walked the streets, easily identified by his khaki pants, the khaki shirt emblazoned with the Georgia Power logo, and the small computer terminal he carried.

He took the terminal off his shoulder and went to the meter of the first house, stayed there a moment, then walked through the yard toward the second house, and then the third.

His pace did not change when he reached the house he sought, one that showed no sign of the ennui that had swept over the neighborhood in recent years, a large house that had been renovated and kept with loving attention. The lawn, as had many others in Atlanta, had been replaced with gravel, but a profusion of flowers bloomed in the borders around the house and in beds along the sidewalk. Late October and flowers were blooming. The side of the house was sheltered by several enormous dogwood trees and large redtips.

The meter reader nodded approvingly. The redtips would provide the shelter he needed.

The meter reader walked slowly along the side of the house, looking at the placement of the windows and their height above the ground, not so much for a place to enter because he would go in through the door. He always entered through the door. He was looking for an emergency exit.

"What are you doing?" came a sudden peremptory voice.

The meter reader looked up. There on the back porch was a big man, well over six feet, with the bulk and muscle of a former athlete; a middle-aged guy, but, as the golf shirt he wore indicated, a middle-aged guy whose muscle had not turned to flab. This was no man to trifle with.

The meter reader thought he knew the man's identity. But he had to make sure. There could be no more mistakes. He smiled and waved the computer terminal.

"Meter reader," he said.

"You a new guy?"

The meter reader shrugged and smiled. "Does it show that much?"

The man on the porch laughed. "I'm sorry, brother. It's just that you obviously don't know where the meter is." He pointed to the side of the house near the porch, an area sheltered by the redtips. "Behind the bush. I don't like for the utilities to be visible. But I let that bush grow too much."

Tony parted the bush. "Here it is." He looked over his shoulder at the man on the porch. "Thanks."

The meter reader turned, held up the computer terminal, and began pressing the keys. His body hid the fact he did not know what he was doing.

"How does that thing work?" the man asked. He hunkered down on the edge of the porch and peered intently toward the meter reader.

The meter reader looked over his shoulder. In a casual voice he asked, "You live here?"

The man nodded. "Name's Vernon Worthy?"

The meter reader held up the terminal and pressed several buttons.

He nodded. "That's the proper name for this address. And the meter number checks out." He looked at Worthy and smiled. "Can't be too careful."

With his right hand the meter reader unbuttoned one button of his shirt just above his belt. For a moment he felt the comforting handle of the knife. His face showed no expression as he turned and held the terminal in his left hand and approached Worthy. "I can tell you what I know about this thing, which is not much."

Worthy looked at the small terminal. It appeared to weigh no more than a pound. Distant alarm bells were beginning to sound. He ignored them. He was bored and wanted to talk to someone. He leaned closer.

The meter reader took another step toward him.

Almost involuntarily the question came: "What's your name?"

The meter reader looked up, a puzzled expression on his face.

"What's your name?" Vernon Worthy repeated.

The meter reader smiled.

Now he was close enough. He raised the terminal. A light flashing on the face of the terminal drew Worthy's attention. The meter reader's right hand snaked inside his shirt.

"Tony," he said softly. "Tony the Dreamer."

Vernon Worthy leaned closer, not sure he had heard what he thought he heard. In that moment the terminal, backed by the Tony's wiry strength, smashed into his nose, flattening the cartilage and causing Worthy a moment of blinding pain. He

grunted, raised his hands toward his face, and tried
to fall backward away from the meter reader.

But it was too late. The *jambiya* had been drawn
and now it had to taste blood. The curved blade,
swung in a backhand motion from left to right as it
was pulled from Tony's belt, darted under Vernon
Worthy's raised arms and sliced his throat from ear
to ear.

Tony jumped to the right. But he could not avoid
the geyser of blood that fanned out of Worthy's
throat. His arm and face and upper body were
drenched. He never paused. He dropped the terminal and quickly shifted the *jambiya* to his left hand,
spun in a circle, and used the momentum of the
turn to shove the blade with great force under Worthy's ribs into his heart.

In that moment the two men came face to face.
Tony was angry. He knew when he looked into the
glazed eyes of Vernon Worthy that the man would
die in seconds. He disliked killing anyone so
quickly. There was so much more he wanted to do.

"I killed your whore," he whispered. "I killed her
son."

Vernon Worthy heard him. His lips twitched and
a glimmer of anger flickered once in his eyes and
then faded.

He could do nothing. He was looking down from
a great height upon an open field. The field was
bathed in a great light—a soft, ineffable light, and
on the field was a young man galloping through a
sea of white faces to score touchdown after touchdown.

Then he died.

29

On a steaming hot afternoon in late October, they came to Barnesville from all over Georgia, even from Florida, Alabama, and Tennessee, to pay homage to a cop killed in the line of duty.

Jeremiah Buie, wearing the kilt with the ancient hunting tartan of Lord of the Isles and cradling his pipes, the bagpipes revered in Scottish history as the Great Pipes of Donald, stood on the slope of a gentle hill on the outskirts of Barnesville and watched the assembly.

A double line of motorcycles, all with their lights turned on, stretched for perhaps a half mile. The motorcycles were escorts for the hearse bearing the body of Major Vernon Worthy, and for his family, the honor guard, and the six officers who were serving as a personal escort for the casket.

Hundreds of police cars came from cities and counties in four states. Their bright headlights looked for all the world like the flashing eyes of great battle horses at a medieval gathering of warriors.

State troopers blocked every road and every side street between the church and the cemetery. The procession, long though it was, flowed and undulated smoothly through the streets of Barnesville and onto the grounds surrounding the cemetery.

The order of events at a funeral for a police officer killed in the line of duty is decided jointly by the family and the police. At a funeral for a police major in the city of Atlanta, it is the desire of the police to pull out all the stops, to have a funeral closely approximating the ceremony and pomp and ritual seen at a military funeral where the deceased was a hero killed in battle. In this instance the family acquiesced. The only family left by Vernon Worthy was his frail and elderly mother, who was too numb to object, and the four brothers and three sisters, who, though they knew Vernon would have preferred a small, simple funeral, were too proud of their brother to deny him these final honors.

The police officers in attendance were caparisoned in splendor. They wore their Class A uniforms, and from a distance they sparkled and glinted in the bright sunshine. From the visors of their hats, down across their buttons and their belt buckles to their shoes, they glinted and gleamed and flashed tiny bursts of light. The uniforms were gray and blue and black and brown and tan, but they were uniforms, and the men and women who wore them were as one that day.

Black tape across their badges united them.

The creases in their sleeves and trousers were knife-like, and their gloves were whiter than choir robes. The officers all wore the same straight-ahead, firm-jawed look. And the faces of more than a few were streaked with tears.

Dean Nichols and Caren Diamond were there, but Jeremiah could not pick them out in the crowd.

Jeremiah waited. Even high on the hillside, not a zephyr of a breeze stirred the humid air. Heat settled over the crowd.

As a rule, Jeremiah liked funerals. But he did not like police funerals. The flags and the uniformed officers and the ceremony plumbed too deeply into his Celtic past. Police funerals, like weddings, reminded him of his own mortality. So he had not gone to the church service but instead had waited on the hill outside of town.

The major would have understood.

After all, Jeremiah had spent more than an hour with his body at the scene of the homicide, an hour in which he had talked softly to the major and played out various scenarios of what might have happened. He also made a confession to the major. "That evaluation you did of my job performance was right," he said. "I should not have been promoted."

Jeremiah did not need to go to the church. He knew what took place. He had been to these things before. Mayor Eldrin Bell, in firm, resonant tones, almost certainly had eulogized Vernon Worthy as a friend and as an outstanding police officer. The chief, wearing a uniform that resembled a lit-up Christmas tree, had done the same.

An elderly preacher talked of how he had known Vernon Worthy as a boy, as a young man, and as a ranking officer who still visited the church of his childhood. Then the old preacher went to the Bible, either to Ecclesiastes and the verses about the silver cord being loosed and the golden bowl being broken, or to Psalm 23 and the verses about the green pastures and still waters.

Whatever verse he used, he preached a funeral that made the welkin ring.

Jeremiah watched as the honor guard, as sharp and crisp and snappy as any military unit, fired a twenty-one-gun salute. Their gold scarfs, gold sashes, and gold stripes down their trousers—bold bursts of color against the deep blue of their uniforms—marked them as a special unit.

From the hillside where he stood, Jeremiah saw the helicopters coming. They seemed almost to stand still as they appeared in the distant haze. Then they began to grow. Five choppers came out of the afternoon sun, low and fast across the gently rolling countryside of middle Georgia. As the choppers approached the cemetery, one pulled up almost to the vertical, then peeled off to the side while the others continued over the open field and the cemetery in the famous missing-man formation. The resonating, thumping thunder of their passage lessened, then softened until there was silence.

And in that silence came the first haunting notes of "Taps," played ever so slowly by the police bugler.

Though it was sundown, the day had not cooled and the sharply creased uniforms were becoming damp and limp with perspiration.

Jeremiah, even though he wore a kilt containing eight yards of wool and a black jacket that soaked up the sun, showed only a faint gleam of moisture at his temples.

The American flag was taken from the casket, folded into a triangle showing only the white stars on the blue background, and then presented to Vernon Worthy's mother. She clasped it to her bosom and stared at the gleaming copper casket.

Then, at a signal, Jeremiah began playing.

The bagpipe is a martial instrument. Music marches rather than flows from its curious shape. The sound that explodes from the pipes is the skirl by which men go into battle, the music of warriors. But yet, in some inexplicable fashion, when a pipe major plays the old, familiar tunes, the sounds of childhood, those songs assume a sweetness and poignancy that can be evoked by no other instrument.

And so it was that when the high, ethereal notes of "Amazing Grace" came marching across the vale, those who had not yet shed tears joined those who had.

Jeremiah paused, took a deep breath, and began the song that would close the ceremony.

The first haunting notes of "Going Home" wafted down the hillside and across the open field, the field where Vernon Worthy, in a game of football, had experienced the great turning point in his life.

The celestial notes enveloped the family and the comrades of Vernon Worthy.

The ineffable sweetness of the notes lingered like a benediction in the vespertine stillness.

And it was then that Jeremiah Buie cried. He

blamed it on the pipes. He cried for his friend and he cried for the daughter he would never see again. And he blamed it on the pipes.

After the funeral he went to the major's elderly mother, clasped her hands between his, and said, "Your son was my friend."

Something in Jeremiah's voice caught her mother's ear. She was an old woman and she came from a time and place when blacks and whites did not socialize together. She was unnerved at the presence of so many white people. She did not know them and she did not know what to say to them.

But there was something different about this man. She stared deeply into his eyes. She looked at the kilt. Her eyes narrowed as she fought to remember.

"Are you the white boy Vernon used to talk about?" she asked slowly. She ignored the people flowing around them, waiting to pay their respects. She held onto Jeremiah's hand and continued to stare with the direct stare that only children and old people can get away with. "Are you the one he called Sissy?"

Jeremiah smiled. He nodded.

"That was a long time ago," she said.

"A long time ago," he agreed.

"And you say my son Vernon was your friend?"

Jeremiah raised his eyes for a moment to stare over the old woman's head. "He was my friend."

With the insight of the very old, she knew he spoke the truth. "Bless you, child," she said, and with surprising strength she put her arms around his shoulders and pulled him close. Then, when his face was pulled down into her neck, she whispered urgently into his ear, "You find him. You find the one who did this. You hear me? Let my soul rest?"

Jeremiah nodded. He pulled away, eyes straight ahead, not hearing the murmurs of praise for the music he had played, and marched toward his car filled with renewed determination to see Tony Soporif burn in hell.

He turned on the ignition, turned the air conditioner on high, and then stepped outside the car to take off his coat and return the bagpipes to the case. As he settled behind the steering wheel, he moved his sporan aside. It was then he remembered his beeper. He opened the sporan and removed the beeper. It was the vibrating rather than auditory sort, and he could not feel its slight tremor from inside the leather sporan. The only number listed on the readout was his office.

The car radio would not raise Atlanta, so he drove up Highway 41 to a service station and wheeled in beside a pay phone.

In Barnesville, a man wearing the kilt draws curious stares. But Jeremiah did not notice. He dialed the telephone and waited until the young police trainee who was manning the office answered.

"This is Sergeant Buie. You have a message for me?"

"Yessir, Sergeant. Just a moment." The young trainee searched through the messages. "Two calls, Sergeant. The first is from DEA, a woman named Sally. She wants to know if her painting is finished."

"Call her for me," Jeremiah said. "Tell her it will be completed in a day or so, and I'll see that it's delivered. Who else?"

The trainee paused. "This might be a joke," he said.

"I don't have time for jokes. Just tell me who called."

The trainee's voice was hesitant. He was intimidated by Sergeant Buie. "Yessir. He called four times. Said it was very important that he speak to you. But he wouldn't leave a number. Said for me to find out when you would be back in the office and he would call you here."

"Does he have a name?"

"Yessir." The trainee paused.

"Well, what is it?"

"He said his name was Fish Sandwich."

30

"Hey, man, I think I seen that dude you looking for," Fish Sandwich said over the telephone. His voice was angry, almost defiant.

"Where's that?" Jeremiah asked.

"At the mosque."

"Al Farook? On Fourteenth Street?"

"Yeah, man. You know where it is. Up near the top of the hill. Big place."

"You sure?"

"Fuck no, man, I ain't sure. I ain't sure of nothing except that white folk want to fuck with us."

"Why do you think it's the man I'm looking for?"

"You said he had a broken tooth, a front tooth, right?"

"Right."

"First time I seen this guy he kept poking his tongue at one of his front teeth. The whole side of his face was jumping in and out. And he reached in there with his finger and poked around a couple of times."

"Maybe he had food in his teeth. Come on, Fish, give me something."

"He totes a knife."

Jeremiah involuntarily sucked in his breath. He leaned closer to the telephone. "Did you see it?"

"Naw, I didn't see the dude's blade. But I don't got to see it to know he totes one."

"Then how do you know, Fish?"

"When he say his prayers, when he . . . what they call prostates himself, he always be adjusting."

Jeremiah was disappointed. "He always be adjusting," he echoed.

"Yeah, when he starts to get up from the floor, he always sneaking in an adjustment. Like he don't think nobody knows what he doing."

Jeremiah sighed. "Fish, maybe he's pulling up his pants. Maybe he's hustling his balls. Maybe he's scratching his ass. How do you know he's adjusting a knife?"

There was a long pause.

"How do you know?"

When Fish Sandwich answered, he was defiant. " 'Cause I tote a blade, too. One you took off me wasn't the only blade in the world. And every time I prostates myself, no matter how tight my belt be, leaning down and stretching out that way pulls the blade loose. I always gots to adjust my blade after I pray. He does it the same way I do."

"Okay, so the guy carries a knife. So do you. So do a thousand other people in Atlanta. And he sucks his teeth. So do a thousand other people. What else?"

"He got the bad eye."

"He what?"

"He don't like black folk."

"Fish Sandwich, I don't think this will be a surprise to you. But a lot of people don't like black folk."

"I know that's right," Fish Sandwich said grimly. "But this dude always be giving us the bad eye. Uppity motherfucker. Talks to them slant-eyed fuckers and them other Arabs, but he don't like black folk."

"Other Arabs? He's an Arab? How do you know?"

Fish Sandwich snorted. "Hey, he ain't no brother. He be an Arab. I mean, he don't wear no bed sheet like some of 'em do, but he be an Arab."

"So he gives you the bad eye. Does he say anything?"

"Naw," Fish Sandwich said impatiently. "He ain't got to say nothing. It's the way he acts. Man, you think I don't know if somebody treats me like a nigger?"

Jeremiah was silent.

Fish Sandwich jumped into the silence with more explanation. "You come down to Vine City and you give me and the brothers a load of shit, but it ain't 'cause we black. I know that. We saw how Mr. Worthy talked to you. He liked you. No brother like Mr. Worthy would put up with some whitey who fucked with the brothers. You gave us shit 'cause you a cop and you just got to fuck with somebody. But this Arab don't like black folks. He gives us the bad eye."

"So where do I find this Arab?"

"Friday. At the mosque. Noon prayers. If he gonna be there, he will be there Friday at noon."

"You know where he lives?"

"Fuck no, man. I ain't following no dune coon around Atlanta. I don't know where he lives."

"If you saw him last Friday, why didn't you tell me the other day when I was in Vine City? Why did you wait until now to call me?"

Fish Sandwich paused. " 'Cause I saw on TV about Mr. Worthy. If this dude you looking for be the guy what done it, then I'll talk to anybody. Even you."

After a moment he continued. "Man, Mr. Worthy was a good brother."

Jeremiah was silent for a long moment. "Yes, he was, Fish Sandwich," he said softly. "Yes, he was." He paused. "You know, he used to call me Sissy."

"I wonder why." Fish Sandwich laughed and poked a finger toward the telephone. "If this dude with the blade is the one you looking for, I hope you catch him," he said. "I don't care if he is a Muslim. He don't like black people. And ain't nothing says that just 'cause he be a Muslim, I got to like the motherfucker."

"Fish Sandwich, I'm not sure just how sound your theology might be, but I agree with the sentiment."

"Say what?"

"Never mind. How is Miss Dinette?"

"She a fine lady." Fish Sandwich was pleased.

"I know she is."

"Hey, man, I got to go. But let me tell you one more thing."

"What's that?"

"Don't send no white cops in the mosque. The emir will snap to 'em in a heartbeat. Keep the cops outside and snatch him when he be away from the mosque."

"How many people in the congregation?"

"I heard a man say that on Fridays there be six thousand faithful there. Maybe more."

"Six thousand! I can't find this guy in the middle of six thousand people."

"Yeah, you can."

"Oh?"

"You got any black undercover people?"

"Yes."

"Muslims?"

"Yes."

Fish Sandwich snorted. "Some black folk will do anything for money. Okay, here's what you do."

A moment later, Jeremiah laughed. "You might make a good police officer one day."

"Fuck that noise, man."

"Fish Sandwich?"

"Man, I got to go. I can't spend all day talking to no white cop."

"Thanks. For Mr. Worthy, I say thanks."

"Yeah."

31

"There's Fish Sandwich," Jeremiah said. "The guy in front of him must be our boy."

Dean turned his head slightly and studied the slender man leaving the crowded mosque. He had seen Tony at close range, but behind sunglasses and under a hat. He studied him.

Caren Diamond, sitting in the backseat of Jeremiah's car, did not hesitate. She had seen Tony from across the squad room. She had seen the tilt of his head, the set of his shoulders, the way he walked, all the identifying traits that in surveillance, especially from a distance, are more important than facial characteristics.

"That's the one. That's him," she said intently. Her eyes followed Tony across the parking lot. "Fucking Arab," she whispered under her breath.

Jeremiah and Dean, both astonished, turned as one and stared at her over the seat. Caren was wearing jeans and a blue chambray shirt. The blue outfit exaggerated the blue of her eye makeup and set off her earrings, which were of lapis surrounded by gold. A 9mm pistol in a black leather holster was snugged high on her right hip.

"Sorry," she said. She smiled and, half embarrassed, shrugged. "That's bred in the marrow of the bones in Jewish kids. From the time we can first understand, our parents tell us that Arabs want to destroy Israel and wipe all Jews from the face of the earth."

"Don't worry about it, Diamond," Dean said. "I'd have sworn Willy was the perp."

"Why?" she asked. Her eyes followed Tony.

"You got to understand something," he said in an emphatic, didactic tone. "The human being is the only animal that has sex in a face-to-face position. It's special. But Willy ain't got the message. He likes to come in the back door."

"You mean you and your wife did it only face to face?" Caren deadpanned.

"Of course," he said. "That's the only way."

"Never tried the Chinese basket trick?" Jeremiah asked. He was watching Tony.

"What the hell's that?"

"How about the—?" Caren begun.

"Stop it," Dean interrupted. He turned around in the seat to face Caren. "I don't want to hear it."

"I'm not surprised she wanted a divorce," Caren said.

"You're a police officer," Dean said. "You shouldn't be talking about stuff like that."

He wiggled his shoulders and settled back in the seat. "Besides, I'm the one who filed. Served the papers myself."

He shrugged. "In about three weeks I'm going to be divorced. And it only cost me twenty-five dollars."

"She gets the house?" Caren asked.

Dean nodded. "I told her I'd come over and cut the grass."

"That's very nice of you," Caren said. She pointed toward Tony. "Right behind him. There's our U.C. guy. We got him."

At that moment the radio crackled and a quiet voice said, "Heads up. I got the eyeball. He's in front of me. Light-skinned black male. Short, dark hair. Five feet ten or eleven. Weight one sixty. Appears to be thirty-five, maybe forty. Brown pants, white shirt."

"We copy," Jeremiah whispered.

"He's not black," Jeremiah said in an aside to Dean and Caren. "He's Arab."

Dean snorted. "What the hell difference does it make? Six of one and half dozen of another."

"I was getting worried," came the voice of the undercover officer. He was whispering into a microphone fastened inside his collar. "Tried to reach you from inside but no answer."

"Yeah, we lost you inside. Wouldn't transmit from in there."

"Allah's influence," came back the voice of the undercover officer.

"Allah owes *us* one now," Jeremiah said. "As soon as this lad gets into a car, give me the description."

"You got it."

Dean shifted in the front seat and chewed on his cigar. "I still think we should have grabbed him in the mosque. All the Arabs are lined up on the floor, looking up each other's asses. Perfect place to pop him."

Jeremiah shook his head in resignation. "You're an equal-opportunity bigot."

Dean nodded. "You got that right."

"He looks just like the composite," Caren said with surprise. "For once they did a good job."

Dean was offended. "Looks just like the picture I took," he said.

"A good picture of a cold-blooded killer," Jeremiah said.

" 'Course he's cold-blooded," Dean said. "He's a fucking reptile."

Jeremiah laughed. "I owe Fish Sandwich a big one. He pulled it off."

Dean watched Fish Sandwich break away from Tony and walk across the parking lot in the other direction. Dean sucked on his cigar. "No big deal. All he did was find the guy and park on the Arab's right side when the Arab kneeled to pray. That eyedeed him for our undercover guy. And we took it from there."

"Yeah, but for a black kid from Vine City, a kid working to become a Muslim, helping out a white cop is a hell of a step. It is a big deal. I owe him."

A cop working extra duty stepped into 14th Street and stopped traffic in both directions, then waved for cars in the parking lot to exit. They came in a steady stream, hundreds of cars.

"We set up?" Dean asked.

Jeremiah, eyes on the parking lot, nodded. "Five other cars. Set up to go either direction on Fourteenth Street. A couple of them will take parallel side streets once he is on the move."

"This puppy is ours," Dean said with a slow

grin. "Maybe he'll eye-dee us, want to duel it out, and I can get his picture in my scrapbook."

Jeremiah held up a silencing hand as the radio crackled. "Okay, he's getting into a brown Toyota" came the rushed voice of the undercover cop who was following Tony. "Four-door. Georgia plates Queen Mighty zero six six six."

Jeremiah wrote the number on his wrist. He flicked his lights, a signal to the cop working traffic that he was getting ready to move. The cop, whistle in his mouth, hands moving furiously as he waved the stream of cars onto 14th Street, nodded once.

"He's yours" came the voice of the undercover cop. "Five cars from the exit."

Jeremiah nodded toward Caren. She pulled the microphone of the portable radio to her mouth and said, "All surveillance units stand by. Subject is Brown Toyota, Georgia plates. Number Queen Mighty zero six six six."

"His tag number is reversed," Dean said. He pulled his cigar from his mouth and looked at Jeremiah.

"What do you mean, reversed?"

"Should be Mighty Queen rather than Queen Mighty. That's what he is."

"Trace the number," Jeremiah said. "See who owns that vehicle."

Dean nodded.

"There he is," Caren whispered.

Jeremiah flicked his lights again, and the cop working traffic blew his whistle and held up his hand to stop the flow of cars from the mosque parking lot. The flow stopped two cars behind Tony.

The brown Toyota, moving fast to keep up with the flow of cars, turned left on 14th.

Caren pulled the microphone close. "All surveillance units. He's moving west."

Jeremiah pulled onto the street, the old car lugging and choking and spitting a cloud of smoke.

"I love police work," he grumbled.

"Next big intersection is Northside," Dean said.

"He'll go left, Caren said.

Dean turned and stared. "How do you know that?" he demanded.

"I know. He'll go left."

"If you're right, I'll let you go with me sometime when I go out to arrest some homeless people."

"I'm beginning to think you don't like homeless people," she said.

"You got that right," he said. "Weren't any homeless people until the city said the loitering ordnance was unconstitutional. We kept them off the streets. Besides, most of those people have been released from mental institutions, are alcoholics, chronically unemployed, or have criminal records. They are the asswipes of society."

"You have an understanding heart," she said.

"And you have an empty head."

Caren pointed ahead. "Northside is over the hill."

The Toyota turned left. Dean shook his head in amazement as Caren pressed the transmit switch on the microphone and said, "South on Northside."

Jeremiah looked at the big four-lane road teeming with Friday traffic. "Now we got room to rock and roll," he said.

The Toyota cruised leisurely south on Northside, a street that, perhaps more than any other in Atlanta, showed the city's polar extremes. A few miles north, beyond I-75, Northside was lined with the great homes of Atlanta. But here, on the city's near west side, it was a zoning nightmare: a commercial melange of cheap boardinghouses and spavined apartment buildings spiced with bars where women danced nude, with boat stores, rib shacks, machine shops, and the greasy, sprawling detritis of Atlanta's commercial underbelly.

Jeremiah glanced at the suppurating commercial pustules and shook his head in disgust. "This town has gone to hell," he said.

"You got that right," Dean agreed. He pointed to a flag, striped in bright colors, that fluttered from the door of an apartment house. "I've seen that flag all over Atlanta. What country is that?"

"That's not a country," Caren laughed. "It's the flag flown by gays. It shows their unanimity."

"United Fag Emirates," Dean growled.

Jeremiah moved in and out of the flow of traffic, keeping the Toyota in sight.

Caren put her hand on Jeremiah's shoulder. She watched the Toyota intently as it approached the tangled intersection west of Georgia Tech. "Don't worry," she said, squeezing Jeremiah's shoulder. "He's going straight home. He won't turn again until he gets to wherever he's going."

Again she was right. The Toyota motored

serenely through the intersection and continued south.

Jeremiah dropped back, allowing other surveillance cars to leapfrog him and accompany the Toyota. He recognized one of the surveillance cars—it was driven by a female officer in civilian clothes—when it came from a side street south of Georgia Tech.

"Okay," Jeremiah said. "Give her the eyeball for a few blocks."

"Three, you have the eyeball," Caren said. Her hand remained on Jeremiah's shoulder.

"Got him" came the woman's voice.

A moment later: "He's continuing south on Northside."

The Toyota passed the domed stadium and Vine City.

Caren smiled in appreciation. "He's going somewhere over around the Clark–Atlanta University complex." She nodded. "That makes sense. He can hide in the big international community that lives around the colleges."

"Can't hide from me," Dean said around his cigar. He patted his gun. "My meat-seeking bullets will go around corners to pop that puppy."

The Toyota turned right onto MLK. As it approached the nexus of Atlanta's black business community—a one-block area containing Atlanta Life Insurance Company, the Citizens Trust Bank, the *Atlanta Inquirer*, and the Atlanta office of the NAACP—it began slowing. The directional lights began blinking.

"He's turning left onto White House Drive" came

the voice of the eyeball. A moment later: "He's looking for a parking place."

Jeremiah held up a finger. But Caren anticipated what he would say. "Three, you keep the eyeball and drive on by," she said into the microphone. "Get the address. Five, you move in closer for backup. Four, if you're close enough, put some people on the ground. Let them do a walk-by and confirm the address. Once he's inside, we'll move in."

Jeremiah nodded in approval. Even Dean was impressed. "Diamond," he said, "we gonna have to take away your training wheels."

She ignored Dean. She was looking into the rearview mirror, into Jeremiah's eyes. "If he killed the major, you know you are probably next on the list?"

Jeremiah laughed. "Maybe. But before I cavort in the Elysian Fields, this lad will have been burning in hell for many years."

Dean was puzzled. "Cavorting in what fields? You sound like a pervert."

Jeremiah laughed. Caren shook her head.

Six minutes later, Tony was observed going into a small house on White House Drive across the street from Booker T. Washington High School.

White House Drive is a street favored by faculty members from the Clark–Atlanta University complex, the greatest collection of black colleges in the world. The street is lined with small frame houses that are neatly maintained and have well-tended yards. The houses are close together, no more than three or four feet.

Five minutes later, officers were in place near

both the front and rear doors of Tony's house. Other officers were watching the windows on both sides of the house.

Jeremiah stopped his car and got out. Caren and Dean fanned out to each side as Jeremiah stepped onto the porch and knocked on the door.

A moment later Jeremiah and Tony were staring into each other's eyes. Tony's right hand drifted toward his waist, toward an opening where a single button was not fastened.

Tony looked to the right of Jeremiah, where a burly cigar-chewing man stood on the sidewalk, hand on his pistol. Tony's eyes narrowed. He had seen the man the day he had gone to the homicide offices. To the left stood a woman he also recognized. She was standing there, legs apart, hand on her pistol, staring at him with great intensity.

Animosity between the two crackled like heat lightning.

"I'm Sergeant Jeremiah Buie with the Atlanta Police Department, and I'd like to ask you a few questions," Jeremiah said.

Jeremiah's antenna were quivering. His eyes were locked on Tony. He knew he was on shaky legal ground. He had no warrant. He did not even know this man's name.

But much could be learned about a person in the few seconds after a police officer identified himself and said he wanted to ask questions. In fact, the nature of the response dictated the course and nature of the interview.

He instantly sensed that Tony was not afraid. Jeremiah could smell fear. If a person were guilty and found himself confronting a police officer, he popped out in perspiration that smelled of fear and guilt. Tony was looking him squarely in the eye. And he was as cool and unruffled as if he had stepped outside to greet old friends.

"What sort of questions?" Tony said.

"Routine." We thought you might help us with an investigation."

"I have no wish to help you with anything."

Jeremiah smiled. The lines were drawn.

"Take your hand away from your waist. Put your hands over your head and turn around," he ordered.

"What?"

Jeremiah spun Tony around. "Put your hands on the wall, mister."

Tony sensed that the other man and the woman had moved closer. He would have no chance if he resisted.

"Am I under arrest?" he asked.

"We just want to talk to you. Routine," Jeremiah said. His hands rapidly frisked Tony. He paused as his hands encountered the knife.

"Weapon," he said over his shoulder.

Dean and Caren pulled their pistols and pointed them at Tony.

Jeremiah pulled the knife from Tony's belt, hefted it for a moment, and smiled in satisfaction.

"Cuff him," he said to Dean. "We're going downtown."

"I do not want to go with you," Tony said. "If I am not under arrest, I want to stay in my house."

"What's your name?" Jeremiah asked.

Tony did not answer.

Jeremiah cuffed Tony's hands behind his back. He seized Tony's arm and spun him around.

"You're gonna talk to me, asshole," he said. "You're gonna tell me—"

Caren saw the storm clouds on Jeremiah's face and stepped forward. She put her hand on Jeremiah's arm. "Be careful," she said.

Jeremiah's face twisted in a rictus of anger as he glowered at Tony. This was the man who had sliced the major's head almost from his body; the man who had killed the major's fiancée and killed Christopher Gowon, Jr.; the man who had killed the Hispanic gang member. This was the man involved in a plot to elect a Muslim who traveled under the name Frederick A. Carr as president of the United States.

Tony smirked. "I do not want to accompany you," he said. "You are taking me against my will."

Dean stepped forward. "Sergeant, we'll take over," he said to Jeremiah. He clamped his beefy hand on the chain holding the handcuffs, looked around the small front porch of the house, and said, "Hey, asshole. Where's your flag?"

Tony looked at him in a quizzical manner.

"You know," Dean said. "The fag flag. Considering your interests, you should be flying the fag flag from your door." He paused. "In your case, the back door."

Tony's black eyes glazed over and his face hardened. "You do not spit in an Arab's beard unless it is on fire," he said softly.

Dean twisted the chain. "I will spit in your beard,

piss on your face, and shit in your hat," he growled. "And you will like it."

Tony laughed. "I thought this was America. I thought that a person has rights."

"The only right you got is the right to sit in the electric chair," Dean said.

"Put him in the backseat," Jeremiah ordered. "Keep a close eye on him. We're going to homicide."

He turned to Tony. "We're gonna ID you. Then I'm taking out a warrant to search this place. After that I'm going to charge you with homicide."

Tony looked up at Jeremiah.

"I know you," he whispered.

He laughed.

32

Dick Head was taking a stand; he was acting like a prototypical rabbit leader.

"Let him walk," he said. "His lawyer is in the hall threatening us with a wrongful-arrest suit. And he's right. You got nothing." He paused and added, "Do you understand that . . . Sergeant?"

Shining one's badge on a man, using his lower rank when addressing him, was a good outline template for getting that man onto the frequency.

Jeremiah Buie wasn't listening. He had gotte over the shock of having the chief drop into homicide—a virtually unprecedented event—when he heard the chief say he was ordering the release from the holding cell—at homicide they called it the "witness room"—of a prisoner named Tony Soporif.

Jeremiah opened the door of his office and glanced down the hall. A slender man of about forty stood up and stared. The man wore a black suit. He had a small and narrow, otter-like face, the eyes of an unsuccessful rapist, and a complexion like the belly of a sewer-dwelling fish. His wispy mustache, which grew in anemic tufts like weeds in parched earth, emphasized the paraphimosis of his nose. His lips were full and cracked and looked as if they had broken apart while trying to shit the nacreous, darting tongue.

It was Fast Eddie, the most famous criminal lawyer in Atlanta, and as he stared at Jeremiah, he wrung his hands in a fruitless effort to wash away the guilt of his past and future sins.

Who had called Fast Eddie? It couldn't have been Tony. He had been locked up.

Jeremiah closed the door. "Chief, this sorry son of a bitch killed the major. I believed he also killed the major's fiancée and I believe he killed her son, not to mention a gang member. I think he should get a medal for the gang member, but the others are personal. And we got him nailed.

He did not mention that he was Tony's next intended victim.

He stood close to the chief and looked down at him. Dick Head could easily be intimidated.

The chief backed up a step. He was wearing a suit today, a custom-tailored suit. He wished he had worn his uniform. It was a benefit in having cops ideate the true nature of the process system.

"Tell me, Sergeant Buie. Tell me exactly what you have. Convince me that Fast Eddie is wrong. Integrate this into the totality of the overview and tell me what you have."

He motioned for Jeremiah to sit down and paced back and forth in front of Jeremiah's desk. Once Jeremiah was seated in a rickety chair against the wall and the chief could look down at him, he held up his fingers and began ticking off the reasons.

"The blood test, which you took illegally, does

not match your best evidence—the DNA sample. Is that correct?"

Jeremiah grimaced. "The sample was switched or altered," he said.

The chief ignored him. "And when you followed this Tony Soporif from the mosque to his house, obtained a warrant, and later searched the house, you found several sets of tennis shoes but none to match the pattern found at two crime scenes. Correct?"

"His tennis shoes were new. He tossed the others. Give me some time, I'll find them and we'll have a match."

"The tennis shoes at the suspect's house did not match the prints taken at the crime scenes. Is that not correct?" insisted the chief.

Jeremiah nodded.

"So both pieces of your physical evidence, your best physical evidence, flopped. You got zero? Is that right?"

When he had to, the chief could talk cop talk.

"We have a partial print."

"Oh, yes. The partial print. I forgot about that. I'm assuming you printed this Tony Soporif?"

"We did."

"And the printing was as illegal as the blood sample?"

Jeremiah nodded.

"Just for the sake of argument, what did you find?"

"We're not sure. There are some similar characteristics. Not enough to go to court with."

He looked at the chief. "We still have the bite mark."

"Ah, the bite mark. And do you place a great deal of credence in the bite-mark evidence?"

"I'll take what I can get."

"You had a dentist take a mold of the suspect's mouth, did you not?"

"I did."

"Did you have the suspect's permission or did you get a warrant?"

"I told him it was part of the processing before being admitted to jail. He didn't object."

The chief folded his hands behind his back, stared down at Jeremiah, and shook his head. "Then it goes in the same category as the fingerprint and the blood test. Fast Eddie will never allow that to be admitted."

"Have you looked at Fast Eddie's conviction record?" Jeremiah said. "He hasn't won a case in twenty years. He has a reputation only because he charges clients a fortune."

The chief waved an admonishing finger. "Sergeant, you made a basic mistake that a recruit wouldn't have made. You took shortcuts on a high-profile case. You didn't follow procedures." He paused. "It is my guess that you did not even obtain his license-plate number."

"Yes, I did," Jeremiah said. "But we got zip. The car was registered to some phony company. It would take weeks to unravel the paperwork."

The chief paced, his fingers steepled and his lips pursed. "Go back to the dentist. Satisfy my curiosity. What did he say?"

"After he took the impressions he went into a back office to let them dry and study them. He wanted to compare the molds with pictures of the bite marks. He came back about the same time you got here, so I haven't had a chance to talk with him."

The chief smiled, a solicitous smile. He shook his head. "To avoid duplicating your talking to the dentist and then writing a report, why not have the both of us hear the dentist in real time? Bring him in."

"Chief, this guy is a bit strange."

"He's part of the process system on this case. Bring him in. I want to hear what he has to say." The chief smiled again. "Who knows, his diagnosis might provide the evidence that will justify your charging this Tony Soporif?"

He rocked on his toes and smiled. "Bring him in. Convince me I should not release Mr. Soporif."

Jeremiah gritted his teeth. Calling a scumbag "mister" was beyond his understanding. He opened his office door. Pinky Green was standing in front of Dean Nichols's desk, talking to Nichols and Diamond. Nichols had a glazed expression in his eyes, but Diamond appeared to be listening— that is, until she saw Jeremiah's office door open. The alacrity with which she stood up and stared at him showed she had been waiting anxiously. She looked over his shoulder briefly, glared at the chief, then her glance returned to Jeremiah.

Jeremiah shook his head and motioned to Pinky Green.

"Doctor," he said across the room. "The chief would like to speak with you."

Pinky Green strutted across the squad room, hand outstretched. It was fitting that he talk with the chief.

"Dr. Green," said the chief after the introductions were made, "it is my understanding you took impressions and made a mold of the mouth of one Tony Soporif and that you then made certain comparisons between the mold and what purported to be bite marks taken from a recent homicide victim."

Pink Green was offended. "They weren't purported bite marks. They were bite marks."

"Very well, what were your conclusions?"

Pinky Green hummed with tension. He stroked his nose, cleared his throat, wrung his hands, and paced in a small circle. Then he pulled at his beard. Finally he stopped, looked at the chief, held up three fingers, and said, "In these cases, you must ask yourself three things."

He pulled one of the fingers down. "First of all, is it a human bite?"

He pulled another finger down. "Second, if it is a human bite, what are the unique features?"

He pulled the third finger down. "Finally, how do the teeth from the mold compare with the bite mark?"

The chief nodded impatiently. "Macro strategic plan linking. The ideation is sound. It gives you a directed point. Now, what are your conclusions?"

Pinky Green stared. He was not sure he understood anything except the question.

He cleared his throat and pulled at his beard. "I'm not sure."

The chief stared at Dr. Green. "You're not sure?" He turned to Jeremiah. "He's not sure."

Jeremiah leaned closer to the dentist. "What do you mean, you're not sure?"

The chief held up his hand toward Jeremiah and smiled at the dentist. "Doctor, proceed. Tell us why are you not sure."

The dentist wrung his hands and continued pacing. For the first time he addressed his remarks to Jeremiah. "Do you remember our conversation in the restaurant, when you first brought this case to my attention?"

"How could I forget?"

The sarcasm was lost on Dr. Green. "Then you'll remember I told you that the incisal edge of tooth number eight was split or jagged. It had a rough edge."

Jeremiah nodded.

"I mentioned also that tooth number five was out of the plane of occlusion, that it was either broken off or missing."

Again Jeremiah nodded.

Doctor Green pulled his beard. "The mouth I just examined was not like that. Not quite. Tooth eight had a smooth edge and the one-tooth bridge at tooth number five was in the plane of occlusion."

Jeremiah stared intently at the dentist. "Are you saying the teeth of the man in there do not match the bite marks I gave you?"

"I think so. But I'm not sure."

"Dammit, man, you're a doctor," Jeremiah exploded. "You said you were a scientist. Be scientific. Stop this mealy-mouth shit. Be sure."

Again the chief held up an admonishing finger. "Sergeant Buie, allow the doctor to finish." He smiled and nodded toward Dr. Green. "Doctor, please continue."

Dr. Green cleared his throat. "The mouth, as it is now constituted, does not match the bite mark. However, tooth number eight has recently been bonded. And the bridge replacing tooth five is new."

Jeremiah's white eyebrows jumped a notch. "Without the new dental work, would the mouth match the bite mark?"

Doctor Green paused. He pulled his beard. He shrugged. "Possibly."

Jeremiah bit his lip and took a deep breath. When he spoke, his voice did not betray the frustration he felt. "Dr. Green, why do you say possibly?"

"I would have to see the X rays that were made before the dental work was done. I would need to see the record of the dental examination, and I would need to talk with the dentist who did the work. He will have molds of the mouth done before he put in the bridgework. Then I could give you a definite answer."

"Dr. Green, how many dentists are there in Atlanta?"

The dentist was pleased with the question. He rocked his head back and forth. "I'm president of the Georgia Dental Association, so I know there are about fifteen hundred dentists in the metro area."

"What percentage of all dentists belong to the association?"

Dr. Green shrugged. "About seventy percent. We're trying to increase that."

"So there are roughly two thousand dentists in the Atlanta area?"

"That's a rough estimate, yes."

"On the man you examined, was the dental work of a complicated or sophisticated nature? Could any dentist have done it, or would it have to be done by a specialist?"

Jeremiah held his breath.

Dr. Green sniffed. "Bonding and a one-tooth bridge? Basic dentistry. Any dentist could do it."

Jeremiah sighed. "I have about two thousand dentists to interview."

The chief stepped in. He patted Dr. Green on the back and escorted him to the door of the office. "Dr. Green, you've been most helpful in assisting us to reframe this case. You've provided a template by which we can format and define our future course. I'm sure Sergeant Buie will be getting back in touch with you. On behalf of the police department, I want to thank you."

Dr. Green, again not sure he understood what was being said, stared at the chief for a moment. "There is some evidence that this person had a parafunctional habit."

The chief was puzzled.

Dr. Green spoke rapidly. "The incisal edges of several teeth, the same ones I mentioned to you at the restaurant," he said, looking at Jeremiah. He turned back to the chief. "Those teeth were chipped, indicating a parafunctional habit."

"Is that important in bite-mark identification?" asked the chief.

Dr. Green thought for a moment. "Not in this case."

"Good day, Doctor. And thank you again for your help."

"One other thing," the dentist said. "If there's any press coverage on this case, I hope you'll remember my involvement."

"Indeed we will," the chief said. "You will receive full and proper credit." He closed the door behind Dr. Green and turned to Jeremiah.

Jeremiah made a final effort to stop the chief from saying the only thing he could say.

"Chief, this guy did it. I know it. He's dirty. He killed a cop and at least three other people. I'm checking with the feds about his background. Give me a couple of days. Let me hold him that long."

The chief straightened his tie and pulled at his cuffs. He opened the door to Jeremiah's office. "Mr. Soporif will walk," he said over his shoulder. "And since you have no evidence against the man, the only comments you will make regarding my decision will be comments of support."

He paused. "Furthermore, you will stay away from Mr. Soporif. You will not conduct any surveillance on him or his residence. You will not install any electronic surveillance device on his telephone, nor will you install any videotaping device near his home. Furthermore, you will not, officially or unofficially, ask any other agency—local, state, or federal—to assist you in doing same. Are we on the same frequency, Sergeant Buie?"

Jeremiah nodded.

"When you brought him in, did you take anything from him?"

"Yeah, a knife. An Arab knife." Jeremiah stared at the chief. "It could take your head off."

"Give it back."

Jeremiah threw up his arms. He was disgusted.

The chief smiled, opened the office door, and walked away. When he saw Fast Eddie, he stopped and turned around. In a voice heard all over the squad room, he fired a final salvo toward Jeremiah. "Sergeant, any deviation from my instructions and not only you but the two officers working with you on this case will be assigned to the traffic squad as part of the Folder Analysis and Review Team."

Dean nodded as he pretended to study his scrapbook. "Always wanted to be on the FART squad," he mumbled under his breath.

The chief smiled, nodded at Fast Eddie, and said, "Your client will be released immediately."

The chief looked at the detectives in the squad room, and smoothed his suit as he walked toward the elevator.

33

Caren Diamond walked across the squad room and stood before a window overlooking the rear of the building. The chief's black car was parked on the curb. He did not park in the reserved spaces of the front parking lot as did other department heads at City Hall East. He had wanted a special parking place only a few steps from the door. So he had the curb at the rear entrance painted yellow, ordered that a single parking space be outlined in yellow, and—just for insurance—ordered the cops who pulled security duty to keep all other cars, both city and privately owned, away from the rear of the building. His shiny black car stood there in solitary splendor.

Caren's eyes roamed the thick bushes that bordered the rear of the building. Nothing. But she knew someone was there. The chief was leaving town that night to consult with senatorial candidate Frederick A. Carr, something about a task force on urban crime, a program to regain the streets.

If the chief was leaving tonight, it would have to happen today. She did not know what would happen, but she knew it would happen today. She had passed along the name "Tony Soporif" to a friend. Actually, the man was not a friend; he had sought her out after she went to work with the police department, told her he worked for the "government of Israel," and asked her to remember him on cases that might interest Israel. Within hours after she had given him Tony's name, he called back asking for more information.

When she met him the first time, she thought he was an unusually taciturn and guarded man, very much in control of his emotions. But when he called back, he was so intense he could barely control himself.

She gave him a physical description of Tony Soporif, which seemed to make him even more excited, and had a messenger deliver a copy of the artist's rendering as well as several copies of Dean Nichols's photographs.

"Israel owes you a great debt," the man—he said his name was Ariel—told her. "We have been looking for this man for years. Now you must tell me everything you know about this man."

Caren felt as if she were being pulled into a maelstrom. But she gave him a quick overview of Operation Bilal.

"I must see the complete document. I must," he said.

"That's not possible," she told him. "There's only one copy. Even the chief does not know of its existence. I can tell you everything that's in it, but I can't allow you to see it."

He paused. Then his voice was deadly serious.

"You do not understand," he said. "I must see the file. Now."

He was so emphatic that she had the impression he would come over and steal the existing copy if she did not provide him with a copy.

Caren Diamond was a poised and tough-minded woman. But this man intimidated her. Possibly because she knew his employer and she knew the people who worked for that employer recognized no legal, moral, or social limits when it came to achieving their objectives. They made the Red Dogs look like a litter of cuddly little puppies.

The night before, she had met him again. He seemed much more hard-eyed than she remembered. She took him to City Hall East. Once inside the homicide offices, she used the key Jeremiah had given her to open his office. She locked the door behind her. The man used a tiny camera and photographed every page in the document. He did it with a speed and dexterity that indicated he had done this before. Many times.

A few hours later, in the middle of the night, he knocked on her door. She was not asleep. It was too hot to sleep. She hated air conditioning, but tonight she had almost turned it on. When she heard the knock, she grabbed her pistol, glided on tiptoe across the room, and looked through the peephole.

She was naked, but the shock of seeing this man at her door was such that she opened the door a crack and peeped around.

"What do you want?" she whispered.

"You must forget you have ever seen or met me," he said. His voice was so intense that she backed up a step. She forgot she had a pistol hidden behind her back. She nodded quickly in agreement. His eyes continued to stare into hers—to probe, almost as if he were reading her mind. Whatever he saw satisfied him. He relaxed a degree.

"People are about to become involved in this matter," he said.

"What peo—?"

He held up a hand. "Do not ask. This chief of yours"—he grimaced and his eyes turned cold—"is no friend of Israel."

Caren's eyes widened. She knew what that meant. And even in the heat she felt a sudden chill.

He stepped closer to the door but made no effort to come in. "I must ask you something. And you must tell me the absolute truth. More is at stake than you can ever imagine."

She nodded.

"Will this Sergeant Buie solve the homicide cases involving the family of your Major Worthy? How close is he to arresting someone? Or will the suspect kill him first?"

"He won't kill Sergeant Buie." Caren's voice was strong. "Buie had the suspect in custody, but the chief ordered him released. Buie will have him again. Soon. And next time it will stick."

"What is this Soporif's address?"

Caren shook her head. "I can't tell you that. This is an Atlanta police matter, not something for the—"

His steely glance stopped her. "You know I can find him."

"Yes, but I ask you not to look. Sergeant Buie will arrest Soporif within the next few days."

She saw the man did not believe her.

"Don't get involved now. Please. Give us a couple of days."

The man stared at her. "Don't you understand? The very existence of Israel is at stake."

Caren nodded. "Why do you think I called you? I understood that from the time I read the report of the Nigerian officer. I realized that the real target of Operation Bilal was not America; it was Israel."

She paused. "If we arrest the perpetrator in this case and hang him around Frederick Carr's neck, Carr will be forced to resign his candidacy. But—"

"We think Carr is an Arab," he said. "We can't prove it, but there are some things . . ." His voice dwindled away.

Caren stared at him. He had surprised her. But in an instant she realized the truth of what he had said. It made sense.

"If you become involved," she said slowly, emphasizing the word *you* so the man knew she was referring to his employer—"then there is a chance your involvement might become known. If that happens, this country might find itself in a religious war. Much is at stake for Israel. But much is also at stake for America. Israel's needs will be met when we arrest Tony. Stay out of it for now. Give us a few days."

The man was not convinced.

Her voice grew more earnest. "Israel has been threatened with more immediate danger," she said. "Remember Saddam Hussein's Scud missiles in the

Gulf War? Israelis died, but Israel stayed out of the war. I'm asking you to stay out of this one. At least for a few days. Give us that long. Then if we don't succeed, do what you must."

The man stared. Caren felt as if the man were reading her mind.

"You are Jewish, and you ask me that?"

"I am Jewish and I ask you that."

After a long moment he nodded. "Two days. After that we take action. But our holding-off applies only to this man you call Soporif. It does not apply to your chief." His eyes hardened. "His sins against us go back many years." He shook his head. "He is no friend of Israel."

The man stepped away from the door and disappeared into the shadows.

Hours later, the events of the evening still running over and over through her mind, she sat up in bed with a start. The man she knew as Ariel was going to move against the chief. Considering the crisis Israel faced, saying the chief was no friend of Israel was the same as issuing a death warrant.

Caren was brought back to the present with a start. She continued looking out the window of the homicide office. The chief's car remained by the curb. No one was in sight around the rear of the building.

She looked at her watch.

Whatever was going to happen would happen within the next few hours.

The clock was ticking.

34

Chief Dick Head straightened his tie and shot his cuffs as he strode rapidly from the rear door of City Hall East. He was preoccupied and more than a little annoyed. His driver cum bodyguard had become violently ill an hour earlier—a stomach virus of some sort, judging by the sudden onslaught of heavy vomiting. The incident called for some reframing, since the chief needed to go to the airport now. He wanted time to prepare an outline template of his meeting with Frederick Carr.

The meeting, scheduled for that evening, would be delicate indeed, but if he could ideate the process system for Carr and then suggest a proactive and self-creative stance for Operation Bilal, he could emerge from this thing as the true prototypical rabbit leader.

It was the culmination of all the work he had done for Tony and the Nigerians over the past years, and he meant to take full advantage of the opportunity.

As the chief leaned forward to open his car door, he noticed a movement out of the corner of his eye. Instinctively he smiled as he stood up and turned toward the young man walking toward him.

The young man was tall and very slender. He

wore black sneakers, jeans, and a gray T-shirt upon which was an image of Martin Luther King, Jr. His eyes were hidden behind dark wraparound sunglasses.

A street kid.

The chief, ready to show that even the mayor's Number One Man can take time to rap with a brother, stuck out his hand, and said, "S'appening, bro?"

"You the chief?"

Dick Head was pleased. He was in civilian clothes, but he had been recognized. He nodded, increased the size of his smile, and said, "Like the shirt."

The young man reached forward and took the chief's hand. But rather than shaking it, he jerked, pulling the chief off balance and causing him to lurch forward. In that moment the young man pulled his head back and with the speed of a striking snake, he slammed his forehead into the chief's nose.

The chief was paralyzed with pain. Tears blinded him, stars danced before his eyes, and his knees wavered. In that moment the young man, still holding onto the chief's right hand, spun him in a circle and snaked his right arm around the chief's neck. He pushed his left arm up high, gripped his left forearm with his right hand, and used his left hand to push the chief's head forward and hold it in the crook of his right arm. He held his head against the back of the chief's head, his face pushed into the chief's hair, and stepped back, keeping the chief off balance. The King's Men had wanted him to use a knife or a gun for his first killing, but he had seen this choke hold demonstrated on television and wanted to try it. Anybody could stab or shoot a dude. That was easy. But to kill a man with your bare hands was something else. With this act he would gather the respect of the King's Men.

The chief's legs flopped weakly a few times, quivered, and were still. The young man whispered into the chief's ear. " 'Nonviolence is a powerful and just weapon,' " he quoted.

It was the last thing the chief ever heard.

He was unconscious.

The young man, oblivious of his surroundings and unmindful that someone could step out the rear door of City Hall East any second, continued to hold on. For about three minutes he held the chief in a choke hold.

By then the chief was dead.

As the young man released the chief, his left hand seized the collar of the chief's coat and stripped it down his left arm. The right sleeve quickly followed.

The young man held onto the cuffs of the coat, put his foot in the chief's back, and pushed hard. The coat was in his hands as the chief fell across the curb.

" 'In order to be somebody, people must feel themselves part of something,' " he quoted. " 'In the nonviolent army, there is room for everyone who wants to join up.' "

He was very proud that he had memorized what, to members of the King's Men, was a quote of extraordinary length.

As the young man slipped on the coat, he noticed a tag sewn over the inside breast pocket on the right side. The tag, which he could not read, said, "Custom Designed for Richard Alpha Martin Head." The label, which he also could not read, said, "H. Stockton—Atlanta."

The young man slipped on the dark blue coat with the faint gray chalk stripe. It fit in the shoulders, but the arms were a bit short. He shrugged, looked over his shoulder toward the door as if daring anyone to emerge, and leisurely strolled away.

He was more than pleased. He now was a full-fledged member of the King's Men. He had earned his colors. At the same time he had earned five keys of crack cocaine for the brothers in the King's Men. He didn't know and he didn't care who the white dude was who had promised five keys of crack. And he wasn't sure who he had killed; the dude was the chief of something, didn't matter what. In fact, it wouldn't have mattered if he were the Holy Ghost. Not for five keys. The King's Men would have offed the mayor himself for five keys.

As the young man, jaunty in the new coat, continued strolling through the parking lot, across the Kroger parking lot toward North Avenue, he idly wondered about the brother he had just killed.

Guy didn't fight back at all. Shit, even a rabbit would fight if cornered. This dude hadn't been much.

The new member of the King's Men shook his head as he remembered the feel and smell of the man's hair.

Whoever the dude was, he sure did have fine hair.

35

"Lot of funerals," Dean Nichols said. "Lot of funerals." He sat in a straight-backed chair by Jeremiah's desk. His tie was loosened and his sleeves rolled over muscular forearms.

Caren paced the floor in the small office.

"Too many," Jeremiah muttered. "Even for a Scotsman." He leaned back, hands behind his head, looking at the ceiling.

"You guys like funerals?" Dean asked.

Jeremiah nodded. "Everyone should attend at least one funeral a week."

"What if your family or friends are not dying at the rate of one per week?" Caren asked. Today she was wearing a red mini-skirt, red boots, and a red wide-brimmed Spanish-style hat. She wore a white blouse and white hose. A heavy onyx pendant nestled between her breasts, gold and onyx bracelets were on her wrist, and she wore large onyx earrings.

"Doesn't have to be family or friends," Jeremiah said. "Can be a stranger. But everyone should attend at least one funeral a week."

Dean licked a cigar. "Why?" he asked as he jammed the cigar in his mouth.

"Keeps you in tune with the eternal verities," Jeremiah said. "Funerals are good. Except police funerals. I don't like them. Police funerals and weddings should be avoided if at all possible." He looked from Dean to Caren. "Speaking of which, what have you got on the chief's murder?"

Dean shrugged. Caren's right hand suddenly clasped the onyx pendant. She hoped no one heard her sudden gulp. The city was in unprecedented turmoil because of the chief's murder. For police officers, all vacation and off-duty time had been canceled. Every cop in town was calling in markers from his snitches. Caren was afraid the dragnet would reveal the involvement of Ariel and his people.

"Price on the day watch is handling it," Dean said. He bit the cigar. "Somebody saw some punk kid walking across the parking lot about that time. He was wearing a dark suit coat—must have been the chief's since his was missing. That would make the kid a member of the King's Men. Only way to get to those geek monsters is to take away their crack."

"Could it have been someone trying to blame the King's Men?" Caren asked. She had stopped pacing and was facing the door. She spoke over her shoulder. She wanted to draw attention away from the King's Men.

Jeremiah and Dean looked at her in astonishment. The King's Men would kill anyone trying to pass as a member of the gang. Besides, who would want to pretend to be a member of the most hated gang in Atlanta? Even the most socially militant black people abhorred the King's Men.

"As a diversion, I mean," she added with a shrug.

Dean glanced around the squad room, grinned, and rolled the cigar around in his mouth. "Personally, I think the son of a bitch who did the chief ought to get a medal," he said. "Chief was a big-time asshole."

No one responded. "I got a great picture of him. Eyes all bulged out. Face purple. If he wasn't so recognizable, I'd put him in my scrapbook."

Jeremiah slammed his fist on the desk. "Goddamn chiefs. Treacherous, perfidious bastards. He was leaking information to Tony. You can't trust a chief. Any of them."

Caren and Dean stared at Jeremiah. They did not know he had identified the information leak.

"If he was leaking information," Dean said, "he's responsible for Major Worthy's death."

Jeremiah sighed. "I know. I know. But it couldn't have been anyone else. I wish it were. The nature of the information and the time frame in which it was acted on mean that only the chief could have passed it on to Tony."

Dean chewed his cigar for a moment. "Sergeant, with the chief out of the way, we got room to go get Tony."

"I wanted the chief alive," Jeremiah said. "Once I had enough evidence and gave it to the feds so they could confront him, he would have sung like a flock of birds. He would have given up everything and everyone."

An uncomfortable silence settled over the three.
It lingered for long seconds. Jeremiah was about to
return to his office when there was a sudden hub-
bub at the elevator.

A black-clad Red Dog, gelid eyes rolling in
fiendish delight, was pushing three handcuffed
young men ahead of him. The three wore the red
and orange colors of the Rod and Gun Club. As one
of them spun around to complain, the insignia on
the back of his jacket was visible—a stylized but
recognizable rendition of an erect penis.

The Red Dog grinned, seized a handful of jacket,
and shoved the gang member hard into the other
two, causing all three to stumble and lurch across
the hall.

The Red Dog looked over the waist-high parti-
tion. He recognized Jeremiah. "Sergeant," he said.
"Understand you want to talk to any of these
young assholes who call themselves the Rod and
Gun Club?"

Jeremiah nodded. "Where'd you get these lads?"

The Red Dog, a steely aura of machismo oozing
from every pore, turned lazily toward the three
gang members. His mouth was creased in a humor-
less smile. With an extended forefinger he poked
the closest in the chest. Hard.

"These sweethearts had their names in the computer at the health department. It seems they have
drippy—" The Red Dog glanced at Caren, hesitated, then continued in a voice of mock sympathy.
"They have sexually transmitted diseases."

He slammed a fist into his palm. "Nobody wants
the job of going after gang members except us

Dogs. We like to take on two or three every morning just to kick-start our pacemakers. So I went out and rounded up these sweethearts."

The Red Dog glanced at Caren. "You could have brought them in by yourself," he said. "Nothing to it."

The three gang members glared at the Red Dog. That they were so docile and meek that even a woman could have arrested them was an implication that deeply offended them.

"You be careful talking that way," one of them blustered.

Without looking, the Red Dog kicked his left leg hard to the side, catching the gang member in the hip with such force that he was knocked to the floor.

"Did anyone speak?" the Red Dog said solicitously. "Did I hear a voice?"

Jeremiah stood up. He looked at the cop's name tag. "Okay, Dorsey," he said. "We'll take care of these lads. Thanks for dropping them off." He pressed the buzzer that opened the half door and motioned for the three gang members to enter.

"We can talk to you here, or we can put you in a cell and talk to you there. Which is it gonna be?" he asked.

The three boys shrugged and tried to pretend it did not matter. But they had spent six hours in a holding cell at the city jail before the Red Dog brought them to homicide. They had seen enough of cells for one day. Besides, the Red Dog had been all too anxious to acquaint them with the majesty of the law. Now they wanted a break.

"Here," one said.

Caren pointed to a row of chairs against the wall. "Two of you sit there," she said. "Keep two chairs between you." She turned to the gang member who had spoken and pointed toward the chair alongside Dean's desk, the one where Jeremiah had been sitting. "You sit there."

The Red Dog waved. "Homicide ever needs any help, call the Dogs," he said. He turned and sauntered toward the elevator.

Jeremiah watched the Dog swagger onto the elevator. "My kind of terrorist," he muttered.

As Jeremiah turned, he noticed that the third gang member was staring with horror at a picture atop Dean's desk.

A picture of Tony the Dreamer.

36

"What's his name?" Jeremiah asked.

The gang member swallowed, took a hesitant step forward, and peeped through the small window into the cold room at the M.E.'s office. Atop the stainless steel table, a sheet folded back from his face, was the body of the young man Dean called the Temple monument.

Jeremiah watched the face of the gang member peeping through the window. The young man wanted to show no emotion, to be blasé and distant about what he was doing, but when he saw the body of his friend, his eyes widened in revulsion and horror and he spun around, back to the door, breathing hard.

"*Jesus Christos*, he's been dead two weeks," the gang member gasped. "He should be in the ground."

"Can't plant him if we don't know who he is," Dean said.

"What's his name?" Jeremiah said.

Without discussing it, he and Dean were settling into a "good guy, bad guy" routine. If the young gang member chose to be a tough guy, he would quickly find that Dean was tougher.

"Where has he been for two weeks?" the gang member asked. He sounded as if he were afraid of the answer.

"Off at school," Dean said. He grinned and studied the cigar he was holding.

The gang member crabbed two steps down the wall. "School! Man, what the hell you talking about school?"

Dean shrugged. "We can only keep him here a couple of days, maybe a week, before he starts stinking. Bad. Then he has to be embalmed. We sent him off to an undertaking school. They fixed that puppy up. Now we can keep him for months."

"Or until someone identifies him and we can bury him like the good Catholic boy I'm sure he was," Jeremiah added.

The gang member was horrified. "You mean people what want to be undertakers practiced on him? They cut him up?"

Dean nodded as he licked his cigar. "About the size of it." He paused. "Speaking of that, they had to cut his pecker off. Only way to deflate the thing." He stuck the cigar in his mouth and reached, as if in commiseration, to pat the gang member on the shoulder. "Don't worry. I'm told the students did a good job of sewing it back on. It ain't straight and it ain't sticking up, but it's on."

The gang member blanched and turned toward Jeremiah. He would look neither Dean nor Jeremiah in the eye as they were, in his eyes, men of power. In the Hispanic culture it is considered disrespectful to look a man of power in the eye.

"Ricky Zapata," he blurted.

"That's his name, Ricky Zapata?" Jeremiah asked.

"Yeah, man, Ricky. Riccardo Zapata."

"You knew him?" Jeremiah asked.

"Yeah, man, I knew him."

"You were with him the night he died?"

The gang member paused.

"Take off your shirt," Jeremiah ordered.

The gang member's eyes flicked across Jeremiah's face. He was confused.

Dean took a deep breath that seemed to make him increase in size, and his face hardened as he reached for the gang member. "You heard the man. Take off the goddamn shirt or I'll rip it off for you. And I won't be as easy on you as the Red Dog was."

The young man, eyes darting back and forth between Dean and Jeremiah, pulled off his jacket. He handed it to Dean, who looked at it in disgust and tossed it to the floor.

"*¡Ivate a la mierda!*" The gang member lapsed into Spanish. "My colors! You don't do that to my colors. We'll—" He quieted as Dean took a step toward him.

"Listen, *pendejo*," Dean snarled. "*El que quiere peces que se moja el culo.* I don't give a fuck about your colors, and I don't give half a fuck about the spic pussies you run with. I'll wipe my ass on your colors, and I'll shoot the first fucking one of you that says a word." He jabbed the cigar toward the gang member. "Now take off the shirt."

The gang member gritted his teeth. His eyes glared at Dean as he defiantly jerked his shirt open and sent buttons flying down the hall. He threw the shirt on the floor.

"*Tener mala leche,*" he mumbled. "That is what you want?"

"Turn around," Jeremiah said.

The young man spun around.

"Do it again," Jeremiah said. "Slowly."

The young man turned.

On his right shoulder was an angry red mark.

Dean and Jeremiah looked at each other.

"Put your clothes on," Jeremiah said.

"That's it. You just want me to turn around. What the hell is with you guys?"

"He told me what happened," Jeremiah said.

"Who told you what?" snapped the gang member as he reached for his shirt.

"Ricky. Ricky told me."

The gang member paused. "The fuck you talking about? Ricky's been dead for weeks."

"I sat in there with him after he was killed. We talked for several hours. He told me what happened that night."

"Crazy," muttered the gang member. He slipped on his shirt, looked with disgust at the scattered buttons, then picked up his jacket, and pulled it on. "Nothing happened except Ricky got killed."

"Ricky told me what happened before he was killed."

The young man stared at Jeremiah. He did not know what to say.

Jeremiah put his hand on the young man's shoulder and walked down the hall. Dean lagged behind.

"I'm going to the bathroom," he said. "I'll catch up with you."

Jeremiah ignored him. "Don't worry about anyone finding out," he told the gang member. "We're not interested in that and we won't tell anyone. All we want is the man who killed Ricky."

The gang member pulled away from Jeremiah. His eyes were wide in fear. "I don't know," he said.

"Yes, you do," Jeremiah said. "His picture is on Detective Nichols's desk." He paused. "I saw your face when you looked at the picture. You know who killed Ricky."

37

The homicide division of the Atlanta Police Department, thinking it was melding technology and law enforcement, tried in the late 1980s to tape-record all confessions and all statements regarding homicides. But the equipment bought by the city was of such inferior quality that the recordings were inaudible. When detectives said that a single tape recorder was insufficient, that the room itself should be wired for better reproduction of the interviews and confessions, the city refused. Then it was found there was no climate- and humidity-controlled storeroom for the audiotapes and that the vitally important recordings, of lousy quality to begin with, were breaking down and becoming useless.

The city decided to take a giant technological leap forward and videotape all confessions and all statements. During the first session the lens fell out of the camera.

So it was back to having victims and witnesses and subjects and perpetrators dictate a statement to a stenographer. Many jurisdictions around the country follow the same procedure. After the statement is taken in shorthand or in notes, it can take a week or a month for the stenographer to transcribe the statement and have it typed. Then it is put aside and forgotten until the trial approaches and the detectives start assembling all the evidence. Each person who gave a statement must be tracked down and asked to sign the statement. Sometimes the person can't be found; sometimes the person changes his mind about signing.

The homicide squad in Atlanta is one of the best in the country when it comes to taking a statement and getting it signed. The procedure is simple. After the victim or witness or subject or perpetrator gives a statement to a detective, the detective calls in a secretary. The statement is dictated to the secretary, who types as the person talks. A detective looks over the secretary's shoulder, always keeping in mind the needs of the courts and the tendency of defense attorneys to muddy the waters.

The detective makes sure the statement is as concise and as relevant as possible—no long, rambling family histories or recitation of what the person making the statement might have had to eat for the past three days—just a clean clear statement that covers the issue at hand and one that defense lawyers will have a difficult time tossing out.

Once the statement is typed, it is signed and witnessed. Everything is tied up neatly.

So it was with the Rod and Gun Club member after he returned from the cold room, where he had identified the body of his friend.

Both Jeremiah and Dean heard the gang member's statement. They did not press him when he said his friend had been raped by Tony but that he had not. Let the boy keep what little pride he might have left. All they wanted was for him to identify Tony as the man who killed Ricky.

Dean remained silent while Jeremiah took the statement. But he remained in the room. It's best to have two detectives listen to a statement. Then the person giving the statement finds it difficult to recant. Both officers saw the gang member pick up a picture on Dean's desk. They saw him pick up the composite of Tony the Dreamer. And they heard him identify Tony as the man who killed the gang member whose body was tossed into the azalea bushes at the temple.

Jeremiah looked at Dean. He signed, wiped the perspiration from his face, then stood up, and went outside. "I don't think I've ever seen it this hot in Atlanta," he muttered to Caren as he pulled out a handkerchief and wiped his face.

"It's very humid," she said, pointing outside, where lowering gray clouds pressed down upon the city. "Severe thunderstorms and possible tornadoes are forecast for this afternoon."

"Maybe it will cool things off," Jeremiah said. He nodded toward the witness room. "I want you to type his statement. Pretend you are a secretary."

Her eyes slammed down in anger and she pointed a threatening finger.

"Before you go nuclear, think about it," Jeremiah said in a placating manner. His eyes widened as he leaned toward her and smiled. "You are capable of logical and rational thought?"

She realized what he was asking. If she took the statement, it would be given before three police officers, a redundancy that would provide irrefutable testimony in the event the gang member wanted to recant. He could not deny he had made the statement. And if he thought she was a secretary, he would be more open than if he thought she was a cop. And because a woman was there, he would never say his statement had been made under duress. Jeremiah was right to bring her in as a secretary.

He realized he had fouled up once on this case. He had let his emotions run away when he arrested Tony without following proper procedures. The chief had been right to release Tony. Lesser mistakes had destroyed homicide cases. On a high-profile case, everything had to go by the book. No more mistakes could be permitted. Jeremiah knew that.

Caren sat down at the typewriter. The gang member smiled at her, stared at her legs, and let his hand suggestively slide to his groin.

"Don't even think it, sonny," she said. She rolled the paper into the typewriter, poised her fingers over the keys, and nodded at Jeremiah.

An hour later it was done. Signed, sealed, and delivered. Locked up tight and ready to go to court.

Dean and Caren came into Jeremiah's office, shut the door, and sat down. They looked at Jeremiah and waited.

"Okay, Diamond," he said. Jeremiah's tie was snugged up tight, his sleeves were buttoned at the cuffs, and he looked as if he had dressed five minutes earlier. But sweat was rolling down Dean's face.

"Nichols, you appear to be in distress," he said. "Is the air conditioner broken?"

"It's overloaded," Caren said. "It's just too hot."

Like Jeremiah, she showed no sign of the heat. In her white linen suit and her necklace, earrings and bracelet of pearls, she was cool and calm and confident.

"When is it supposed to rain?" Jeremiah asked. "That will cool things down for a couple of hours."

"This afternoon," she said.

"If there is a God," Dean mumbled.

"Okay," Jeremiah said. "Recap. Tell us what we got."

Caren held up the statement, gathered her thoughts, and in her intense fashion began speaking. "We have the statement of—"

Jeremiah held up his hand. "Just a minute," he interrupted, "before you do that. Nichols, where are we on the investigation into the chief's homicide?"

Dean leaned forward. His white shirt was sodden and stuck to his body. "Two things. First of all, the city is in so much turmoil over his homicide that no one will bother us on this case. We are free to go after Tony without having to worry about the bosses. Second, I talked to Price about an hour ago. It was one of the King's Men, no doubt about that. Price is rousting those puppies. He has a name, a new member of the gang, but he can't find him."

"Motive?"

Dean shook his head. "That's the problem. Price said it appears to be a random killing except for the victim and the location. When the chief gets killed at the back door of city hall, that's not random. But we can't figure out why a gang member, even a geek monster, would kill the chief. Price is working on it."

Jeremiah nodded. "Okay, Diamond, go ahead," he said.

Without missing a beat she continued. "We have the statement of an eyewitness who saw this guy Soporif—that's not his real name—kill Riccardo Zapata. He identified Soporif as the perpetrator. He also said Soporif threatened to do the same thing to him that he had recently done to, and I'm quoting, 'that Nigerian boy.' Soporif mentioned details that were not known to the public—the choking and the homosexual rape—details that could be known only by the perpetrator."

"What's his real name?" Jeremiah interrupted.

Caren was puzzled. "Whose real name?"

"You said Soporif is not his real name. We knew that. What is his real name?"

Caren looked at the statement in her hand.

"I don't know. He is known to several intelligence agencies as Tony the Dreamer." She shook her head in annoyance. "I guess that's the reason for his using the name Soporif. He's a real cutie. He's known to have been associated with militant Islamic groups for almost twenty years. But he always stayed in the background until about 1985, when a Muslim government came to power in Nigeria. Soporif is suspected of killing dozens of people in the aftermath of that coup. And he became a bit more public after that. Whenever there was violence or an assassination, his shadow was seen."

Jeremiah's eyes widened.

"He is an Arab, as we know. Either Iranian or Iraqi," Caren continued, "a Shiite Muslim who was hired by the Nigerians and since then by other

Muslim causes. He is suspected in dozens of homicides, including a DEA agent in Lagos, several CIA agents and . . ." she paused for a moment, "other agents."

Dean stared at her open-mouthed. "That puppy is a real bad ass," he said. He patted his pistol. "He needs one of my meat-seeking bullets to put him out of his misery."

Jeremiah studied Caren. She met his gaze. But deep in her eyes he saw a faint flicker of fear. "You've been doing your homework," he said.

She shrugged. "I just found this out in the past couple of days. I was putting it all on paper for you. You know what the chief used to say."

Jeremiah nodded. "If it is not on paper, it hasn't happened."

"Where'd you find all that out?" Dean said. "If it's true, that information had to come from the CIA."

"That's okay, Nichols," Jeremiah said. He held up a hand to stop him. His eyes remained on Caren. "I think I know where it came from," he said slowly.

"You're certain about the coup in Nigeria?" he asked.

Caren nodded. "My source is quite certain."

Jeremiah sighed. Too bad the major was not here. He nodded toward Caren. "Continue. What else do we have?"

Relieved, Caren rushed forward. "This morning while you were out, I located a dentist in Snellville who did the work on Soporif's teeth. Soporif, Tony the Dreamer, whatever his name is. I took a picture out and the dentist identified Soporif. Then I put Dr. Green in touch with this dentist. Now Dr. Green says the bite marks on Christopher Gowon, Jr., were definitely made by Soporif. Says he will testify in court to that effect. He also says the bite mark on the gang member was made by the same mouth, by Soporif, and that he will testify to that."

Jeremiah smiled. "Pinky Green must be in dental heaven."

"Boss, we got this guy good," Dean said. "He's locked down tight."

Jeremiah nodded. "I can't understand why the DNA sample didn't match. Somewhere along the line, the sample was altered."

He thought for a moment. "Justice rides a slow horse. But we finally got this guy, and we got him because he wanted to make a point; he wanted to impress some gang member with an object lesson, to show what would happen if he were crossed. He wanted someone to know how powerful he was. I've seen it before. His ego caught him."

"Just in time," Caren said.

Dean looked at her. "What do you mean, 'just in time'? You talking about the election?"

"Yes," Caren said quickly. "The election. It's just a few days away."

"I think where I made a mistake was in the beginning, when I thought this guy was not organized," Jeremiah said. "There were too many clues for these to be organized and carefully thought-out homicides."

He shook his head. "Whatever this guy's name is, he's smart. He had us going in circles." Jeremiah nodded in reluctant admiration. "He is the smartest bad guy I've ever gone up against."

"Boss, a smart crook is rare as cow shit in a carport," Dean said. "But it doesn't matter how smart he is. We're about to bag him. And this Arab business about electing a senator is about to go down the toilet."

"Before we go after Freddy Carr, we've got to get this guy Soporif," Jeremiah said. He looked at his watch. "It's noon, Friday. He's probably at the mosque. I can get a warrant in an hour. We'll catch him at home." He looked at Dean and Caren.

"I'm going to have the SWAT people there," he said. "But I'll make the arrest. You two will be my backup." He looked at each of them. "Be careful."

Caren looked at Jeremiah. "I thought if SWAT came in, they were in charge," she said.

Jeremiah nodded. "That's SOP," he said. "But I know the lieutenant. He will let me make the collar."

Dean snapped his fingers and stood up. Jeremiah and Caren looked at him. "Gotta get my camera," Dean said. "I got a feeling this puppy is going to get blown halfway to hell and I want a picture."

Jeremiah looked at Caren. "You up to this?"

"I have to change clothes."

"But are you up to it?"

She nodded.

Jeremiah smiled. "Then let's go fight some crime."

38

"SWAT people in place?" Jeremiah asked.

Caren nodded. "They are."

"Soon as the rain slacks up, we can pop him," Dean said.

The three of them sat in Jeremiah's car. They were parked on MLK about three blocks from Tony's house.

Shortly before noon, the thunderstorms that had threatened Atlanta all morning had unleashed a frightful display of lightning and thunder, of strong wind and heavy rain that fell in such semi-tropical fury that visibility was limited to a hundred feet. The rain still was falling, and the mist that rose from the hot pavement caused the streets to become veiled and shrouded.

An inner perimeter had been established around Tony's house. It was manned only by tactical personnel, those who would take part in bringing him down.

The residents of every house between Tony's house and MLK had been called and told to lock their doors and stay inside. Two blocks away was a command post and an outer perimeter controlled by uniform officers. The one weakness in the perimeter was directly across the street from Tony's house: Booker T. Washington High School. But the front door of the school had been locked, and an unmarked van filled with SWAT members was parked in front of Tony's house to prevent him from running toward the school.

White House Drive had a frozen, surreal nature. The street was a rain-soaked tableau. The nearest activity was a block away, at the corner of MLK, where, inside a small shack, Old Black Joe stood, wiped the condensation from the windows of the shack, looked over the vacant lot where his chitterlings and barbecue and ribs and brunswick stew were cooking. The smoke filled the shack with a rich, pungent aroma that he still found, after all these years, to have an undeniable and magic appeal.

The barbecue pit and the giant pots were covered by a carport-like structure, the roof of which pressed the smoke from the pits and the pots toward the ground, where it was held prisoner by the heavy humidity. The scene had a smoky and veiled rather mysterious appearance.

Old Black Joe did not notice. He was waiting for the string of cars driven by hungry whites who would begin arriving in a few hours. Rain really brought the white folk out; they loved to eat barbecue after a storm, especially on a Friday. He sold twice as much barbecue on a rainy Friday as he did on a Friday with good weather. Old Black Joe looked at his cash register and nodded in anticipation.

Nearby, two police helicopters were on the

ground inside the football stadium at Morris Brown University. The pilots had been forced down by the thunderstorm and were waiting for the rain to abate. They could be on the scene in seconds.

"Shoulda used the Dogs on this guy," Dean growled.

"One terrorist is enough," Jeremiah said. "We don't need them."

The SWAT team, in place in the alley behind Tony's house, ignored the rain. They were anxious, like ravenous rottweilers straining on their leashes, as they sweated testosterone and hoped the bad guy would make a move on the homicide sergeant. Then they could shoot the son of a bitch.

Jeremiah, Dean, and Caren wore tactical radios on their belts. They each wore an earplug attached to a featherweight boom microphone. Every word they uttered would be heard by the SWAT team and by the officers at the command post. Dean's camera dangled from his shoulder.

They sat in Jeremiah's car and waited. Ironic that here in the very nexus, the living, beating heart of Atlanta's black community, Adamu Zahir, a.k.a. Tony the Dreamer, had been run to ground.

Jeremiah looked through the window and nodded with approval at the now lightly falling rain. Through the trees a patch of blue sky could be seen to the west. He nodded. "It has slowed enough that we can do it," he said. "Alert SWAT and the choppers. Tell them we're moving in."

The old car, made more asthmatic than usual by the high humidity, lurched and jerked and wheezed and smoked as Jeremiah wheeled onto

White House Drive, pressed the accelerator, then slammed on the brakes in front of Tony's house. Jeremiah, Dean, and Caren jumped out, leaving the doors open, and ran across the rain-slick sidewalk.

Jeremiah walked softly across the small porch to the front door, where he spun around, back to the wall, and faced outward. He pulled his 9mm from his belt and held it in both hands, barrel straight up.

Caren tiptoed to a corner of the porch so she could see the front door as well as the right side of the house. Dean stepped onto the porch with a heavy footfall, taking up a position to see the front door and the left side of the house.

It was Dean's footfall that alerted Tony. He paced swiftly from the rear of the house to the almost empty front room, dark behind pulled blinds, and saw two silhouettes—all with their guns drawn— on the front porch. He knew intuitively that the back door was covered by additional armed men.

He was boxed in.

Tony fingered the knife at his belt. He had one chance. He ran into the hall, reached overhead, and pulled a heavy cord that dangled from the ceiling. A set of steps going into the small attic appeared. He was in the attic when he heard the front and back doors simultaneously kicked off the hinges.

The dormer through which he exited onto the roof ran perpendicular to the front-door-back-door axis of the house, so he was invisible to the SWAT team in the rear as well as to the cops out front. But he would be in open sight the moment he began moving.

Tony never paused. The survivalist instinct that had warned him of a hundred dangers over the years told him his safety lay in fleeing, in getting away from the homicide cop who had arrested him earlier. Tony wanted to stay and confront him; he knew the white guy was Vernon Worthy's partner, the man who had been next on his list.

He could kill the white cop later. Now he had to run. Tony crouched and eased onto the roof. He took a deep breath, then quickly, with flexed knees, crabbed down the roof and jumped to the next house. He was halfway across the roof before he was sighted by a SWAT team member, and was onto the next house before the SWAT man radioed what was happening.

Jeremiah cursed and ran for the front door. "SWAT team, take the back yards," he barked into his radio. "I've got the street." He raced down White House Drive, gun in hand, followed closely by Caren and Dean.

"Might have known it," Dean grumbled. "Willy has got to rabbit."

The SWAT lieutenant in charge of the team was annoyed that Jeremiah was giving orders. SWAT was in charge. He had agreed to let Jeremiah make the arrest only because it was personal between the sergeant and the suspect. The suspect was known to be armed and was suspected of killing a cop and two other people. The SWAT team would bust his chops.

But Sergeant Buie's orders had been correct. Buie and his team were already racing down the sidewalk. The SWAT lieutenant motioned for two of his men to take to the roof and follow the suspect. The remainder of the team could scale fences and cut through flower beds as quickly as most people ran down an open street. They would corner the suspect before the homicide cops arrived.

The lieutenant watched as two men, M-16s slung over their shoulders, were boosted atop the shoulders of their companions and onto the roof. Crouched low, rifles in hand, heads locked in the direction of the suspect, they took off.

"Choppers One and Two, the suspect is on the roofs running toward MLK," the lieutenant radioed as he dashed across the backyard in pursuit of Tony. Five seconds later, the snarl of the helicopters was heard as they leaped out of the stadium and raced across the treetops at full power.

Jeremiah caught a glimpse of Tony as he crossed the crown of the fourth house down the block. He was almost at the corner. If Tony got onto MLK, with all the pedestrians and traffic and noontime activity, he might escape.

"Faster," he yelled over his shoulder.

Caren was beside him, running easily in tennis shoes, but Dean was huffing and puffing and falling behind.

The two SWAT team members on the rooftop raced pell-mell from one roof to another, quickly closing the gap, confident the two of them would bring down the suspect. Tony heard them coming. He paused. The detectives on the street to his left could not see him because of the trees. They were rushing to cut him off at the corner. The SWAT team members on his right were charging through backyards, grunting, leaping fences, and pushing their way through thick shrubbery. They could not see him, either. He made his decision.

He raced over the crest of a roof, and before he started down the slope, he seized a lightning rod to slow his descent. He crabbed past a dormer and hid behind a wide brick chimney. He took a deep breath and waited.

The SWAT team members atop the roof were traveling almost as fast as the men on the ground. The suspect was now only one house ahead. They saw him when he ran over the crest and grabbed a lightning rod to keep from falling; obviously he was an older guy.

The two young cops wanted the glory of this arrest. They wanted it badly. The homicide sergeant had insisted the bad guy be taken alive. But if SWAT reached him first, he might easily be provoked into resisting. If he did, he was history. The two men increased the pace, one right behind the other, as they raced down the back slope of the roof. The suspect was not in sight. Already he had cleared the next roof. The two cops had to hurry or the guys on the ground would be the ones who popped the suspect. The two cops did not bother to fan out as they saw a dormer and a chimney.

The helicopters were pressing the attack, the sound filling the air as the first chopper dropped toward the running black-clad men on the roof.

The first SWAT team member was traveling too fast, his body overrunning his feet as he prepared to leap toward the next roof, when Tony sprang from behind the chimney, knife slicing upward.

The SWAT team member never had a chance. The knife sliced into his heart. He grunted and his knees crumpled. Tony twisted savagely and jerked the knife from the cop's body. He reached out with his other hand and pulled the M-16 from the cop's limp fingers.

The second SWAT team member almost lived. He was young, highly trained, and had extraordinary reflexes. The body of his partner was tumbling over the edge of the roof when he, still running full tilt, raised the muzzle of his rifle. He was going too fast to stop, so at the edge of the roof he leaped into the air, spun around, and pressed the trigger. But as he leaped, his boot caught on the edge of the gutter and threw him off balance. His first shots slammed into the side of the house, breaking two windows and demolishing an upstairs bedroom.

He continued firing, though he knew he was a dead man. Tony crouched and squeezed the trigger. The high-velocity bullets caught the SWAT team officer in midair, causing his body to jerk and twist as he tumbled toward the ground. After he hit the ground, he did not move.

Tony swung the M-16 toward the first helicopter. The pilot cursed. He knew it was too late, but he racked the cyclic hard over as he twisted the collective and pressed hard on the left rudder.

He was right. It was too late. A burst from Tony's M-16 shattered the canopy, killed the pilot, and stitched a row of bullets along the gas tank. The stricken helicopter plummeted toward the athletic field behind Washington High School. The helicopter hit with a surprisingly small "plump" and rolled to the side. All was silent for several seconds.

The rear doors of the unmarked van in front of the school flew outward as SWAT team members raced toward the downed aircraft. Then a few tendrils of smoke curled upward as leaking gas spread across the hot engine. The gas ignited in a white blaze and the tanks exploded, sending first one and then another column of orange fire and greasy black smoke high into the air.

The SWAT team members who had sprung from the van stopped and held up their hands to ward off the immense heat. They backed up.

Tactical radios crackled. "Chopper One is down" came the urgent voice from the second helicopter pilot. "No apparent survivors."

"Back off," ordered the SWAT lieutenant. "I don't want to lose another crew. We'll take care of him."

"Roger that," said the pilot. He climbed higher and pulled away. Already the street was hazy in the mist.

The sound of Tony's gunfire caused the detectives on his left to pause a split second. The SWAT team members running across the back yards instinctively sought cover, a place from which to return fire.

Tony caught a glimpse of several black uniforms, pointed the M-16, and held down the trigger as he sprayed the yard to his right. Groans and curses told him he had found several targets. He continued firing. The bullets from the M-16 chewed up shrubbery and caused divots of red clay to turn into dust as they flew through the air. The M-16 ceased firing. It was empty.

Now Tony had to move fast. He had to get out before the cops recovered. He dropped the M-16 and backed up the roof line a few steps. Two quick paces and he leaped to the next roof, moving around to his left to keep the roof between him and the SWAT team members. The end of the block was coming up. He was going to make it.

The SWAT lieutenant searched the roof line. Nothing. He turned toward his sergeant. "Get medics in here and get help for those men," he ordered. "Now." From the corner of his eye he caught movement on a roof much nearer the corner of MLK than he had expected. The suspect was on the move and making good time.

"Move it," the lieutenant shouted. "Follow me." He raced toward the corner. But as he crossed the second yard, he suddenly held up his left hand and skidded to a stop. Ahead was a fourteen-foot wall, part of the rear of a store that once had been on the empty lot. The wall abutted a house to the left. To the right the wall ran all the way to the next building.

The SWAT lieutenant cursed. It would take his team two or three minutes to round the barrier and reach the homicide sergeant. He waved his men to the right. They could intercept the perp if he got past the homicide sergeant and made a run for it down MLK.

Jeremiah rounded the lawn of the last house on the street just as Tony jumped from the roof onto

the high wall and from there onto the ⬛
small barbecue shack at the rear of the empty⬛

The roof sagged and collapsed. Tony fell thro⬛
He landed atop the small counter at the front of th⬛
shack, shook his head, and jumped to the floor. He
clutched his waist. The *jimbaya* was there. Bloody,
but still there.

"What the hell you doing?" shouted someone behind the counter.

Tony looked over his shoulder. The old man presented no threat. He reached for the door.

"Hey," said the old man. "I know you. You the
sumbitch what throwed that trash in my chitterlings the other day. I recognize you. Get your sorry
ass back in here."

Tony ignored the old man. He opened the door.
A few yards away were several great vats filled
with chitterlings and something called brunswick
stew. To the side was a pit where barbecue and ribs
were being cooked over a smoking, smoldering fire
of hickory chips. The air was filled with smoke.

The street was only a few steps away. Tony ran.
Then from the corner of his eye he saw the big
homicide sergeant, pistol high in the air, race
around the corner. Close behind was the woman
whom he had loathed at first sight.

He pulled the *jambiya* from his belt and held it
low, hidden beside his leg, as he changed direction
and ran for the other side of the lot.

Where were the other cops, the ones who had
been at the back door? They had to be coming up
the back way and angling to cut him off.

Tony had run no more than two or three steps

ed to the ground by a heavy
his legs.

o stop" came the petulant voice
o had been in the shack. "You
owed trash in my chitterlings.
dirt and your black ass is going
to jail."

Tony had been slammed behind the knees by a wooden oar used to stir brunswick stew. The old man had jerked it from the steaming caldron and thrown it spinning through the air toward him. Hot, steaming pieces of pig meat and vegetables were on his leg. He wrinkled his nose in disgust as the odor of the pig meat filled his nostrils. He would have to throw away these trousers.

Jeremiah was only a few steps away. Already the woman was fanning out to the side, raising a pistol. Over her shoulder Tony saw another cop, red of face and slow of gait, loping around the corner.

Tony looked for his knife. It was on the ground behind him. He scrambled for it, then stood up. If he moved quickly and acted decisively, he could get past the cops.

He crouched, knife behind his leg, and was about to feint with the knife when his right arm was numbed by a hard blow across the forearm.

"I done told you twice to stop" came the strident voice of the old man. "You can't throw garbage in my chitterlings and get away with it. I'm a businessman."

Tony looked over his shoulder in disbelief. The old man had struck him with the oar from the big vat of chitterlings. The stench of lard and pig entrails caused him to retch.

Before Tony could turn around, Jeremiah, coming in at a dead run, swung his left hand with all his strength, caving in Tony's stomach, folding him over, and knocking the breath from his body.

Tony bent over, eyes wide and gasping for breath. Jeremiah's foot caught him under the chin with such force that he was knocked backward, arms flailing, feet struggling for purchase as he backpedaled across the unpaved lot.

He fell across the enormous vat in which chitterlings were being cooked. Virtually paralyzed, he lay there a moment, gasping for breath, struggling to regain the strength to move. The pain of the hot vat reached his brain, and with a moan, he tried to roll to the side.

Jeremiah anticipated him. The big cop stuck his pistol into his belt, scooped up the oar, and shoved it behind Tony's legs. With a triumphant cry he straightened up, flipping Tony backward into the boiling lard. Only his lower legs and feet were exposed.

The lard sizzled and cracked and then was silent for a few seconds before it began bubbling and sizzling again.

Jeremiah leaned over, hands on his knees, gasping for breath.

"I'm . . . too . . . old . . . this . . . shit," he panted.

"You done fucked up my chitterlings," the old man shouted. He was almost apoplectic. His eyes were round with anger.

"Impossible," gasped Jeremiah.

"All personnel, scene is secure," Caren radioed. She stepped closer to Jeremiah and turned off the radio at his waist.

Old Black Joe stepped closer to Jeremiah.

"What the hell you mean, 'impossible'?" the old man demanded. "What do a white man know about chitterlings?" The old man was talking a mile a minute, dancing from one foot to the other and swinging his arms. He glared at Jeremiah, then at Tony, then back at Jeremiah. He pointed at the steaming vat from which Tony's legs dangled. "Look at that. Ain't nobody gonna buy no chitterlings with a nigger in them. Chitterlings supposed to be inside niggers, not niggers in the chitterlings. I'm calling the police."

Caren holstered her pistol, grabbed Tony by the cuff of the pants, and pulled hard. She gasped and pulled again. The steam and the heat and the odor were overpowering. She put her foot on the vat and heaved again, jerking Tony's body from the vat. She backed up and continued to pull until Tony's body was away from the fire.

The SWAT team rounded the corner and fanned out in tactical formation. They charged across the empty lot as Caren sat down, leaned to the side, and vomited.

Joe's eyes widened as he watched the phalanx of cops charging across the empty lot. "Damn," he said to the SWAT lieutenant. "Police got here before I called. I ain't believing this shit."

Dean, panting hard, ambled up, looked at Tony, and announced to no one in particular, "He tripped. I saw it."

He moved to the side, unlimbered his camera, and began snapping pictures.

Jeremiah gasped for breath. Caren cleared her throat and wiped her mouth.

"Wonder where the nearest bathroom is," Dean said, looking around.

He pointed toward Tony's body and looked at Old Black Joe. "How much you charge for crispy critters?" he asked.

39

It was Friday night.

Jeremiah Buie stared into the amber depths of a glass of single-malt Jura scotch and tried to recover from the adrenaline rush of that afternoon and the subsequent fatigue that had settled into the marrow of his bones.

Now he had plenty of time to drink. Two hours before, Mayor Eldrin Bell had suspended him for a month without pay. The mayor had become almost apoplectic when he learned Jeremiah had called Frederick A. Carr's press secretary and demanded that the candidate be told an Atlanta cop was holding a copy of a Nigerian intelligence document outlining the particulars of Operation Bilal. "Tell him unless he resigns, I'm linking three Atlanta homicides to his senatorial campaign and tying the whole thing around his neck," Jeremiah said.

The press secretary called Mayor Bell and told him of Jeremiah's threat. Jeremiah had anticipated this. A guy running for senator could not be bluffed by a city cop.

Already he had called CNN and the bureau chiefs of the national newspapers and news magazines in Atlanta. He explained in a long interview how a young man, his mother, and an Atlanta police major had been murdered by an assassin known to various intelligence agencies as Tony the Dreamer. He told how Tony had worked for Carr in Atlanta years earlier. He said Carr was suspected of being an Arab who, upon being elected president of the United States, was going to operate by a hidden agenda that would bring great harm to America.

CNN immediately aired the story. Now the story was being updated and verified and fleshed out on an hourly basis by CNN reporters. The updates made it clear that CNN had sources inside several intelligence agencies. The story had taken on a life of its own, and momentum was growing by the minute. The national press corps was in a full-fledged feeding frenzy; a mountain of facts and corroborating data was being put together by the best news-gathering organizations in the world. By Sunday this would be the lead story in every newspaper and on every TV station in America. Carr would not be able to explain it away. Already on CNN the speculation was not whether Carr would resign, but when he would make the announcement.

Jeremiah turned up the small crystal glass and sniffed the scotch. The only truly expensive items in his house were the glasses from which he drank scotch, heavy, leaded crystal that revealed the colors and focused the "nose," showcasing yet cosseting the scotch. Jeremiah sipped the liquid gold of Scotland. He held it in his mouth for a moment, savoring the smooth, peaty flavor.

He also savored the agony that Frederick A. Carr

must be going through at this very moment. To be so close, just days from the election, and to have this happen must be agony and frustration and anger beyond description. The Nigerians and Arabs had invested billions in this scheme, and now they were watching it vaporize. They would not be happy that Carr had failed. The wrath of Islam was about to descend upon Carr.

Jeremiah swallowed the scotch. Tony had met an appropriate end: scalded and drowned in a vat of lard, surrounded by entrails of pigs. His soul would never find rest.

Major Worthy's death had not been avenged, but the fashion in which Tony had come to an end was as close as Jeremiah could get.

He stood and hoisted his glass toward the ceiling. "To you, Major," he said. "I hope you've found a relief pocket."

He downed the remainder of the scotch, looked at the empty glass for a moment, then murmured, "There's no one left who calls me Sissy."

He reached for the bottle of Jura and poured himself another drink."

He walked across the room and opened a red velvet-lined case and stared at his bagpipes. He was reaching for them when the telephone rang. It was Caren, and through the forced lightness and bonhomie of her congratulations, he heard an intensity that weighed him down even more. It was almost as if she felt guilty about something.

"You did more than you know," she said.

"Yeah, I'm Mr. Wonderful."

"No, I mean it. A lot of people owe you a great deal."

"Okay, Mr. Extra Wonderful."

She laughed. "Are you in the scotch?"

"Deeply."

"Why don't I come over and join you?"

Jeremiah paused. He sensed the proximity of the Celtic hounds. They were circling somewhere in the background, low growls coming from their throats. In an hour or so they would be in full bay. The black dogs roamed on Friday nights. They loped through his brain, dragging tattered and twitching memories.

God, he hated Fridays.

"I thought that after sundown Friday was a very special time for you," he said.

"It is," Caren said. She paused. "That's why I want to join you."

He fingered the tartan-covered bag on his pipes. MacDonald, Lord of the Isles, the oldest and most noble of all the clans of Scotland.

"We still have two problems," he said. "The DNA sample and the chief."

"Easy," she said. Her voice was cheerful. "The sample was substituted or altered. Nothing else fits. Whatever happened, it doesn't matter now." She paused. "As for the chief, his homicide is still under investigation. Price has information that his suspect is dead. He's trying to verify that. We may never know the motive."

"Maybe not," Jeremiah said. He sighed. "I like things neatly sewn up." He did not speak for a moment. "I'm going to put on the kilt and play the pipes."

"I enjoy the pipes."

"Sad, mournful music is what I'll be playing." He paused. "All our songs are sad."

"What songs?"

" 'Flowers of the Forest' for the major, and for . . . for someone else."

"Your daughter?"

"Yes."

"I think you should. But you also know happy songs, don't you? Some reels and marches. Can you play those?"

"You want me to stay away from the pibroch, to play the little music. Well, I know a few marches. In fact, I'll probably do a bit of marching tonight."

"Then I better come over so I can talk to the officer who answers the complaint calls."

Jeremiah laughed. "Do you like scotch?"

"Yes."

"Not that blended sewage that passes for scotch; I mean good single-malt scotch; I mean the gold of the western isles."

"Yes."

"I'll be looking for you."

Jeremiah hung up the telephone and stood there for a moment staring at his bagpipes. He looked around the room as if expecting to see the Celtic hounds hiding behind the furniture. Nothing. He was surprised. The conversation with Caren had pushed the black dogs far back into the darkness. He no longer felt their looming presence.

He walked across the room and picked up his glass of scotch and sipped it.

Maybe this time it would be different.

Caren heard the skirl of the pipes even before she turned off the ignition of her car. High and clear the sound came, and it was not a lament. She recognized the tune as 'Scotland the Brave.' The music had an exultant, driving thrust. It was a song of triumph, a song of joy, a song one plays when one goes into battle with dragons and expects to win. Hard, confident, exultant, glorious music. Music of affirmation.

She was smiling when she stepped from the car.

ABOUT THE AUTHOR

ROBERT CORAM is an Atlanta writer and a
part-time instructor at Emory University.
He is a former reporter for *The Atlanta
Constitution* where he was twice nominated
for the Pulitzer prize.